Blood
Beneath the
Pines

Sylvia,
Enjoy the Read to
on your way England,
London, England,
Be Blessed
Tammy Partlow

TAMMY PARTLOW

ISBN 978-1-64416-036-7 (paperback)
ISBN 978-1-64416-037-4 (digital)

Christian Faith Publishing, Inc.
832 Park Avenue
Meadville, PA 16335
www.christianfaithpublishing.com

Printed in the United States of America

Chloe Parker hurried into the diner and settled into the booth nearest the door, pushed the red-checked curtain aside, and looked down the street. The white Nissan was still there.

She removed her coat and placed it in a sunken area of the booth's seat. She didn't need the one-page menu propped between the salt and pepper shakers. Snow Valley, Wyoming, had been home to her and the café for as long as she could remember.

"Town's kind of dead this morning, isn't it?" Alice asked as she arrived at Chloe's table.

"Guess we have a little time before the tourists take over." She placed her usual order and tried not to think about the Nissan that had been following her all morning. She might not have noticed the car at all had it not been so out of place.

She looked around the diner. The reading club was meeting in the corner. A local rancher and his son were eating their lunch.

Chloe glanced out the window again. The man was still sitting in the car. She could see his blond hair and the top of his wire-rimmed glasses above the map covering most of his face.

"What's got your attention this morning?" Alice asked as she placed a bowl of steaming hot stew and a smaller bowl of strawberries on the table.

Chloe dropped the curtain and turned toward Alice. "You don't know anyone in town who bought a Nissan, do you?"

"I don't think so." Alice propped her hands on her slender hips and twirled her blonde hair around her index finger. "Jim Bookman bought a new Dodge Ram, but he's the only one I know with a new ride. Why?"

Chloe smelled the beef and potatoes in front of her. She lifted her spoon and scooped up a large bite to cool. "A white car has followed me all around town, and I don't recognize the driver. I know you keep up with everyone's business."

"Hey, are you calling me a busybody?" Alice asked.

Chloe sampled the stew for coolness and then ate the bite in her spoon. "No, I'm just saying you're here all the time, and I wondered if you knew."

"Well, I can't say I've seen many cars at all around here lately. Where did you see it?"

"It's parked down the street now," Chloe said as she continued to eat her lunch.

Alice went to a window and pushed the curtains completely apart. She looked up and down the two-lane road. "Girl, the only car I see is parked over by the jail. And I know who it belongs to—the deputy's ex-wife. It's been parked there since she caught the bus out of town last fall."

Chloe lifted the curtain near her booth and looked out again. The car was gone.

Alice turned to walk away. "If you see it again, give Sheriff Bob a call. He can be your busybody."

"Yeah, he can sure do that!" Chloe started to take another bite of her stew when her cell phone rang. She listened to Hank inform her that the ranch hand left the gate down near the barn. All the heifers due to calf were heading toward the main road. Chloe knew the old man, and the idiot drifter couldn't get the cattle up by themselves. She thanked Alice for her half-eaten food. "I'll see you later. I gotta run."

"But you didn't finish your stew. You're too skinny now. You need to—"

"Can't. Herd's out." She pitched her money on the table and grabbed her coat and cap. "I don't know why Dad can't just sell that herd. Seems I'm always cleaning up his mistakes."

"You be careful out there and call me if you need anything," Alice said. She removed the bowls and the bills from the table and wiped down the area.

Chloe stepped out into the cold Wyoming mountain air. She pulled her gloves from her pocket and put them on, pulled her beanie over her ears, and then drew the coat collar up around her neck. She never looked to see if the car was anywhere around, but she checked her coat pocket for the .38 she always carried.

*****

Willie B. Wilson held the door open for Elizabeth Lee to roll her wheelchair into her room at the Gentle Breeze Assisted Living Home in Bishopville, Mississippi. "Don't run into the coffee table," he joked.

"I won't. Don't worry. I'm old, but I can still see," Elizabeth said. "I need to rest for a while, so help me to bed."

"Yes, Ms. Lizzie." Willie B noticed the Clorox smell of the freshly made bed as they pushed and pulled until she was comfortable.

Elizabeth pointed to her recliner. "Hand me my Bible before you leave. Will you?"

He picked up the well-worn Bible and gave it to her. "Here you go." A photograph of a young brunette girl stuck out of the top of the Bible. "Any word from Sam yet?"

"No," Elizabeth replied, "not a phone call or anything. I hope he doesn't get shot this time. Sam's a bright boy, but Wyoming's too wild a country for a city kid like him." Elizabeth found her glasses in the top drawer of the dresser next to her bed and placed them on top of her Bible. "I wish he would call."

Willie B took a seat in the only chair at the tiny kitchen table. He didn't say it, but he remembered this was Sam's third trip to Wyoming.

"You don't believe Sam will find her this time either, do you?" Elizabeth asked, interrupting his thoughts. She opened her Bible and placed her reading glasses on her nose. "We have to have faith. This is the last chance. I am not going to be here forever."

"Now, Ms. Lizzie, don't go talkin' that way."

"You know it's true. If Sam doesn't find her and get her to come back with him, it's over for this lifetime."

"Then we'll just have to pray harder, won't we?" Willie B asked. He leaned back in the hard-oak chair and looked around the room. Even though Elizabeth had been in the nursing home for a couple of months, the decorations were few. A vase of faded plastic roses sat on the small coffee table along with a framed picture of Morgan, Elizabeth's deceased husband. A frail brown-haired girl sat on his knee. A small wooden cross, Willie B had hand carved, hung on the wall above the table.

The sun brought its morning rays through the window. Willie B looked at his watch. It was almost ten thirty. He needed to get his seeds in the ground before the day got too hot. "Ms. Lizzie, I meant to be gone by now."

Elizabeth looked up from her Bible. "You go on. Maybe Sam will call with good news soon," she said.

Willie B struggled to his feet. "All right, Ms. Lizzie. I'll see you tomorrow."

"Go on." She looked out the window. "Get those seeds in the ground," Elizabeth said then turned her eyes back to the scripture.

"You know me too good, Ms. Lizzie. Them seed are callin' my name."

Willie B stepped out into the hall. As the door closed behind him, he hoped he would see her tomorrow. She was fading fast, and he knew it.

His doubts about Sam finding the granddaughter were growing by the hour, and it was hard to hold a mustard seed's worth of faith in Sam's tracking abilities.

Willie B walked out of the nursing home, got into his old blue truck, and headed home. No matter what happened in Wyoming, he would support Ms. Lizzie's wishes, like always, even if he thought they were impossible.

*****

The man watched the Dodge pickup as it pulled away from the corner parking spot near the diner. He had moved his Nissan to the south side of the café where the snow had been mostly cleared off and ice melt had been generously applied to the sidewalk.

Mounds of dirty week-old snow lined the streets. His decision to wear the new cowboy boots he had purchased the night before was a poor choice, and one he now regretted. At thirty-one, he crept like an old man toward the building.

As he stepped into the diner, he spotted a thick welcome mat and wiped the soles of his boots. A group of loud women sat in the corner, and the only waitress was handing back their change and receipts. She nodded toward him, and he acknowledged her as he took a seat in the nearest booth.

"Be safe," the waitress called to a cowboy and young kid as they neared the door of the restaurant. The wind howled and forced its way in as the two exited the cafe.

Alice arrived at the man's table with a cup and a pot of coffee. "Would you like a cup?"

"Yes, please," the man said.

Alice poured him a full cup and set it in front of him. She placed the one-page menu on the table. "You let me know when you're ready to order, hon," Alice said.

"I'll have a cheeseburger and fries, if that's not too much trouble," the man said with a slight Southern drawl.

"All right, darling, coming right up."

He detected a hint of seduction in her voice. If he played his cards right, she might give him the information he needed. He smiled and handed her the menu. "Someone as lovely as yourself shouldn't be working this hard. Don't you have any help?"

Alice took the menu. "No, it's me and one old cook." She pointed to the white-haired man behind the kitchen window. "We're it," she said as she turned to walk away.

A few minutes later, several women from the group stood and gathered their coats from the pile they had made in a nearby empty booth. The ladies didn't leave right away as he hoped. They stood around wrapping themselves in coats, gloves, and hats and giggling.

Alice delivered his food. "Enjoy," she said. She walked to the women's booth and began picking up their dishes.

The cheeseburger was juicy and fresh, unlike the fast-food burgers he was used to. He listened to the women chat and laugh about the local news as he ate. He noticed a sign over the door that announced: "We only serve local Angus beef, and we're proud of it!"

The last woman out of the booth pulled her coat tightly around her very pregnant belly while Alice gathered the remaining dishes from the table. "Alice, be sure to tell Chloe Parker that I'm sorry I couldn't get out of the booth earlier to speak to her. Next time she's in town, tell her to give me a call. Maybe I can meet her for lunch."

The man stood quickly. He marched over to Alice and the other women. "Excuse me. Did you say Chloe Parker?" The man's blue eyes rested on Alice with a hint of hope dancing in them.

Alice stood speechless for a moment.

The other woman blurted out, "Yes, do you know her too?"

"No, but I'm about to. Excuse me." The man turned and dropped some folded bills near his plate and left.

Chapter 2

Living so far up the mountain wasn't the most convenient, but Chloe loved the higher elevation and the solitude. Between her horses, the Rockies, and the wildlife, her mind was occupied most of the day, but deep down, Chloe knew something was missing. She was never sure of herself even with four years of animal science behind her.

Chloe turned off the main street out of Snow Valley and headed north toward the ranch. The snow-packed switchbacks weren't easy to maneuver, so she shifted into four-wheel drive. As she neared the vista, her cell phone rang. She answered to Hank's voice.

"Hi—we—but—"

"Hello." The phone dropped the call. Chloe placed it on her dashboard and hoped that Hank would try her again. She wanted to reach the ranch before the cattle wandered too far. She had promised her father everything would run smoothly while he was in Montana. She intended to keep the promise, no matter if it killed her. Free rides didn't exist on her father's ranch. Not for anyone.

An hour later, Chloe turned onto the ranch road and caught a glimpse of the sun reflecting off a car's windshield behind her. She couldn't believe what she was seeing.

As Chloe neared the end of the drive, she met a neighbor's pickup and horse trailer. She recognized the driver and began to reduce her speed. She let her window down as she approached the pickup.

"Hello, Abbot," Chloe said.

"I was just up to your place," Abbot said with a mouthful of chew. "Had to help the foreman get your cattle up. They were coming right down this road and heading for the base of the mountain when I drove by." He adjusted his cowboy hat and leaned back in the seat.

Chloe didn't say anything. She watched as he spat his tobacco into a paper cup.

"Yeah, I figured you was gone somewhere again," Abbot scoffed.

Chloe cringed at the thought of him thinking she was out running around and letting the ranch go. She was very responsible, and it didn't sit well that Abbot was implying differently. Chloe knew he would run his mouth to her dad as soon as he had the first chance. She still hadn't forgiven him for the last time he made her look bad at the local ranchers' get-together.

"They could have waited till I got here," Chloe said.

"No, ma'am. I don't think so. You're lucky I just happened by."

Chloe shifted in her seat. "I had to pick up meds for some sick cattle. Like I said, I could have taken care of it, but thanks for your help." Chloe didn't bother with any more niceties. She hated explaining her actions to her nosy neighbor. She let her window up and proceeded to the ranch. She watched her side mirror and saw the Nissan move over to the edge of the snow to allow the pickup to pass.

Since a crazy person would be the only one dumb enough to take a two-wheel-drive car up a mountain covered in packed snow, Chloe decided he was a crazed stalker. As she pulled up to the property, she did not see any signs of the foreman or the drifter. She stopped near the side of the barn and went into the office. She hadn't gotten her coat off when she heard a voice calling her name from the other side of the door.

"Hello, I'd like to speak to Chloe Parker, if I may."

How does he know my name? She peered through the miniblinds and saw the man who had been following her. He didn't look angry. He didn't look like a killer or some disturbed weirdo. In fact, he reminded her of the young John Denver she'd seen on her mother's favorite albums for years. He even wore the same wire-rimmed round glasses.

"What do you want?" she asked.

"Hi, are you Chloe? I need to visit with you for a few minutes. Look, Ms. Parker," the deep voice said from outside the door, "I need to give you a message from your grandmother."

Chloe was puzzled. Her father's mother had been dead for many years, and she had never known her mother's side of her family.

"What are you talking about?" Chloe asked.

"Do you mind if I come in? I have a rather important situation to discuss with you, and it's cold as ice out here. Look, my name is Sam Green. I am from Bishopville, Mississippi. I attend church with your maternal grandmother, Elizabeth Lee." Sam drew his wallet from his jacket pocket. "This is my driver's license from Mississippi. Take a look." He held it to the window of the office door and waited. The wind blew, and the snow was falling again. His hands began to shake from the cold. "Please, Ms. Parker. Could you at least look at my ID?"

Chloe opened the door. The blond man stood looking at her and shaking. "Come in," she said.

Sam walked into the office. "Thank you. I'm not used to this kind of weather, especially on the first day of May. I'm about to freeze." Sam replaced his wallet and pulled his thin jacket up around his ears.

Chloe noticed his Southern accent. She folded her arms and placed one hand inside her jacket. She nodded to the extra barn coats hanging on the rack near the door. "Take one of those. They are a lot warmer than that thin jacket you're wearing."

Sam took one and wrapped it around him. "Mind if we sit down?"

She unfolded her arms and pointed toward the chair on one side of the office desk. Chloe sat opposite him. She wasn't sure what his angle was, and she wouldn't tolerate a lot of nonsense.

*****

Elizabeth woke to a sunny afternoon. In her earlier years, napping after lunch was for the lazy souls. But things were different now. The cancer treatment made her extremely tired, and she was glad to rest when she could.

A light tap came from her door, and a nurse pushed it open. Within a few minutes of the nurse's arrival, Elizabeth was sitting upright in her wheelchair with a light shawl over her shoulders and a thin blanket across her lap. The nurse pushed Elizabeth down the wide hall and out into the garden. She could smell the sweet fragrance of the magnolias as soon as they exited the building.

"Thank you," Elizabeth said and patted the nurse on the hand. "I want to stay out as long as I can."

She watched as the nurse clipped a bouquet of pink peonies. The assisted-living home was beautiful and newly built. Elizabeth looked at the kaleidoscope of colors in the courtyard. If only she could see her granddaughter before she left this world for the next, she would be at complete rest. For now, she fought the regrets that lingered in her mind. The course her life had taken after that one decision was more than she could bear some days.

"Mrs. Elizabeth," the nurse called near the French doors of the nursing home, "are you okay as you are? I could bring you something if you'd like."

"No, I'm fine, dear. I'm enjoying the warm air. You go on in, and I'll wait here for Willie B."

"Okay, I'll be out in a while to check on you," the nurse said. She disappeared through the French doors.

The oaks surrounding the courtyard were stately trees. A light breeze blew their branches causing a wind song in the leaves. Elizabeth thought of sitting on the front porch of her old home in the Pines Community. Morgan had worked so hard building the house only to see it lost to a tornado. A massive oak near the home had given protection from the winds and lent its mighty branches for tire swings, but the happy memories were overshadowed by the destruction the tree left as it blew over the house during the storm.

Regrets had a way of changing her mood, and Elizabeth wished she had brought her Bible outside with her. The Word gave her hope and shut down some of her anxiousness.

"You're a rose amongst the thorns, Ms. Lizzie," Willie B said as he stepped from behind her wheelchair. He handed her a beautiful orange rose he had cut from a nearby bush. "Don't worry, I trimmed off them thorns, just like I always do."

She took the rose and smiled. The soft petals brushed her nose as she breathed in the fresh scent. "I didn't know if you would make it back before dark or not with all that gardening to do. Have you heard anything from Sam?"

Willie B sat next to her in a wicker chair. "No, but I know he will find Chloe and talk her into comin' here. He ain't the best lawyer in town for no reason, you know."

"Why would she want to come here? I'm old and dying. She won't come. I have nothing to offer her." Elizabeth looked out across the lake and wiped her eyes with her bony fingers. *Sam has to convince her to come.*

Willie B slid to the edge of the wicker chair. He patted her on the arm. "It's goin' be okay. Don't worry, Ms. Lizzie. Sam's a good man. I know he'll get the job done. Now let's see what we can do to get your spirit up."

Chapter 3

Chloe *watched as* the fair-skinned man blew warm air over his ungloved hands. Not many men in Snow Valley had perfectly manicured hands. She wished hers looked as good as his. "What did you mean when you said you had a message from my grandmother?" Chloe asked.

"It's a long story. I've been trying to find you for years. We all knew it would be a long shot, but I agreed to try again."

Chloe got up and walked to a nearby coffee maker. She put on a pot and removed her jacket.

Sam continued. "I have been to Wyoming two times in the past two years. When your grandmother found out she had cancer, we went on a mission to find you. An old postcard your mother sent Elizabeth years ago is all we had to go on, and it only shows the state the card was mailed from. I didn't have any idea what town you were in or even if you were still in Wyoming."

Sam took a battered postcard from inside his jacket. "This is the card Elizabeth's daughter, Anna Lee Parker, mailed her about fifteen years ago." He handed Chloe the postcard.

She reached across the office desk and took the card. She recognized Yellowstone National Park and Old Faithful on the front. Chloe flipped it over, and there before her eyes were words written in her mother's handwriting. It had been fourteen years since her mother's death, but the handwriting was imprinted in her mind like the mountains were engraved in her heart. Chloe looked at the canceled stamp. She could only make out Wyoming.

"Why . . . how . . . how did you know to come to Snow Valley?" Chloe slid the postcard back across the desk and searched Sam's face for answers.

"I didn't. I've been all around the Yellowstone area looking for you. This was my last hope, and frankly, I didn't think I would find you. I was trying to accommodate a dying lady's wish. When I heard the two ladies at the café say your name, I couldn't believe I might have actually found you."

"I saw your car everywhere in town this morning. Why risk your life to drive up this mountain road? You could have stopped me in town," Chloe said.

"I saw the Parker name on your ranch pickup. But, I didn't want a repeat of last year's event, when I got shot at by another Wyoming girl I walked up on. If she'd been a better aim, I wouldn't' had to worry about snow covered roads." Sam flashed a million-dollar smile her way. "Anyway, when I stopped in at the diner this morning, I heard one of the customers ask about Chloe Parker. I knew I had the right gal. I couldn't lose you. Snow covered roads or not."

"How much longer does the old lady have? I can't drop everything and go to Mississippi, even if I wanted to." She turned the coffee pot off. "Want some?"

"Sure," Sam said. "If you wait too long, your grandmother might be gone. She tries to look strong, but I can tell she's going down. Elizabeth has always meant the world to me, and I know you would love her too if you met her."

Chloe walked back to the office chair and placed the cups on the desk. Sam took his cup and held it in his white-knuckled hands.

"Do you hear that?" Chloe asked. The tranquil mood was broken by the piercing sound of two patrol cars speeding toward the barn. "What is going on?" Chloe got up and walked around the large office to open the door. Before she reached it, the door came flying open and hit her in the shoulder. She fell back to the floor.

Sheriff Bob bolted into the office. He waved his gun around wildly and screamed something she couldn't understand.

Sam walked in Chloe's direction.

Sheriff Bob yelled for him to kiss the floor as he pointed his gun toward Sam's face.

Sam fell to his knees.

"Get down!" Sheriff Bob screamed again. He walked behind Sam and pushed him to the floor. "And stay down!"

A deputy rushed in behind the sheriff.

Sheriff Bob was on top of Sam with handcuffs in one hand and a pistol in the other still screaming at him.

Chloe finally found her voice again and began yelling herself, "Bob, Bob. It's okay. Get off him."

Sheriff Bob had the handcuffs on Sam and had lifted him off the floor in no time. Sam struggled to get free, but the sheriff tightened his grip.

"Let's go, Floyd." He pushed Sam toward the door and out into the cold.

"What do you think you're doing?" Sam demanded. "My name isn't Floyd. You've got the wrong man. I'm an attorney from Mississippi."

Chloe got off the floor and went after Bob. She grabbed at his arm but missed.

Sam continued to struggle to free himself from the sheriff. "I don't know who you are looking for, but it isn't me. Get these handcuffs off me now," Sam demanded.

Bob wouldn't listen. He swung Sam sideways, shoved him into the back seat of the Durango, and slammed the door shut.

"You come on down to the police station tomorrow, little lady. We'll get your statement. You should call Alice in the meantime and thank her. She might have saved your life." Bob walked around the Durango.

Chloe tried to get a word in over Sheriff Bob, but it was hopeless.

"Yes, sir, she's on top of it. She spotted this pervert at the diner and called us the minute she laid eyes on him. I know he will match the wanted poster I got the other day. Looks like we got us a winner this time. He won't escape our jail, not on my watch."

Chloe could hear Bob continue to talk to himself as he climbed into the Durango. She watched as the two police officers drove down the driveway.

A light snow blew across Chloe's face, and she turned to allow the wind to brush her hair out of her eyes. She stood watching the flashing lights disappear down the gravel road as she rubbed her shoulder. Chloe turned to walk back toward the office. *What in the world has Sam meant? A dying grandmother? In Mississippi?*

How could she have relatives in the South? She had almost no memory of her mother, and she surely didn't recall her ever talking about Mississippi. She didn't even know where Mississippi was.

Chloe got into her Dodge and drove to the main house. She gathered the groceries, took them into the kitchen, and grabbed her phone to call her father. She would see if he knew anything about her mother's family. Then she would call Alice and give her a piece of her mind for not tending to her own business.

*****

Sam attempted to convince Sheriff Bob he wasn't Floyd, but Bob ignored him. Now Sam sat in a Wyoming jail with a stubborn old man eying him like he was a winning ticket for the next re-election.

"Look, I tried to tell you. I've never been to Cheyenne. I'm a lawyer from Mississippi. Won't you at least call and check with my law firm?" Sam asked.

"Save it, pretty boy. I don't have any use for your type," Sheriff Bob said. "And you can knock off that phony accent." He turned to the deputy who was cleaning his rifle.

"You watch pretty boy while I'm gone tonight. He moves wrong, you shoot first and ask questions tomorrow. He may have escaped from them fellows down in Cheyenne, but he won't escape us. No, sir."

"Sheriff, I know you know the law. I get one phone call, and you know it." Sam watched as the sheriff walked out the door. "Hey, Sheriff," he yelled, but the man never looked back.

"Deputy, can you obey the law here and hand me a phone?"

The deputy turned up the television, swung his swivel chair around, and went back to cleaning his gun.

Sam grabbed the bars and shook them as hard as he could. "Come on, man. I'm a lawyer. You have to give me the phone."

The deputy increased the volume again.

Sam sat on the cot. He knew it was pointless.

Chapter 4

Elizabeth opened the lower cabinet door and pointed out the vase she wanted Willie B to use for the roses he'd cut before they came back into the room. Willie B had managed to help improve her mood as he always did. It had been a lovely afternoon sitting outside in the shade. Elizabeth knew nightfall was coming fast, and Willie B would need to leave.

"Thank you for cutting the roses. They look beautiful," she said.

Willie B poured water into the vase and placed it on the tiny kitchen table. "You're welcome," he said.

"Willie B, I need to tell you something in case Sam doesn't talk my granddaughter into coming to Mississippi."

"Stop worryin' now, Ms. Lizzie. I told you he will get her here. You just wait and see."

"In case he doesn't, someone needs to know the truth about Morgan's death, and it might as well be you. I mean, you already know most of it. I simply can't die without telling my story," Elizabeth said.

"Ms. Lizzie, you ain't goin' nowhere. We done talked about this. You goin' be okay. Them doctors are doin' all they can to fix you."

"I can't allow Kimball Mitchell to win this battle. He has won most of the rounds over the years, but he can't have complete victory. I won't let him. I need you to know exactly what to do. You get your grandson to take care of it for me." Elizabeth rolled over to the small coffee table and picked up the framed photo of her late husband and her daughter. She rubbed Morgan's face trapped under the glass.

"If I die and Chloe comes later, you don't let her around Kimball Mitchell. He'll be too strong for her."

"Well, he ain't too strong for Stump," Willie B said as he beamed with pride.

"No, I don't mean physically. Kimball's outsmarted or paid off law enforcement around here for years. I don't want Chloe to come to the South and only hear the bad rumors about her grandfather. I want her to know the truth. Since Morgan's death, that's plagued me the most. I want her to know about the events of what happened on that day thirty-eight years ago. I was hoping a blood relative would bring the Mitchell family down once and for all. But Chloe can't do this alone."

"Them Mitchells have been around a long time, but Kimball's the end of 'em. It was a blessin' from God that Corbin only had that one bad seed before his wife ran off."

"Yes, that boy could have done so much good if he hadn't been so full of hatred toward his mother. He can grow anything on any kind of soil."

"It was in the paper that he got Mississippi Farmer of the Year again this year," Willie B said.

"He did?" Elizabeth asked.

"Oh yes, ma'am. Big write up in yesterday's paper. I meant to bring it for you to read but forgot," Willie B said.

"I'll check out the one in the community room. I think his greed drives him to produce so much corn and soybeans."

"I know, Ms. Lizzie. People look at the surface, but they don't know the real Mr. Mitchell. These folks would never give him an award if they knew what we know."

"No, they wouldn't. That's why I need you to know the full story. You are going to be around a long time yet. Get over here and copy down these directions so you can go home before dark. And there's something else I want you to know."

Chapter 5

Chloe finished her headcount, slammed the gate shut, and latched it. *Wait till I find that idiot drifter.* She wished she had someone she could count on. Her dad was absolutely no help. He might as well not exist. She wondered what kind of man didn't even know where his wife had been born.

She stormed into the calving barn hoping to find the drifter. After her talk with her dad over the phone, she was in the perfect mood to fire someone. She heard a tractor coming and ran out of the barn to see if it was the hired man. Instead she saw Hank driving toward the haystack and flagged him down.

He turned the John Deere off and opened the cab door. "Howdy, little miss."

"Hey, Hank, I did a headcount, and we are five head short." Chloe pulled her cowgirl hat off and let her hair drop down onto her shoulders. "Do you know where that no-good ranch hand is?" she asked.

"No. He might be gone as far as I know," Hank replied. "He wasn't anywhere around when Abbot dropped by. I didn't look for him after that. I figured he'd quit and run off after the chewing I gave him. Are you sure we are short? I didn't see any more strays when we got them up."

"Yes, I'm sure. Did you even count the cattle?" Chloe shook her head as she looked toward the corral. "Worse yet, one of them is the expensive heifer Dad bought a few weeks back. I have to go look for them before it gets dark. She's due to calve any day. Her unborn calf is more important to Dad than I am."

"Now, Ms. Chloe, you don't mean that. Do you want me to saddle up and go with you?" Hank asked.

"No, I'll do it. It's my job, and you have your feeding to do. Night will be here soon."

"When I get finished, I'll come help you if you're still out there by then."

"No, I'll be fine. You need to check the calving barn for newborns since the night calver is now MIA. I'll be taking the ranch dogs with me, so no need to worry."

"Okay, I'll get on with my feeding then." Hank cranked the John Deere, and diesel smoke from the exhaust filled the cold air.

Feeding was a never-ending process. Hank was a good hand but slow from old age. If only she could find one more person like him that was at least twenty years younger, she'd be set. Finding someone as loyal as Hank was impossible.

Chloe drove her Dodge over to the horse stables. She went into the barn and saddled one of the mares and rounded up the ranch dogs. The strays couldn't be too far from the ranch. As long as they hadn't walked over any snowdrifts and wandered away, it shouldn't take her long to find them. She walked the horse out of the barn and was surprised to see Alice standing near her old Jeep.

"Hi." Alice threw her hand up. "I wanted to tell you in person that I didn't know he wasn't a stalker, so don't be mad at me."

"Alice, what are you doing here at this time of the evening?" Chloe asked.

"I told you. I wanted to apologize. I didn't know Sheriff Bob would arrest him."

"Yeah, Sheriff Bob got his man all right," Chloe said. "Too bad, he never seems to arrest the right person. He should have tracked down the no-count drifter that cut out on me." Chloe threw herself into the saddle.

"You lost another hand? Good grief. Why are you so mean to these guys? That last one was hot."

"Hot or not, he wouldn't do the work, and looks don't get calves birthed or cattle fed." Chloe shifted in the saddle. "I really wished you hadn't called Bob."

"I thought you were in danger. At least, that's the way you made it sound in the diner."

"No, I didn't. And besides, I think I could handle a city boy from the South."

"I'm sorry, okay?" The ranch dogs ran behind Alice and jumped up on her jacket.

"Get down," Chloe yelled. The dogs heeled behind her and then curled up on the gravel road.

"It's okay. I love these dogs," Alice said. She reached down and petted both of the collies on the head.

"Don't encourage them," Chloe snapped.

"Are you still mad at me?" Alice asked.

"I'm not mad. Bob is a nervous cat waiting for something to move, so he can pounce on it. Anyway, I have to round up some strays. If you want to wait in the house, I'll be back soon."

"Are you kidding? I'll go saddle a horse and come with you," Alice said.

"You don't have to do that. I'll take care of it."

"You hold on. You could use my help. I'll be right back." Alice ran to the barn.

Chloe knew she might as well wait. Within a few minutes, Alice came out of the stables on one of the sorrel horses.

"Yahoo, let's go," Alice said as she rode past Chloe.

"Yeah. Really? Yahoo," Chloe said with little enthusiasm. She spurred the horse and caught up with Alice. Chloe wished she could get excited about ranching again like she had been when her mom was alive, but between the cattle she loathed and the overload of responsibilities, fun was a rarity.

Chapter 6

Willie B's eyesight was worse at dusk than any other time. He turned off the main road onto the gravel road and came within inches of crashing into Kimball Mitchell's Ford parked crossways in the road. Before he could comprehend why the Ford was parked there, Kimball Mitchell stepped out of the shadows and was standing next to his door.

"I tell you what, old man, I'll give you credit," Kimball said as he spat his tobacco onto the ground. Kimball slammed his fist into the side of Willie B's truck. "Either you're as stubborn as a monkey or just plain dense. Didn't I tell you to stay away from that old bat? Now I find out you're hanging around the nursing home."

Willie B shifted in his seat. The older model truck had roll-up windows, and with his crippled hands, he knew it would take him a while to crank the handle to get the glass back to the top. He reached his arm toward the handle and placed his hand on the crank.

Kimball Mitchell stepped closer to the pickup door and grabbed Willie B's collar. He pulled Willie B's head halfway out the window. "Go ahead, turn that crank. See how high you can get it and still breathe."

"Please, Mr. Mitchell. I'm listenin' to you. You don't have to hurt me. I'll listen."

"Come on, roll it up a couple of times. Let's go."

Willie B's left arm had been pressed against the door. He couldn't turn the crank with it at all, and arthritis in his right hand had robbed its strength.

"I can't do it, Mr. Mitchell. My hand is really swollen today."

"What am I going to do with you two old pests? You just won't die." Kimball shoved Willie B back in the seat. He pulled his revolver from the small of his back, propped his arm across the opened pickup window, and inspected the cylinder of his gun.

Willie B spoke softly. "Mr. Kimball, I can't help when God has us down on his time card. We'll go when he's ready, I guess."

"You getting smart with me, old man?" Kimball twirled the cylinder around and checked for bullets. "Who cares about God's time? I can take you out right now, if I want." Kimball grinned and revealed tobacco residue on his teeth.

"What'd me or Ms. Lizzie ever do to you? When you goin' leave us alone, Mr. Kimball?"

"You think I'm ever going to leave you alone? As long as that old bat's alive, I'm going to keep you both in my crosshairs. And if I get sick of watching y'all, I'm going to pull the trigger."

"She's very sick. Can't you let her die in peace?"

Kimball pointed to the north. "You notice a fire around these parts lately?"

"Yes, sir, Mr. Kimball. I saw a huge pillar of smoke over your place the other day."

Kimball took a photo from his shirt pocket. It was burned all around the edges and so brittle that some of the edgings fell away as he handed it to Willie B. "You be sure to give this to the old bat for me, will you?"

Willie B looked at the burned photograph. He recognized Anna Lee, Elizabeth and Morgan's only daughter.

"That came floating out of the ashes in the sky when I torched her house trailer. You be sure to tell Elizabeth where it came from for me." Kimball turned and walked to his pickup. "You remember, when I get ready to help God out you won't be able to stop me. Got it, old man?" He placed the revolver behind him for a second and walked around his Ford. Then without warning, he whipped his gun out and shot the front tire of Willie B's pickup.

"Oops. I hope you got a cell phone, old man. It's a good walk back to your place." Mitchell got into his pickup and spun out as he drove away. A rock flew up and zinged Willie B's windshield.

Willie B was glad to see Kimball driving away. He would not show Elizabeth the photo, nor would he tell her about the trailer. He slid the photograph in the glove compartment and took out his cell.

Chapter 7

Chloe and Alice rode down the driveway. Chloe searched the area for a place the cattle could have trailed off away from the others. Near the end of the ranch road, she noticed a ditch where the deep snow had been disturbed. In the distance on the east side of a group of willows, she could see a few tracks that the wind hadn't blown smooth yet. Chloe was sure that would be the area the cattle had wandered into.

"Look." She pointed in the direction of the tracks. Alice nodded, and they turned off the road. The wind was blowing harder, and the sun was perched on the horizon waiting to slide down the other side.

Chloe didn't want to get trapped out in the dark, but she didn't want to leave the cattle out either. Her father would have a fit if anything happened to the registered heifer or her unborn calf. She rode farther into the pasture. The ranch dogs started barking and ran ahead of her. Chloe sat straight in the saddle and looked into the mixture of cottonwoods and willows. The broken limbs covering the ground and the knee-deep snowdrifts made the trek harder than she hoped. There was very little light left when she finally spotted a pair of Black Angus cows in the trees.

"Over there!" Alice yelled about the same time Chloe had seen the cattle. The sound of Alice's loud voice startled the strays, and they cut out in a run. The dogs followed barking.

Chloe wanted to throw her hands up, but she knew she had to get moving. She turned the horse into a small clearing and set chase. The cattle moved farther into the darkness. Chloe endeavored to circle around them as the wind blew and the snow began to fall. It stung Chloe's face as she galloped out into the opening. The dogs had turned the cattle, and they were coming back toward her. She cut to the side to let the heifers pass.

A scream came from behind her.

Chloe turned in the saddle for a moment, but it was the wrong moment. The horse jumped over a ditch at that precise second, and Chloe came flying off the horse. A snowbank broke her fall, and for that, she was thankful, but her horse was nowhere to be seen. She stood and dusted the snow off herself.

Once again she heard Alice yelling for help. She looked toward the sound of Alice's voice but couldn't see her. Chloe whistled for her horse a few times, but she knew the wind swallowed the sound as soon as it left her lips. She figured her mare was well on its way back to the ranch by now. She hoped the dogs wouldn't let up on the cattle.

Chloe walked toward the sound of Alice's voice in the knee-deep snow and wished she'd taken the time to put on the coveralls she had left hanging in the barn. Her thermals and jeans weren't cutting it, and the snow numbed her legs as she walked.

"Chloe, over here. Help me."

"Alice, what have you done?" Chloe asked as she neared her. She could see Alice lying in a pile of cottonwood brush.

"The horse stumbled as we crossed this mess. I tried to hang on, but he lowered his head, and I went over it."

"Are you okay?" Chloe asked.

"I think so, but my boot is hung up in this brush, and I'm twisted in this mess. I can't get up."

"Hang on." Chloe moved broken tree limbs around and freed Alice's boot. She helped her to her feet. "I told you not to come. I could've handled it without you."

"I see the dogs are earning their keep," Alice said while brushing the snow off her rear. She pointed toward the direction of the willows. The dogs had pushed all five head down the creek bank and along the willow row.

"Thank goodness for something," Chloe said. She and Alice got behind the small herd and pushed them toward the barn.

"What a wreck," Alice said.

"Thank goodness you have a job in town," Chloe said.

"Hey, I'm not the only one without a horse."

"Yeah, well . . ."

"Well, what?" Alice asked.

"I would have never fallen off my horse if I hadn't been trying to look out for you."

"Whatever. Blame it on me."

"I'm just saying you should stick to the waitressing job. That's all."

"If that's true, what should you stick to? You're not any better at this kind of work than I am, and you do it full time," Alice said.

Chloe didn't answer. She walked alongside Alice in the dark pushing the cattle toward the barn. She wished she knew what she was good at. Alice was right about the only thing she got right was taking care of the horses and her beautiful flowers that bloomed all over her yard. To make matters worse, those were the things her father paid the least attention to when he was around.

*****

Chloe stopped in at the diner at five minutes after eight on Saturday morning. She had fully expected Sam to still be locked up in the jail across the street. To her surprise, she found Sam sitting in the corner booth eating his breakfast. Chloe walked toward his table and waited for an invitation to sit. It didn't come.

"Morning," she finally said.

"Morning," Sam replied without looking up from his cup of coffee.

Chloe noticed he looked a little less put together than the afternoon before. He hadn't shaved, and his thick blond hair was tossed instead of combed.

She slid into the booth and waited to be asked to leave or stay. He never said a word.

Alice came out of the kitchen. "Morning. Will it be your usual, Chloe?"

"Yes, that's fine," she said.

A long silence occupied the time until Alice returned with Chloe's oatmeal and peaches.

"Thanks," Chloe said. "How's your ankle this morning?"

"It's fine. A little sore. If you need anything, let me know," Alice said.

"I'm good."

Alice left the two sitting in silence once again.

"Look," Chloe spoke first, "I didn't call the sheriff, and if you had to spend the night in jail—"

Sam interrupted her, "I did spend the night in the jail." He looked at his watch. "I've been out a full half hour." He turned his cup up and finished off the coffee.

"I'm sorry about Sheriff Bob. He can be unreasonable sometimes, that's all," Chloe said as she looked across the table.

"Yeah. Your unreasonable sheriff finally called Cheyenne this morning," Sam said. "He was shocked to find out they had already captured their fugitive, and he was sitting in their jail. The stubborn goat didn't want to release me even after he called my law firm and got verification on my ID."

Chloe noticed a touch of anger in his blue eyes. "Yes, I agree. He's hardheaded as they come. Kind of like talking to a signpost," Chloe said as she ate the last of the peaches. "I called my father this morning and spoke to him about what you said yesterday."

"I hope you discovered I was telling the truth," Sam said.

"My father doesn't know a lot about my mom's past. She was a runaway and never talked much about her earliest years. Dad said she was a Jones when they first met. But he does remember seeing Lee on her birth certificate when they married. He also recalls seeing some town in Mississippi as her birthplace. He thought it began with the letter *b*, but he couldn't remember the name."

"I can tell you that your grandmother is a wonderful person and has wanted to meet you since she first found out about you."

"How long has she known about me?"

"Elizabeth learned about your mother's death about a year before she found out she had cancer. But there were a few things that Elizabeth didn't know."

"How did she learn about me?"

"Your mother called Elizabeth after you were born, but along the years, she was given misinformation and led to believe you were in Montana with your father after your mom's death. This caused a problem in tracking."

"If she knew my mom died and I existed, why didn't she come to the funeral? Why didn't she come to meet me then? Why did she wait till she's dying to send someone for me?" Chloe sat the coffee cup down harder than she expected. The coffee splashed out on her hand.

Sam quickly wiped it off with a nearby napkin.

Chloe pulled her hand back and wiped it with her own napkin. "I'm not a child. I can take care of myself. Thank you."

"Of course, sorry," Sam said. He blushed.

"You haven't answered my questions."

"Look, there are circumstances that you are not aware of that complicates this situation. Elizabeth would have come for you back then, but she didn't know where your family lived. She hired a company to find you, but they took thousands of dollars she didn't have to give and then disappeared."

"Looks like she could have figured it out if she cared."

"You don't know the whole story. It's one your grandmother can share with you if you'd like to meet her."

"I don't know."

"That's fine. But my flight to Mississippi leaves tomorrow out of Cody. I have a meeting on Monday and have to get back to my office," Sam said. "Listen, I think a lot of your grandmother. She has been like my own grandmother over the years. I'm here for her. Elizabeth needs you right now, and you should decide quickly. I don't know how much time she has remaining, but the doctor isn't giving us a lot of hope."

"I'll talk to my dad. Someone has to run the ranch. I lost another workhand this week, so there's one ranch hand and me holding down the fort. Plus I've already made plans for the summer, so I don't know if I can do this Mississippi thing. There's so much going on right now. It's poor timing," Chloe said.

Sam pulled a card from his wallet and handed it to her. "Death never has good timing. Does it? You give me a call when and if you decide to interrupt your busy summer. I'll be glad to meet you at the Memphis airport.

Chloe leaned back in the booth. "You know, I didn't mean it like that." She searched Sam's face for understanding. "The ranch can't run itself." She twirled her spoon in the oatmeal. "I need the next couple of days to sort this out. I'll let you know on Monday. I promise."

Sam stood and placed a twenty-dollar bill on the table. He looked toward the police station. "I see Sheriff Bob has my rental parked over at the police department."

"Look, I'm truly sorry about the confusion with Sheriff Bob," Chloe said.

"I've survived worse." Sam moved a few steps away from the table. "Not to put any more pressure on you, but your grandmother's seventy-eighth birthday is this coming Wednesday. It would be great if you could manage to be at the party and then return to Cody the next day, if you must."

"Like I said, I'll let you know." Chloe reached her hand out. Sam stepped closer to her and took her hand. Chloe smiled but then thought about how her calluses must have rubbed his manicured hand. She let go and said, "Again, thanks for coming out this way." She noticed the anger in Sam's eyes had been replaced with warmth, and he didn't seem to be appalled at her rough hand.

"Remember, Elizabeth's time is nearing, and if you want to know your grandmother, you better not wait too long." Sam turned and walked passed Alice who had been staring over the bar on a regular basis. "Ms. Alice." Sam nodded as he opened the door. He looked back at Chloe again. "I'll be waiting for your call. Ladies, it's been interesting."

Chapter 8

Sunday morning's sunrise brought color to the mountain peaks. Chloe stepped out onto the upstairs deck and watched the light walk its way down the slope. The snow never looked brighter than the moment the sun's first rays shined their beams onto the peaks. Shades of pinks and purples would follow as the sun rose. She wished she never had to leave the balcony, but she looked toward the barn and knew the heifers would have to be checked. She wondered how many calves had been born since Hank's last watch at three in the morning.

Chloe walked into her bedroom and closed the door behind her. She finished dressing in her jeans and flannel shirt, pulled on her boots, and went down the stairs.

Night calving was the worst job on the ranch, and she hated waking up all hours of the night. No good drifter couldn't have stayed long enough to get the rest of the herd calved out. She only had ten more to go. Maybe less if some were born since midnight.

As Chloe entered the kitchen, she turned the coffeepot on and threw a bagel into the toaster. While it was toasting, she sliced a banana and an apple in a bowl. The doorbell rang, and Chloe went into the living room to answer it.

She swung the massive oak door open and saw Alice standing on the porch. She was wrapped in her biggest winter coat.

"Alice, what are you doing here this early?" Chloe opened the door wider and moved over for Alice to enter the house.

"I thought I would come a little early and help out. I know I really messed things up with Sheriff Bob, and I wanted to make it up to you. Plus I know you are trying to decide if you should go to Mississippi or not. So I thought I could be your sounding board this morning."

Chloe turned toward the kitchen. "Close the door and come on in. You want a bagel?"

"Sure, and some coffee if you have it." Alice dropped her bag on the couch. She pulled the coat off and tossed it over the bag. She walked into the airy kitchen and took a seat at the bar.

"We can exercise the horses later," Chloe said. "There is a ton of work to be done before we can ride."

"I know. I came to help. When my mom and dad had their ranch, calving was my favorite thing, believe it or not."

Chloe placed the light breakfast on the bar and poured each of them a cup of coffee. She turned and placed the pot back in the coffee maker. "You didn't have to come so early. I don't need you getting hurt, *again*."

Chloe knew the herd was gentle, but the newest member was a registered Angus heifer from a bloodline that was known for being overly protective mothers. She remembered the registered heifer wasn't due for another day or two and decided Alice might make the dreaded chore go faster.

"How's your bagel?" she asked then poured them another cup of coffee.

"It's fine," Alice said as she ate the last bite.

"You know," Chloe said, "I'm glad you came up early. I think calving is my least favorite thing, next to working on the fence line around here."

Alice smiled and then finished off her coffee. "Does this mean you're not mad anymore?"

"I wasn't really mad. I was upset because I didn't hear what Sam had to say. You know how Sheriff Bob is. No one can get a word in when he's on a rampage."

Chloe finished her breakfast a few seconds later. The two bundled up and then headed out to the calving barn.

"I'm so excited," Alice said. "It's been forever since I helped with calving."

"Don't get hurt. My dad would kill me," Chloe said. "I'll have to tag anything that was born since three AM. So watch yourself."

Tree branches sparkled like diamonds from the morning's heavy hoarfrost. Chloe breathed in the crisp mountain air as she walked past the horse stables and toward the calving barn. She loved everything about the horse operation, but she tried to leave the cowherd to Hank. Chloe wanted to go to Mississippi. She wanted to feel excited about something. But once again, her responsibilities to the ranch held her back.

They neared the calving barn, and the rich smell of manure overpowered Alice's perfume and everything else Chloe could smell. They entered through the south end of the barn, and Chloe retrieved her small calving bag. She checked for tags and other supplies before entering the calving area. As soon as she entered the middle of the barn, Chloe glanced around the open space for any signs of a new birth. She noticed one calf on the hay in the center of the barn near the divider.

"I have to push this pair into a stall," Chloe said. "You stay here by the barn door. I don't want you in the way."

Alice threw her hands in the air. "Come on. I've done this before. I know it's been a while, but I used to be great at this."

"Fine, but if you get injured, it's your own fault."

"You're more likely to get hurt than I am," Alice said.

"Go open the stall door, and I'll push them. Okay?" Chloe gently walked the pair toward one of the open stalls. The older cow had been in their herd for a long time, and Chloe knew she was a good mother. Once she had the pair in the closed area, she took the tagger out of her small calving bag and tagged the tiny calf. She checked to see if it was a heifer or a bull and called out to Alice to record that is was a bull. She poured iodine on the navel then wrapped the weight tape around the calf's leg above the hoof. Chloe gave the information to Alice, eased out of the stall, and then closed the gate behind her.

"Let me see what's going on at the other end of the calving barn," Chloe said as she walked through the gate that divided the north and south ends of the barn. The latest newcomer to the herd stood with her head down licking her newborn calf. The calf wobbled to its feet and went to its mother's side to nurse. *Oh great. She had to deliver today.* Chloe walked back to the gate. She picked up her bag. "I don't know anything about this new heifer. She wasn't due for a couple more days, so you watch her while I tag the calf."

Chloe went back through the center gate and turned to close it. She looped the chain over the bars once and started to flip the chain again.

"Look out!" Alice warned from the other side of the gate.

Chloe turned in time to see the thousand-pound heifer coming straight for her. She dropped her bag and climbed the steel panel that made up the divider. The heifer rammed the panel and knocked Chloe off the top rail onto the ground on the other side.

"Man," Alice shouted. She ran over and helped Chloe to her feet. "That was close."

"I have to say, I'm glad you were here. I could have been killed. You never know when one of these heifers is going to change into a psycho momma." Chloe dusted the hay off her jeans. She turned back toward the divider and noticed her bag on the ground on the other side of the gate. "Rats. I'll have to open that gate enough to get my bag out."

"You better not do that," Alice warned.

"I have to. Can't leave it laying in there with all the glass bottles of meds and sharp tools in it. You watch the heifer and let me know if she comes at me again."

Chloe walked to the gate. The mother cow was back by her baby's side on the far north end of the barn. There were three stalls lining both sides of the barn. Chloe figured she could open the gate, reach the bag, and get back across the gate in enough time to close it before the heifer could run the thirty-six feet across the barn.

"Let's do this," Chloe said. She opened the gate hoping it wouldn't make any unnecessary sounds. She made a mad dash for the bag, grabbed it, turned quickly causing her foot to slip on a pile of wet manure, and down she went. Chloe heard Alice screaming.

She dug her bootheels into the dirt, lifted herself off the ground, and sprinted for the open gate. She slammed it shut just in time to get a face full of sprayed snot from the heifer that was tossing her head back and forth in front of her.

"Dang," Alice yelled, "girl, you can move."

The heifer turned and went back to her calf.

Chloe doubled over. She needed a second to reply to Alice. "That heifer's not a borderline crazy. She's completely deranged."

"Tell you what," Alice said, "if I can get this calf tagged, would you promise to go to Mississippi and let me stay here on the ranch for the week you're gone?"

"What? There are so many things wrong with that. First, you already had your vacation. Secondly, you don't know any more about calving than I do. And third . . ."

"Yes?" Alice asked.

"My dad."

"Look, I know you are burned out. You need a break. Your dad hasn't played fair by dumping all this work on you. And now, you got one chance at meeting someone you'll regret not meeting if you don't go. Besides, I can do this." Alice's eyes sparkled. "I really want to be a true friend and help you here. It'll only be for a few days, long enough for you to make a fast trip to Mississippi and back."

Chloe leaned into one of the stalls. "You really want to do this?"

"Yes. It's been slow at the diner. I know I could get off a few more days. And I miss being on the ranch. Last week brought back so many wonderful memories for me. Why do you think I come here all the time?" Alice asked with a chuckle in her voice. "It's not to see you."

Chloe thought for a minute and then straightened her shoulders. "Elizabeth's birthday party is Wednesday. If I flew out early that morning, I could make it to Mississippi before her party that night. Then I could visit through the weekend and fly back on Sunday."

"There you go."

"Do you think you could get off Wednesday through Sunday?"

"I'm sure I can."

"My dad's not going to like this idea."

"I'll make Mr. Parker like it. Who can resist me?" Alice asked as she turned her nose up and fluffed her blonde hair.

"I guess, that takes care of everything except one little thing." Chloe looked back at the heifer that was still eying them as if they were marked for death.

"In case I die," Alice said, "you have to promise me something. Give that blue-eyed lawyer a chance to know the real you while you're in Mississippi."

"What makes you think he'd want to know about me?" Chloe asked.

"It was written all over his face. Now, move over and let me show you how this is done."

*****

Chloe watched as Alice walked over to the office wall on the opposite end of the barn from the psycho heifer. She took down a rope then made her way into the last stall on the right side of the barn.

"You keep your eyes on that crazy heifer," Alice said. She threw the rope over her right shoulder and carried the calving bag in her left hand. Alice made her way up and over the row of stalls until she reached the north end of the building.

The heifer watched Alice from the open area in the center of the barn. The calf was lying down. Alice straddled the top rail of the metal panel. She leaned over and opened the gate. The heifer lowered her head and snorted at the hay on the ground. Alice knew she could rope the calf from where she was perched on the rail, but the mother moved in front of the calf about the time she pitched her loop. Alice let the rope go limp. She recoiled the rope and waited. The heifer didn't move.

"Chloe, I want you to shake the divider gate and get the heifer's attention so I can rope this calf," Alice said. "Shake it as hard as you can but wait till I tell you to do so."

"Okay," Chloe answered. She wondered why she hadn't thought to go through the stalls herself.

Alice readied herself and then yelled at Chloe to shake the gate.

Chloe shook the gate with all her might and screamed at the heifer. The heifer turned and looked at Chloe but didn't move.

"Chloe, do it again," Alice called.

Chloe shook the gate and then jumped up and down waving her arms at the heifer. "Come on, you demented cow." The heifer looked at Chloe and then back to Alice, but she never left the calf's side. Chloe couldn't take it any longer. She opened the gate and walked into the open calving lot before Alice had time to say anything.

"Hey, come get me," Chloe yelled at the heifer.

"Are you crazy? Get out of there now!" Alice screamed.

The heifer lunged at Alice who was still yelling at Chloe. Alice saw the heifer coming toward her and swung her leg over the top rail just as the heifer slammed into the panel. Alice jumped sideways, landed on her feet, and stood up.

Chloe screamed toward the heifer, "You think you're going to win this? I've got news for you. You can't stop two cowgirls on a mission." Chloe glanced over at Alice and saw that she would be able to line up a shot at the calf that was now standing alone."

"Alice, I think you have a shot. Take it," Chloe yelled.

Alice climbed back on top of the panel. She threw the rope, and it landed on the calf's neck. The heifer charged the panel again, but Alice was prepared and held her grip on the metal rail. She dragged the calf into the stall. The heifer snorted and rammed the panel a third time. Alice jumped down off the top rail and dragged the calf to the side of the panel nearest her. The heifer scooped up a head full of hay and tossed it in the air.

Alice tagged the calf at her fastest speed ever. Then she removed the rope from the calf's head.

Chloe watched and yelled for Alice to wait for the rest of the calving process. At least the calf was tagged, and there would be no mix-up later.

Alice climbed up and over the same stalls and entered back into the open lot on the south end of the barn.

Chloe ran over to her. "That was insane."

"See, I told you I could handle this ranching business," Alice said.

"Yeah, you rock."

"Do you think we'll have that kind of motherly instinct when we have kids?" Alice asked.

"I don't know. Doubt if I'll ever have kids." Chloe took the rope and calving bag from Alice. She walked to the office, hung up the rope, and then dropped the bag on the desk. "Let's go."

"Why not?" Alice asked.

"Why not, what?"

"Why do you think you won't have any kids? I plan on having a bunch of them if the right guy ever comes along."

"That's it. You have to love someone to want his kid. I don't think I'm capable of that anymore."

"Yes, you are," Alice said.

Chloe walked outside the barn and attempted to wipe the manure off her boot heels in the snow. Most of it rubbed off. "I don't think so," she said. "Doesn't matter anyway. There's not that many great guys left to pick from around here." Chloe looked at her watch. She couldn't believe it was almost nine o'clock. "Come on, we're not going to have long to ride before I have to come back here at noon."

"I'm glad you're going to Mississippi. Maybe you'll find what you've been looking for," Alice said.

"Who said I was looking for something? I have everything I need right here."

"Yes, and I'd love to change places with you. But I know you're not happy."

"There's a lot on me, that's all. Dad doesn't want to sell the cattle, but he doesn't have time for them either. I think he thinks of me as an extra arm and leg that can get the work done for him when he isn't around."

"You go to Mississippi and have a great time. Don't worry about the ranch. I know I can handle it."

"Thanks, Alice. You're a great friend. But seriously, I'll have to check with Dad to see if it's okay with him first."

Chapter 9

*K*imball Mitchell drove to the post office. He pushed a kid out of his way as he opened the door to the main lobby. Monday was his biggest mailing day of the week. He returned to his truck carrying an armload of mail and a large manila envelope tucked under his arm.

Kimball closed his pickup door and started the engine. He flipped the envelope over and noticed the postage. Kimball knew right away it was from his man in Wyoming. He ripped off the end of the envelope, dumped out the contents, and found a handwritten note.

> Don't know if you recognize this person. Heard he was from Mississippi. Thought you would be interested in anyone from that area visiting with our little Ms. Chloe. Let me know if you need any further assistance on this matter.
>
> X

Kimball picked up an eight-by-ten photo from his lap. It was a picture of a young brunette and a blond guy sitting together in a diner. He recognized them both. *What in the world is Sam Green doing with Chloe Parker? What is Green doing in Snow Valley, Wyoming, for that matter?* Kimball's light complexion turned a bright red as he read the note from his associate a second time. Obviously, Sam had made the acquaintance of his long-hidden secret.

Kimball threw the pickup into reverse and drove to Sam Green's law firm downtown. He didn't stop at any of the red lights and nearly caused a crash at 5th and Presley Street.

He backed his truck into a parallel parking space in front of the law practice. The law firm occupied the largest of all the old homes on the street. Located on the corner, it commanded attention. The house was adorned with ample lattice trim. White wicker patio furniture displayed pastel blue and green striped cushions and was arranged perfectly on the veranda.

Blue impatiens, in full bloom, were planted in huge terra-cotta pots. Two risers at the top of the steps held the arrangements. The pot positioned at the left of the steps had the misfortune of being too close to Kimball's swinging arm as he stormed up the steps. The container landed upside down as he walked by, and the tender flowers lay in ruin under the weight of the massive vessel.

He threw the office door open and marched over to the young receptionist. "Where is Sam Green?" He demanded as he leaned across her desk.

The pudgy-faced lady's eyes glared at him. "Excuse me, but could you lower your voice, please?" She spoke in a well-mannered tone. "We do have people waiting in the lobby."

Kimball looked around and realized he wasn't the only person in the office. He placed his hands on the mahogany desk and pressed forward. In a chilling tone, Kimball asked through his clinched teeth, "All I want to know is, where is Green?"

"He isn't in now."

"Which way is his office?" Kimball demanded.

"Sir, do I have to call the police? Would you please leave?" She picked up the phone's receiver and pressed nine before Kimball reached across the desk and grabbed the receiver.

In almost a whisper, Kimball repeated himself as he replaced the receiver on its base. "Listen, I want to see Sam Green now. Either you can show me his office, or I will knock on every door in this joint."

The receptionist stood and raised her voice, "I'm telling you, he isn't here."

A muscular man stepped out of the office to the right of the receptionist's desk. Kimball recognized him right away as one of the partners of the firm. He returned to a standing position.

"Hello, Mr. Mitchell," the partner said. "Can I be of assistance?"

"I need to speak to Sam Green."

"I'm sorry. He isn't in, but if you would like to make an appointment, I'm sure he'll be happy to meet with you."

"Don't bother. I'll catch up with him." Kimball turned and walked out the door. He noticed the broken flowerpot and the smashed small branches of blue flowers then scolded himself for the show he had put on in the office lobby.

In Kimball's early years, his reputation hadn't meant so much to him. He allowed his tempter to get the upper hand too many times. Now that he was in his fifties, he still had to beat down the beast that could expose who he really was. Kimball's father fooled many a man with his calm demeanor. Kimball was only beginning to get a handle on his rage.

Chapter 10

C*hole took a* deep breath and waited for Sam's voice to come over the receiver. She took a seat near her dresser and looked in the mirror.

"Good morning, Chloe." Sam's deep voice was clear and expectant. "I hope you have good news for Elizabeth and me."

"Morning, Sam," Chloe slowed her voice. "I wanted to get in touch with you as soon as I could."

"Did you get a chance to speak to your father yet?"

"Yes, he won't be able to get home until Wednesday afternoon. But Alice, the gal you met at the diner, offered to come to the ranch and help with the chores until Dad gets here. So it looks like I'll be flying down for a few days. At least, I can meet Elizabeth and be there for her birthday."

"That is wonderful news," Sam said. "I'm excited to hear this, and I know Elizabeth is going to be so happy."

"I'm only going to be there for a few days. So—"

"Elizabeth isn't going to believe it."

"Dad remembered where my mom's documents were filed," Chloe said. "I was able to locate her birth certificate and verify that indeed she was born in Bishopville, Mississippi, to an Elizabeth and Morgan Lee."

"I'm glad. Guess that settles it. I finally found the elusive Chloe Parker, daughter of Anna Lee. Now, maybe the next time I go to Wyoming, I won't get shot or thrown in jail."

"I could bring my .38 with me if you'd like," Chloe said. She rearranged her brush and makeup supplies as she smiled to herself.

"That's okay."

Chloe stood and walked to the window. Snow was falling again, and the mountains were shrouded in clouds. "You know, maybe you could help me," Chloe said. "I don't understand why my mom left Mississippi if Elizabeth and her husband were as nice as you say they were. I don't think people run away from great situations. I can't help but wonder why my mom felt the need to leave them and then never speak of them again."

"Look, as I said the other day, you don't know all the details. There is a reason she needed to flee Mississippi, but that's for you and your grandmother to talk about."

"When I was ten, my mom died. For a long time, I wondered what her family was like and where they were. But I finally decided if Mom hadn't thought enough of them to tell me, then something had to be wrong with them. So I stopped thinking about it." *What am I letting myself into?* Chloe walked back to her dresser and picked up a framed picture of her mother.

"If you're still curious, come to Mississippi with an open mind and allow Elizabeth to share all the details with you."

"Oh, I'm still curious. I don't think my dad really wanted me to leave the ranch, but he finally agreed to it. And I'm looking forward to seeing Elizabeth."

"Do you have a flight booked, or would you like my secretary to hook you up?"

"Yes, in fact, I do have a flight booked. I'll be flying into Memphis at three o'clock on Wednesday afternoon. Do I need to rent a car and drive to Bishopville, or is your offer to pick me up still available?"

"The offer stands, but let me check my schedule, if you don't mind. Can you hold a minute?"

"Sure," Chloe said. She looked carefully at her mom's fine features in the old photograph. She had her mom's brunette hair, but that was all. She didn't think she favored either of her parents. Her father was tall, and that was the only thing she took from his genes.

Sam's deep voice came back over the receiver. "Looks like that will be fine. I'll be at the baggage claim at three."

"Okay. I look forward to seeing you again."

"Be safe," Sam said.

The moment Chloe hung up the phone, she rehearsed her conversation, and then she second-guessed herself. She would call Alice and check to see if she had made a fool of herself.

Alice was far ahead of her in the relationship department. She had talked about nothing but the Southern gentleman since Sunday. Given the same amount of time, Alice would have already pulled together every bit of information about Sam there was to be known.

Chloe looked around her bedroom and wondered what the trip would hold for her. She was more excited than she had been in a long time. She knew she couldn't stay but a few days, enough time to see the old lady and wish her a happy birthday.

She picked up her suitcase and went to her closet. What would she pack? How warm was it in Mississippi in May? Would she regret going? Could she get a sense of her mother as a young girl?

Chloe walked to the bedroom window and watched the large snowflakes shift with the wind. A white blanket had covered the ground beneath her. The fir trees dotting the lawn were bent low from the extra weight of the wet snow. She wondered how nature had become her only source of peace. Chloe took a deep breath and hoped Mississippi's beauty could match Wyoming's, but she doubted it was possible.

Chapter 11

Willie B walked into the cafeteria and found Elizabeth eating a bowl of soup surrounded by a group of friends.

"Ms. Lizzie, I've got some great news."

Elizabeth looked up at Willie B. She hadn't heard him at first but noticed the huge smile on his wrinkled face. "Oh Lord, Chloe's coming, isn't she?"

"Yes, ma'am, she is."

"Oh glory." She let out a loud whoop. "I'm so happy I could dance on this one good leg." Elizabeth pushed her wheelchair back away from the table and reached toward Willie B for a hug. They embraced as the others cheered them on. Sam miraculously finding Chloe, and now to know she was coming to Mississippi. She was overwhelmed with joy.

Elizabeth sat back in her wheelchair. "Girls, we have lots of planning to do. I want to have a party right here in the cafeteria or the gym. It will be for my most special friends. I can't wait to show her off. I know she will favor Anna. God rest her soul."

Willie B pulled up a chair. "I'm so happy for you, Ms. Lizzie."

"When will she be here?"

"Sam said she'd be in Memphis at three o'clock on Wednesday. So I'm guessin' she'll be here maybe around six o'clock or so. And, Ms. Lizzie, do you member what day Wednesday is?" Willie B asked.

Elizabeth thought for a few minutes. "It's my birthday. Oh Lordy. This will be the best birthday I've ever had. This doesn't give us much time, does it? We have to get our seventy-year-old bodies moving." Elizabeth looked at the ladies sitting around the table. "Girls, we have a lot to do. We must plan a welcome-home party for my granddaughter. Who wants to help?"

Everyone at the table raised their hand. Smiles were all around. Elizabeth would make this the best party the nursing home had ever seen. Chloe would know she was welcomed in her mother's hometown.

"I will have a list of the things we need and who is in charge of what in a few minutes," Elizabeth said. She turned to a friend and asked if she would locate one of the head nurses to bring her some paper and a pencil, and then she turned to Willie B. "You're a good helper, but you're as old as dirt like me. We need someone with energy and strength. You get Stump on the line. It's time to take advantage of his twenty-year-old body. And you tell him we will need his help."

"Yes, Ms. Lizzie, I'll give him a call. Maybe he'll bring a couple of his friends to set up tables and the heavy stuff." Willie B stood from his chair, walked over to Elizabeth's wheelchair, and placed his hand on her shoulder. "I wasn't supposed to tell you, but me and Sam already planned you a small birthday party. We got a cake ordered and everythin'."

"Willie B, y'all shouldn't have done that. You are so thoughtful."

"You just worry about plannin' for Chloe. I reckon we got the rest taken care of?"

"All right, I'm glad you told me. I'll get some special things for Chloe."

"I'll tell Sam I told you about the party, so he'll know," Willie B said.

An attendant delivered a notebook and a pencil to Elizabeth. She made a short list of items she needed: a banner she wanted to be printed and a grocery list of items that could be easily prepared by old hands. Elizabeth asked another friend to find the number of the local bakery. She couldn't wait to order a beautiful cake for her granddaughter. She decided this celebration would have to make up for all the events they had missed over the years. Elizabeth had longed for this day since she found out her daughter, Anna, had given birth to a baby girl twenty-four years earlier.

Before leaving the cafeteria, everyone at the table had a job. Elizabeth was reaping the fruits of all the years she had labored at her local church helping plan parties and other events for her friends. Now it was Elizabeth's turn to celebrate. All her friends would come together and help her.

"You go through this list, Willie B," Elizabeth said, "and call anyone who hasn't been contacted yet."

"Yes, ma'am."

"And, Willie B, you call Bertha from the church too. Tell her my hair needs a new do first thing on Wednesday morning. Tell her I'll expect her here at 8:00 a.m. I don't care if she has to cancel the mayor's wife's appointment," Elizabeth said. "She owes me big time, and you tell her I'm calling in the marker. I can't have no granddaughter of mine seeing me looking like this." Elizabeth pulled her long gray hair down from the rolled-up ball it was in and then rerolled it. She tucked it in and stuck the bobby pins back in the twisted ball of hair.

"Yes, ma'am."

"And, Willie B, do you have a new wood carving that you could give Chloe as a welcome-to-Mississippi gift?"

"I don't know, Ms. Lizzie. I hadn't had much time this spring to do any carvings. I'll look around when I get home. Surely I got somethin'. I'll call Bertha as soon as I can, but I think I'll do that from home too, if you don't mind. I gots to water my plants."

"Yes, that's fine. And be sure to call those names from the Pines Community. And please go to the trailer and get a few things for me. I have some items that I would love to share with Chloe, like my canned goods and homemade crocheted pieces. She needs something from her grandmother to take back with her when she leaves."

Willie B dropped his head.

"What's the matter? Are you sick?" Elizabeth asked.

"No, ma'am. I just gotta tells you somethin' that I had rather not. You . . . you member I asked if you had everythin' you wanted out of the house trailer?"

"Yes."

"Well, what I didn't tell you was Kimball Mitchell burnt the place to the ground the other day. There ain't nothin' left there but a bunch of melted metal. He burnt the trailer twice."

Elizabeth dropped her head into her hands. "Oh my sweet Jesus. Why in the world do people have to be so evil?"

"I'm sorry," Willie B said. He placed his hand on Elizabeth's shoulder. "I surely didn't want to tell you. I know Kimball's won another round, but you gonna win the victory in the end. 'Member, we figured we'd never find Chloe, and now she's on her way home to Mississippi."

Chapter 12

When *Kimball picked* up Rodger Riverton, an attendant at the Gentle Breeze Assisted-Living Home, Rodger joked about spending Tuesdays with Kimball. Kimball didn't laugh. For the two months Elizabeth had been in the home, Kimball Mitchell had been supplying Rodger Riverton with all the beer he could drink at the local pool hall. Of course, Kimball expected a return on his beer outings, and he finally got one.

Well into Rodger's fifth bottle of beer, he dropped the news that he had been asked to work late on Wednesday night due to a huge party.

Kimball had lowered himself to the pool table to take his winning shot when Rodger finally got the words out of his mouth that the party was in honor of Elizabeth and her long-lost granddaughter. The cue ball hopped into the air and flew off the table as the pool stick drove into the cloth.

Kimball let out a slew of words that could have been uttered by someone who had lost a serious tournament.

"Why haven't you already told me this?" Kimball asked. He marched over to the nursing attendant, grabbed him by the collar with one arm, and shoved the drunken man into the jukebox. "Why do you think I've been paying you? I told you I wanted to know everything about the old bat from the day she moved in."

"Sorry, Mr. Kimball. I meant to tell you."

"What time is the party being held?" Kimball asked as he shoved the end of the pool stick he was holding under the fat man's double chin.

"It's at seven tomorrow night. Maybe a little earlier, whenever the granddaughter gets in from Wyoming."

"Find your own way home," Kimball said as he let go of Rodger. He swung his stick against the side of the pool table. It cracked in half. He dropped the piece in his hand and stormed out the door.

Kimball decided he would give his man in Wyoming a call and see if he had heard anything on his end about Chloe leaving Wyoming.

*****

Wednesday couldn't have come fast enough for Elizabeth who had awakened early that morning. She had done little else since Monday than prepare for Chloe's homecoming. There was still so much to do that she feared she wouldn't have the strength to do it all before the party.

She said her morning prayers, read her Bible, and praised Jesus that she was finally going to meet her granddaughter. Then Elizabeth prayed for Chloe's safety. She knew Kimball would not be happy once he found out.

At 8:00 a.m., her friend from church arrived with all her beauty tools. She gave Elizabeth a manicure and fixed her hair. Elizabeth thanked her friend for coming to the rescue and for making her look as lovely as possible.

She spent the rest of the day ordering people around. Stump and several of his friends had come the night before and set up tables and chairs in the gym. Sam had hired an event planner to take care of the main details, but Elizabeth had managed to exasperate the woman to the point that she fled the building under the cover of running errands.

Willie B came to the gym around noon. Decorations had taken over every table in the place.

"Oh, Willie B, it's about time you got here. We have so much to finish."

"Ms. Lizzie, it's goin' to come together, just you slow down now." He pushed her wheelchair toward the courtyard area. "Let's go outside and rest awhile. It's such a pretty day."

"No, you push me right back in the gym. If I'm not in there, it won't get done right." Elizabeth turned her wheelchair around herself.

"Ain't no need in arguin' with you. Already learnt that," Willie B said as he pushed her back to the food area. "What happened to that party person Sam hired?"

"Oh, she's busy. I don't have time to wait for her. Let's see what else has to be done," Elizabeth said. She pulled the handwritten list from her duster pocket and moved her swollen-knuckle fingers down the paper. "Looks like I've got someone taking care of every detail. Chloe will love it."

"What do you need me to do now?" Willie B asked. "Everyone has been called in the Pines Community."

"I wanted you to go out and cut some beautiful roses from the courtyard. You know the ones I like."

"Didn't that lady bring flowers with her?"

"Yes, but I don't care for daylilies," Elizabeth said.

"Okay, Ms. Lizzie." Willie B turned to leave.

"Don't get any that look like they have seen forty days of bad weather. I want the nicest ones for Chloe."

"Don't I always pick the nicest ones for you?" Willie B asked as he neared the doorway.

He left the room, and Elizabeth found the other flower arrangements the planner had purchased. She blended the six bouquets into three and sat the empty containers aside for the roses from the courtyard.

Elizabeth found some extra ribbon and tied more streamers to several bunches of balloons while she waited for Willie B. Within ten minutes, he came in carrying a large armful of long-stem orange and white roses. Elizabeth told him to place them on the table near the empty vases. She began placing the flowers in groups to make three arrangements.

"Did you find a carved piece that we could give Chloe?"

"No. I had some, but none of them seemed just right."

"Why don't you go work on making her one. Everything is covered here if I can stay on top of things. But don't stay gone long. I might need you for something I can't think of right now."

"Yes, Ms. Lizzie. I'll hurry back."

Elizabeth noticed someone folding napkins. "Oh my," she said. "Go on. I'll see you back here in a while. I have to go show this young'en how to fold napkins."

"Don't be too hard on her," Willie B said as he turned to leave.

Elizabeth pushed her way over to the tables and showed the young lady how she wanted the napkins folded.

Chapter 13

The baggage-claim area was crowded, but Chloe didn't have any trouble spotting Sam. She noticed he looked more at home in his starched white dress shirt and khaki slacks than he had in the new Western boots and jeans she'd last seen him wearing. He was definitely a city boy.

"Chloe." Sam waved as he walked toward her.

"Hello, again," Chloe said as they met.

"How was your trip?"

"Not too bad. I had a long layover in Denver. Not a lot of turbulence. That's always a plus."

"Do you fly often?" Sam asked.

"Not really." Chloe looked at the conveyor as it began to turn. She moved her leather purse from her right shoulder to her left and shifted her feet. She wished she had taken some lessons on small talk from Alice.

"You make those boots look good. I could never manage mine for long, but yours suit you," Sam said as he eyed her square-toed leathers. "In fact, you rock that whole cowgirl look."

"It's not a look. This is who I am. I'm not trying for a fashion statement."

"No, hey, I didn't mean it like it came across. You look nice. That's what I was trying to say."

"I noticed I'm the only one in the entire Memphis airport wearing boots," Chloe said as she looked around the terminal. "I didn't realize how many people wear shorts and flip-flops when they fly."

"We are enjoying a long spring this year. It's very nice outside."

"Great. I'm looking forward to warmer weather," Chloe said then smiled. "Hey, there's my bag." She pointed to a black canvas bag with a pink ribbon tied to the handle.

"Oh, allow me." Sam reached to pick up her suitcase. "This thing's light. You don't pack like most women I know."

"They wouldn't do well in Wyoming then. Besides, I will only be here a few days."

Sam led the way toward the exit.

"I have to get home as soon as possible. I left the ranch in Alice's hands, and I'm a little concerned about that," Chloe said.

"I'm glad you were able to break away for a few days." They exited the building and walked to Sam's Charger. He placed the luggage in the trunk and opened the door for her.

"Sweet. Haven't had a door opened for me in years, maybe ever. I didn't know guys still did that sort of thing."

"You're not calling me old-fashion, are you?"

"No, not really."

Sam closed her door and went around the car. After he turned on the ignition, the radio blasted an old tune over its speakers. "Sorry." Sam turned down the music and drove out of the parking lot.

Chloe said, "I only packed jeans and a couple of thin tops. Hope that wasn't a mistake."

"If you need anything while you're here, let me know. The mall isn't too far from my office. I'll be glad to take you," Sam said. He drove to the exit booth and paid the parking ticket.

"Thanks. I'd like to see a little of Bishopville while I'm here," Chloe said. "But I want to spend every minute I can with Elizabeth."

"Of course. I meant if you needed something." Sam pulled out into the Memphis traffic. "We'll have to stop for some famous barbecue before heading for Bishopville. Is that okay with you?"

Chloe laughed a nervous chuckle. "Yes. I didn't mean we don't have time to eat! It's just that my dad really didn't want me to take these five days away from the ranch. After travel time, I'll only have three days to talk to my grandmother, and I want to use my time wisely."

"Your grandmother is so excited to see you. She isn't going to want you to leave come Sunday. She has waited for this day for a long time. I'm grateful she's still well enough to visit with you."

"I hope I'm not a disappointment."

"You could show up bucktoothed and bowlegged, and she would think you were the Queen of Sheba."

Chloe smiled.

"But trust me, there's nothing to be disappointed in," Sam said.

Chloe glanced at Sam and then out the window. She pushed her thick hair back from the side of her face.

Sam switched on the car's blinker. "We're here. The best BBQ in Memphis! Heck, maybe in the world. You're gonna love this place."

"If you say so."

Sam pulled into a crowded parking lot. The building looked like an old log cabin. A porch stretched the full length of the front. Several sitting areas were arranged under ceiling fans that turned at a steady slow pace. Flowers of all colors lined the walkway leading to the establishment. Trees with dark leaves and huge white blooms adorned the sides of the building.

The smell coming from the restaurant was more than Chloe could take. She could feel saliva building up in her mouth. She might order more than a snack.

Sam opened the door, and Chloe walked in first. A young Southern man greeted them and showed them to a wooden table with a red-and-white-striped runner across the middle. A mason jar full of freshly cut white daisies sat in the center of the table. Chloe couldn't believe the crowd at three thirty in the afternoon. She thought of Alice and the Slick Fork Café back home. It would be lucky to have one person, if that many.

Over the course of the meal, Chloe ate faster than usual and listened to Sam explain about his Southern way of life. She adored the pulled pork, and the coleslaw was the best she'd ever had. As they left the diner, she was thankful for the time they had taken to stop and eat. She had learned a few details about her grandmother and the Pines Community.

A half hour later, there were no signs of the busy multiple-lane roads. They had left them behind as they entered Mississippi. Traffic had funneled down along with the lanes of which there were only two now. Pines lined both sides of the ditches and blocked out the hot Mississippi sun. Chloe was used to the wide-open territory where she could see for miles, but she enjoyed the cozy feel from the rows of pines.

Within two hours, Sam had taken her deep into a world of rolling hills covered in lush green grass. As they drove past a few small towns, Chloe formed her impression of life in rural Mississippi.

She relaxed and enjoyed the scenery as Sam named the plants and trees she pointed out to him. From what she had seen, Mississippi was a beautiful and peaceful place. The cold mountain air was behind her and the warmth of the Southern sun was ahead.

Chapter 14

Kimball Mitchell sat on his back porch shooting at the squirrels that jumped from limb to limb in the pines behind his house. Fortunately for the squirrels, by sunset Kimball had finished off all the beer in his house. He decided he was too drunk to shoot straight, so he leaned his rifle against the porch. Since the night before, he had thought of little else but the party for Elizabeth and Chloe.

Kimball couldn't understand how Sam found Chloe. He knew Sam was very intelligent, but there had been little information as to where Anna and Chloe were living. He had personally seen to it that Elizabeth had been fooled into believing that Anna had been living in Montana at the time of her auto accident.

He remembered the week after Anna's death. He had found an article about a woman the same age as Anna who had been killed in a head-on collision in Helena. He proudly hand delivered the photo of the wreckage to Elizabeth with the news that her only daughter was dead.

As long as Chloe stayed in Wyoming, he hadn't been too concerned. Having her in Mississippi would cause nothing but trouble for him. He was sure of that.

He couldn't understand why Elizabeth was so stubborn. His warnings to the old bat to leave the kid where she was had gone unheeded. He wondered if she didn't believe his threats anymore.

Fifteen years earlier, she hadn't listened, and he taught her a lesson that cost her daughter's life. Looked like he would have to teach her another lesson.

He picked up his rifle and stepped off the porch. He watched as a squirrel ran down a pine tree and stopped to eye him. The squirrel sat motionlessly for a second and then darted to the other side of the tree as if it knew the man had it marked for dead.

Chapter 15

Chloe couldn't decide if the nauseous feeling in her stomach was coming from butterflies or if the barbecue wasn't agreeing with her. Peace had been replaced with an anxiousness she didn't enjoy. Throwing up in Sam's new Charger couldn't happen.

She wanted to meet the grandmother she had only dreamed of as a child, but she was not sure if she could take the emotional drain of getting to know someone who was dying. She tried to take her mind off her nerves.

"I sure appreciate the quick tour while driving through Mississippi today and the barbecue."

"It was my pleasure," Sam said.

Chloe looked out the window toward the west. It was almost seven. Traces of orange-and-red streaks stretched across the horizon. The colors reflected off the pond in front of the assisted-living home as they pulled into the entrance's parking lot.

"I don't think I can do this. My stomach is in knots," Chloe said.

"You'll be fine." Sam parked the Charger in a space marked with a huge bouquet of balloons for the guest of honor. He looked at Chloe and then took her hand that was resting on her thigh.

She didn't resist.

"Listen to me. Your grandmother is going to adore you. Shoot, she already does."

"Thanks Sam." Chloe let go of his hand and turned to open her door. "Oh my gosh, I forgot to pick up a small gift while we were in Memphis. I can't go in without something for her."

"It really isn't necessary, and besides, it's almost time for the party to begin," Sam said as he glanced at his watch.

"I think flowers would be nice," Chloe insisted.

"Okay, look, there is a mini-mart right across the street. Could you get something there?"

"Do they sell flowers?"

"No. But, there's a grocery store about five miles down the road. I think they have a floral section. And it's near the checkout lanes."

"That will have to do then," Chloe said.

Sam placed his hands on the steering wheel and drove out of the drive into the traffic. They were in and out of the grocery store within a few minutes. Sam drove to the assisted-living home while Chloe admired the daylilies in her hands. Sam tried to turn into the parking lot again, but a large Ford pickup cut him off. The driver came to a stop crosswise to the entrance. Sam attempted to pull around the side of the truck, but there wasn't enough room. He stopped the Charger and blew his horn. He waited for the pickup to move out of the way. It didn't.

"What's going on with this guy?" Chloe asked.

"I don't know."

Chloe watched as a lanky man walked around the side of the pickup.

"Sam Green! Get out of the vehicle," a voice rang out.

Sam adjusted his wire-rimmed glasses and squinted to get a closer look. "I think that's Kimball Mitchell." Sam leaned back into his seat. "I heard he showed up at the firm the other day and make a total scene."

Chloe reached into her bag and then remembered the .38 wasn't with her. Rarely was she without her gun, and now she needed it. It was in her gun case almost 1,500 miles away. "You don't have a pistol in the car, do you?" She asked.

"Uh, let me think, NO," Sam answered.

The man yelled again, "Get out of the car!" He raised the rifle toward them.

"We could sure use a gun right now," Chloe said and ducked down into the leather seat.

Sam threw the car into reverse and clipped the front-end of another car as he backed out of the nursing home and onto the highway.

Rounds flew over the car.

"Stay down," Sam yelled as he maneuvered the vehicle until it broke free of the second car. He pushed the accelerator to the floor, and then picked up his phone and dialed 911.

As they drove across town, Sam and Chloe met two patrol cars with lights and sirens blaring.

"I'm going to pull into this bank and wait for a few minutes." We should give the officers time to investigate before we go back," Sam said. He threw the Charger in park and leaned back in the seat. "I can't believe Mitchell actually shot at us."

"What about the residents of the home? Do you think they are okay?" Chloe asked. "Why is that guy so angry at you?" Chloe tried to slow her breathing.

"If it was who I think it was, he is your grandmother's old landlord. And, the way she tells it, he's a killer. I've never fully believed all the stories Elizabeth told me about Mitchell, but I'm starting to."

"If he's that dangerous, why isn't he in jail?"

"It's a long story. I'll let Elizabeth fill you in on all the details. But for now, he's a second-generation adversary of the Lee family." Sam looked at his watch. "Let's wait a couple more minutes."

"Why was he shooting at you?"

"I don't know. I haven't seen him since the last time he was in the same courtroom as me, which was at least two or three years ago. He was being sued for shooting a man's dog. Supposedly it was sitting in the back of a pickup in a restaurant parking lot. Story goes; Kimball thought the dog was barking too much. He got his gun and shot it."

"What happened?" Chloe asked.

"Nothing," Sam said. "The day of the trial, the dog's owner didn't show. No one has seen the man since. The mock investigation into the man's disappearance was just that."

Chloe looked at the yellow daylilies in the vase she was holding. "I can't stand to think something might happen to Elizabeth before I meet her. Maybe we should go back now."

"Yeah, you're right. Maybe everything is okay." Sam pulled the car around and reentered the highway.

Chapter 16

Kimball threw the rifle onto his leather couch. He withdrew a small address book from his desk drawer, picked up the phone, and dialed the long-distance number.

His man in Wyoming answered, "Hello."

"Listen, you find everyone who saw Chloe Parker and Sam Green together while he was in Wyoming. I want them questioned. Find out what he was doing there and anything anyone knows."

"Yes, sir, Mr. Mitchell. I'll get right on it first thing tomorrow morning."

"You'll do it now. Do we understand each other?" Kimball said in a deadly tone.

"Yes, sir, that's what I meant. I'll get right on it."

Kimball hung up the phone. He threw the address book like a baseball into the mirror above his bar and watched as the mirror shattered into a hundred pieces. He wished he had killed the old bat years ago when she reared her ugly head and threatened him with some evidence she had against him. Now there were two heads to crush instead of one.

*****

Chloe saw patrol cars parked everywhere when they drove back into the nursing-home parking lot. She looked in every direction for the black Ford pickup, but it was no longer there. It was almost 8:00

p.m. Her upset stomach had turned into stress in her neck muscles, but this time she was ready to meet her grandmother.

Sam spoke to several officers standing around the nursing-home entrance. He told them he couldn't be a hundred percent sure who the man in the driveway was because he was standing in the shadows. The dark made it impossible to make a positive identification, but he was ninety-nine percent sure it was Kimball Mitchell.

Chloe listened patiently as a policeman told them that the suspect had already driven away when they arrived. Another officer walked over and warned them to be on guard and call 911 if they saw the pickup again.

Sam thanked the officers and then opened the door to the nursing home.

Willie B was standing beside Elizabeth's wheelchair. On the opposite side, a heavyset male attendant held the handle of an oxygen-tank cart.

"Willie B," Sam called to the man.

Willie B turned around and walked over to Sam and Chloe. "Sam, thank goodness, y'all are all right. We heard shootin' outside, but we didn't know if anyone was shot. Elizabeth's just plain worried sick." He looked at her wheelchair. "She had been sittin' near the doorway when the shots rang out. She was looking for y'all to pull up and saw the whole thing."

"Is she okay now?" Sam asked.

"Yes, I think so, but she's on oxygen," Willie B replied.

"Chloe, I'd like for you to meet Willie B. He is your grandmother's most loyal friend and sidekick."

Chloe shook Willie B's hand. "It's great to meet you."

"Well, come on, and let's get you over to Ms. Lizzie—I mean—Elizabeth. She's been waitin' forever to see you," Willie B said.

The three of them walked over to Elizabeth who sat in a wheelchair facing away from the door. The oxygen mask was pressed over Elizabeth's nose. Chloe noticed how frail she looked. Her thin hands looked transparent holding the mask. Elizabeth lifted her head. Chloe saw a sparkle in the blue-gray eyes of her grandmother. She recognized the features of her face as if she'd seen them before, only the features were wrinkled and old. Chloe knew she was looking at the mature version of her mother. She was so happy the elderly lady was still alive.

Elizabeth took the mask from her face and wiped her cheeks. "Oh my dear goodness." Tears formed in her eyes, and she reached her shaking hand toward Chloe.

Chloe bent down and gave her a gentle hug. "Hi, I'm Chloe." Her long, brown hair fell around Elizabeth's knees. She crouched beside the wheelchair. "I am so glad to finally meet you. You look a lot like my mom. I guess, it's correct to say that my mother favored you."

The attendant took Elizabeth's hand holding her mask and pushed it back to her nose. "You should keep this mask on," he insisted.

Elizabeth put her hand back in her lap. "I'm fine." She turned and glared at the attendant. "I tried to tell you that. I want to talk to my granddaughter, now take this away."

The attendant checked her oxygen level. "Fine, but I'll be back in a while to check on you." He walked away with the oxygen cart.

"Oh, I know they think they are helping," Elizabeth said in a weak voice, "but sometimes I want them to leave me alone. I know how I feel, and I don't need that tank." Elizabeth looked at Sam. "How can I ever thank you for bringing my girl to Mississippi?"

"No need, ma'am, I'm glad you finally met each other," Sam said and then grinned.

"I have so much to tell you, but our party has been on hold too long. Did you hear there was a crazy person shooting outside, dear?"

Chloe looked at Sam and grinned. "Yes, ma'am. Glad everyone is okay."

"Yes, me too." Elizabeth sat up as straight as she could. "Let's get things going before everyone falls asleep," Elizabeth said. She let go of Chloe's hands and turned her wheelchair to go out into the crowd of friends.

The police had left, and only a couple hung around the front entrance of the home.

Willie B called out for everyone to gather around. The hall filled with elderly people and staff members. "Everyone, be quiet, Ms. Lizzie's got somethin' to say. Now hush up."

Elizabeth reached for Chloe's hand again. She spoke in as loud a tone as she could. "This here is my granddaughter, Chloe Parker. All the way from Wyoming."

The crowd of people broke out in applause. There were even a couple of whistles from elderly men who could manage them.

"I want you to welcome her and treat her like the princess she is." Elizabeth grew quiet. "It's been a long time since our dear daughter, Anna, was alive and even longer since I last saw her. Morgan would have loved that Chloe is with us tonight. Rest his soul." She looked up at Chloe. "Chloe looks so much like her mother that I can hardly keep from crying." Her voice softened to a whisper. "But the Lord has brought fullness to my heart. So tonight I'm going to rejoice with my family and friends."

Everyone clapped again. Elizabeth asked Chloe to push her to the serving tables. Chloe noticed that there was enough food to feed a hundred people. She wished she hadn't eaten the barbecue.

Chapter 17

A*lice stepped outside* of the calving barn into the night air at ten minutes after nine. She congratulated herself on the last birth of the season, and she was thrilled that she wouldn't have to come back at midnight.

The final cow/calf pair had been turned out with the rest of the pairs into the calving lot next to the barn. Alice was glad Hank had helped her get the psycho pair out the day before. Now the barn was empty, and she could relax.

Alice bent over and stretched her back. All she wanted was to soak her sore muscles in the hot tub.

She headed toward the main house and brushed against a fir tree next to the barn. A noise came from beyond the trees, and she froze. She thought about Chloe telling her of the dangers of hungry bears wandering into the ranch looking for food. Alice turned to go back to the barn and noticed a pickup parked down the road with its lights off.

She struggled to get her feet in motion. She ran into the dark opening of the barn and lunged straight into the arms of a huge, black shadow.

The large man wrapped one arm around her waist and pressed a cloth over her mouth with his other hand.

It happened so fast she didn't even scream. All she could do was struggle to free herself from the man's massive arms.

When Alice awoke, a scarf had been placed over her eyes, her hands tied together with a zip tie, and her mouth taped shut. She labored to free her hands, but the nylon cut into her wrist. As Alice strived to loosen the ties, she banged her head on the side of something very hard. She decided it was too painful to move around, so she relaxed her body. Alice could feel hay underneath her on the ground. She assumed she was still in the barn.

A voice came from Alice's left side. "You're going to tell me everything I want to know. You don't, you're a dead lady."

Alice thrashed about for a few minutes, and then a hand ripped the tape from her lips. The pain was great, but she refused to scream. Alice licked her hurting lips and said, "I don't know anything about anything. What do you want with me?"

The voice spoke slowly and with no emotion, "I want to know everything you know about Sam Green."

"Who the heck is Sam Green?" Alice asked.

"Okay, we are going to try this once more. I want to know everything you know about Sam Green and Chloe Parker. I won't ask a third time." The man placed the edge of a knife's blade to her throat.

Alice attempted to pull her head away from the blade. Her head hit something metal again. She decided she must have been tied to one of the stall panels. "Wait, please, just give me a minute." Alice tried to raise her body enough to get away from the tip of the blade. "Are you talking about Sam, the Southern gentleman from Mississippi?"

"Now we are getting somewhere."

"I don't really know anything about him, except he's gorgeous." The steel of the knife-edge pressed into her throat a little farther. Alice was sure it caused her throat to bleed. She decided this probably wasn't a good time to be a smart mouth. She slowly pulled her head back. "Seriously, Sam only came in the diner where I work a couple of times," Alice said.

"You know Chloe Parker, right?"

"Yes, but she doesn't know Sam either."

"You are friends, and I want you to tell me everything she and Green talked about."

"All I know is she has family in Mississippi, a grandmother. Sam asked her to come down to Mississippi and meet the woman."

"What else?"

"The old lady is dying from cancer. Her name is Elizabeth something or other, and she sent Sam here to find Chloe. Chloe didn't even know she had a grandmother in the South. She was curious about the old lady and wanted to meet her."

"How long is Chloe gone for?" The man asked as he moved the knife blade farther down Alice's throat toward her chest.

"She told me she would only be gone till Sunday. She flew out this morning. Please, that's all I know. Really, that's all I know." Alice struggled again to free her hands.

The cold edge of the knife left her body, and then she felt the blade touch her hands behind her back. Within seconds, her hands snapped apart from each other.

"Leave the blindfold on your eyes, and I won't have to kill you after our little fun is over," the emotionless voice whispered into her ear.

Alice wasn't going to sit there and wait to be attacked. Enough was enough. She decided to make a run for it. She was very athletic and knew she could jump to her feet in a matter of seconds. Chills ran down her neck as his cold hands touched her face. Alice leaned forward slowly. She knew in order to escape his grip, she would have to take the guy by surprise.

Alice waited for the sound of his voice so she could know his exact location. As soon as the man spoke again, she head butted him as hard as she could. She lifted the blindfold off her face. The barn was dark. The man was bent over in front of her holding his head. Alice bolted to her feet and ran through the barn toward the calving lot. She slammed the gate closed behind her and noticed the man running at full speed for her.

She ran along the edge of the fence until she reached the haystacks. She climbed through the wire fence, and as she exited the calving lot, she heard a scream for help in the darkness behind her.

Alice stopped and listened as the screaming rose above the sound of the psycho cow snorting and bellowing. She knew the attacker would be busy fighting for his life while she ran to save hers. She made it to her Jeep and offered up a silent *thank you* for the crazy heifer as she cranked the engine.

She grabbed her cell and dialed 911. She glanced around the haystacks for any sign of the attacker. He was nowhere in sight. Alice threw her Jeep in gear and flew down the driveway. She passed the pickup at the end of the drive and slowed long enough to take a picture of the license plates with her cell phone.

She pulled off the gravel road onto the main highway. She drove the familiar road but kept an eye in the rearview. The only light she saw was the moon above. No one had followed her.

Chapter 18

The worthless man cried like a baby when Kimball tied him to the back of his Ford pickup.

"You sure you don't have anything else to tell me, Rodger?" Kimball asked.

"I don't know anything else to tell you." He pulled on the rope. "Look, Kimball, I don't know what you want. I'm sorry I forgot to tell you about the party."

Kimball scoffed. "Have it your way. He walked around the truck and started the ignition and pulled his pickup forward.

Within a matter of seconds, Rodger screamed and begged Kimball to stop.

Rodger offered up the nursing home's schedule, and he told Kimball that security had been beefed up since the threat. It was an added bonus Kimball hadn't expected. Kimball knew he couldn't leave Rodger alive. And the way he figured it, it would be a righteous kill. Besides, Rodger should have known he was as good as dead the minute his dirty hands were tied to the bumper.

Kimball's country-club friends of Bishopville would scowl upon his midnight activities, but he didn't care. In the dark of night, he could be himself. It was only in the public eye that he had to be sophisticated and polished.

When he drove out of the trees and around the pool hall in the early morning hours, Kimball wasn't the least bit worried about the body being found.

Kimball's cell phone rang. He tried to pull the cell from his pocket but dropped it. The phone fell between his legs. Kimball managed to get one bloody hand on the phone before it stopped ringing.

"Hello," he slurred.

"Mr. Mitchell," the harried voice said, "I had a chat with one of the locals."

"Oh yeah," Kimball said. He heard a series of groans on the other end of the receiver. "What's the matter with you, man?"

A weakened voice spoke, "I almost got trampled to death. That's all. I may need to see a doctor."

"I don't have time for games." Kimball reeled as he drove down the paved road.

"She's . . . Chloe is the old woman's granddaughter. Looks like she is planning on staying a few days. The grandma sent Green here to get her."

"That's all you got? I already know all this," Kimball said.

"You mean I almost got killed by a crazed animal for nothing?"

"Get me something new," Kimball screamed over the phone and hung up. Thirty minutes later, Kimball drove to his ranch, fell out of the truck, and stumbled his way into the house.

Chapter 19

Chloe's cell phone rang Thursday morning around six thirty. "Hello," Chloe said in a sleepy voice.

"I hope I didn't wake you, Chloe," Alice said. "But I couldn't wait any longer to call you."

Chloe sat up in the bed. Her mind immediately went to the horses. "What's the matter?" Chloe asked.

"Everything is okay, but—"

"But what?" Chloe demanded.

"Everything is fine at the ranch, but I do have to tell you what happened to me last night."

Chloe relaxed. "Alice, surely, you didn't call me this early and scare me half to death just to tell me about some man, did you?" She stood and went into the bathroom.

"Yes, yes, I did, but this wasn't the kind of man I usually tell you about. I was attacked last night."

"What?"

"Yeah, I came out of the barn after pushing the last pair out into the calving lot, and next thing I know, I'm tied to the metal stalls with a knife to my throat."

Chloe placed the plastic glass of water she had picked up back on the counter. "At the barn? No way," Chloe said in disbelief.

"Oh yeah, it happened, and I got bruises to prove it." Alice summed up the events of the previous night for Chloe.

"Do you think the psycho got him?" Chloe asked.

"No. Sheriff Bob has been here all morning. He found some blood, but that was all. I tried to take a picture of the man's license plate, but it was too blurred to read."

"Are you really okay?" Chloe asked.

"Yes. Hank is going to stay in the guesthouse until your dad comes home on Saturday."

"You mean Dad didn't get in yesterday afternoon?"

"No, he called and said he wouldn't make it until Saturday. Didn't he call you?"

"Of course not." Chloe turned the water up and drank it. "Does the sheriff have any clues as to who it was that attacked you?"

"No, but he collected some evidence and took it with him."

"Are you sure you are okay?" Chloe asked.

"I told you I am fine. I have a hen-egg-size knot on my forehead, but this hard head of mine might have saved me from being raped or killed," Alice said.

Chloe breathed a sigh of relief. "Did you recognize who it was? Do you think it was the drifter I fired?

"No and no. I'm telling you, I don't have a clue who he was. He was very tall and very well built. His arms were huge."

"I'm so glad you got away from him."

"Yeah, I'm kind of amazed at how I handled the situation," Alice said.

"I'm proud of you too. You call Sheriff Bob if you need help. As we already know, he'll be there in a flash. They both had a chuckle. Stay in after dark and lock the doors." Chloe hung up the phone and then decided to call Sam. He agreed to meet her for breakfast and then run her by the assisted-living home to meet with her grandmother.

Chloe dressed in a pink, cotton shirt and a pair of jeans. She pulled on her boots and thought about how out of place she was. She didn't own a sundress to her name. For that matter, she didn't own any dresses. Chloe thought it might be nice to go with Sam to the local mall since he had offered, but she wanted to visit with Elizabeth more than anything else. She decided to rent a car and go where she pleased.

Chapter 20

A few hours after Kimball had passed out in his living room, he awoke to dried bloodstains on his hands and shirt. He showered and then made himself a pot of coffee. A trip to the nursing home to check out the information he had gotten from the attendant was next on his agenda.

Within an hour, Kimball was sipping water from the nursing home's fountain. He looked around for staff members, but the schedule appeared to be right. Other than the receptionist, the staff was nowhere to be seen.

Kimball glanced at the directory. He knew Elizabeth's room was next to the game room. It was on the first floor and to the right like the attendant had told him. He used his cell to dial the nursing home's number. When the receptionist answered the phone, he went past her desk and down the hallway. Kimball hung up immediately. He heard "Hello, hello" behind him as he continued walking forward.

He slipped into Elizabeth's room and closed the door. Elizabeth was lying on her side facing the window. He quietly walked by the recliner, picked up a pillow, and then moved to the edge of her bed.

She turned toward him. Before Elizabeth could say his full name, he pressed the pillow over her face.

"If you're quiet, I might be able to tell you what I need to say before you smother yourself."

Elizabeth struggled under his weight.

"I said be still, old bat." He felt her body relax. "Good. I told you years ago when we first found her that if she ever stepped foot into this state, she was as good as dead. Do you think I lied?"

Elizabeth threw one of her arms out from under the cover.

"It wasn't enough for your daughter to die. Now, you have all but killed your granddaughter as well. I have to admit, I underestimated you. I should have killed you years ago. I regret not paying more attention—"

The door opened, and Chloe stepped into the room. "What are you doing?" she yelled.

Kimball let go of the pillow and moved in her direction. He grabbed her by the throat and threw her up against the bathroom door. "You're next, little gal. You're next." He held her to the wooden door until her face turned red. Then dropped her to the floor. Kimball knelt beside her choking body. He took a handful of brunette hair and pulled her face near his mouth. "You're next," he whispered. Kimball stood and left the room.

Chapter 21

Chloe struggled to get breath back into her body. She coughed and rubbed her neck. Finally able to rise, she staggered over to Elizabeth. She removed the pillow and hoped she would find her alive.

Elizabeth was unconscious. She looked paler than ever. Chloe bolted for the door and yelled for help. She ran back to Elizabeth and shook her lightly. "Wake up. Please wake up."

A nurse arrived within seconds. Elizabeth had coughed a couple of times and was coming back around. The nurse hooked her to the oxygen machine in the room and buzzed the nurse's station for additional help.

Elizabeth came back to herself. She was very irritable and pushed the nurse away as she tried to help.

The room began to spin, and everything seemed to dim. Chloe knew she needed to sit down before her light-headedness caused her to faint. She took a seat near the door and watched as several nurses poured into the room. One asked if she needed anything.

Chloe refused any help. "I'm fine. Please check on my grandmother."

Elizabeth was pulling at the oxygen mask and yelling for everyone to leave her alone.

Chloe explained to another nurse what had happened. She didn't know him, but she thought he was the same man that had been there the night before. The nurse picked up the phone and dialed 911.

Chloe called Sam on her cell phone. The dizzy feeling was going away, but she was very angry. *How dare this man threaten me and my grandmother? I will find out who he is, and he will pay.*

Elizabeth continued to yell at the staff. "I'm not going any-where. I'm fine."

"Listen, you need to be checked out to make sure there hasn't been any damage to your heart. Did you know the man who was in your room?" Chloe asked.

"Oh, yes. I know him. That was Kimball Mitchell in the flesh."

"I wondered if it might be him."

"It was, and if you hadn't come in, he would have killed me."

A couple of officers walked in the door ahead of the paramedics. "Elizabeth, these fine gentlemen are going to take you to the hospital and get you thoroughly evaluated," the nurse said in a slow tone. "I want you to go with them, and don't give them any grief."

"I don't need to go to no hospital. I'm fine."

Chloe stepped closer to her bed. "I want you to feel your best. Please go with these guys, so they can make sure you are okay. You were almost suffocated. We need to be sure you didn't suffer any heart damage. I'll even go with you. All right?"

"Okay, I'll go for you," Elizabeth said.

"We will meet you at the hospital to question you about the events leading up to this," a detective said.

Chloe nodded at the officer.

Paramedics loaded Elizabeth onto the gurney and into the ambulance. As Chloe stepped into the vehicle, she called Sam a sec-ond time and told him to come to the hospital instead of the nursing home. She was still furious. She decided Kimball Mitchell wouldn't get away with this.

*****

The hospital emergency room was crowded for a Thursday before lunch. Chloe looked around the ER floor and surmised that there were about as many people in the waiting area as in the entire town

of Snow Valley. She listened to babies crying and old people coughing until she wasn't able to take it anymore. She stood from her seat
and walked down the first hall she found. She saw an indoor garden
at the far end and took a stroll in its direction while she dialed Alice's
number.

She shared what had happened and asked Alice for an update
on her attack. She learned no arrest had been made in the case, and
no one had seen the sheriff or his deputy all day.

Chloe saw Sam as he walked into the waiting area. She waved
to get his attention, but he didn't see her. She walked down the hall
to where he was standing at the nurse's station.

"Are you okay?" Sam asked. "I'm sorry it took me so long to get
here."

"It's okay. Let's walk to the garden area. There are way too many
people in this waiting area for me," Chloe said. She led the way,
and Sam followed. "Like I told you over the phone, the doctor said
Elizabeth didn't suffer any real damage, but he wants her to stay overnight for observation. She is asleep right now, and Willie B is with
her, and he refuses to leave her side."

"Is this where he grabbed you?" Sam lightly touched her throat.
"Did you get someone to examine you like I suggested?"

"No, but I told you I was fine. It looks bad, but I'm okay."

"It's a huge bruise. I want you to get someone to take a look at
you before we leave."

"Trust me, it's nothing but bruising. I've had worse from a horse
kick before."

"Not to the throat, I hope?"

"No, but you know what I mean. I'm okay. So let it go." Chloe
pulled her shirt collar up and flipped her hair around her shoulders.
"Kimball Mitchell doesn't know it, but he's done squatted on his own
spurs. Who does that man think he is, coming after an old woman in
a nursing home? And threatening to kill me?"

"He knows he's Kimball Mitchell. The man that has gotten
away with murder, rape, and you name it. One way or another, he
always wins."

"He isn't going to win this time."

"What did you tell the police?" Sam asked when they took a seat in the courtyard.

"I told them what I saw when I came into Elizabeth's room and how he attempted to kill me."

"Did they question Elizabeth at all?"

"No, the hospital staff rushed her into the examination room as soon as we got here. The officers said they would come back later. I'm supposed to make a statement and look at some mug shots. But I asked them to wait until you got here."

"Is anyone from the police force watching Elizabeth's room?" Sam asked and then stood.

"No, and I don't think they understood this man could have killed us." Chloe rubbed her neck.

"We'll see about this," Sam said. He pulled his cell from his suit pocket and dialed the commissioner. "Hello, Frank, this is Sam Green."

Chloe listened as Sam explained the situation. She watched as he walked around waving his arms at an invisible person. She was impressed at how quickly he handled the matter.

Sam hung up the phone. "Okay then, that solves that. He is sending a couple of officers to watch her overnight. He also asked about you."

"Wait, what? No, thank you. I can handle myself."

Sam walked over, touched her chin, and lifted it slightly. "Is this how you handle yourself? If so, I don't want to think about what Kimball Mitchell could do to you if he decided to really hurt you."

Chloe pulled her head away. "Listen, first of all, I didn't expect to be attacked in a nursing home. And for that matter, I didn't expect to see Elizabeth being smothered by a pillow." Chloe stood and picked up her bag.

"Okay, sorry, all I'm saying is I don't want to see you hurt. After all, I'm the one that came to Wyoming and begged you to come down here."

"There's more," Chloe said. "Do you recall my friend, Alice, from the diner?"

Sam nodded.

"Someone assaulted her last night too."

"What?"

"The man told Alice he would kill her if she didn't tell him everything she knew about us."

"Us? Are you serious?"

"Yes, I am. Alice was very shaken by the whole thing." Chloe threw her bag over her shoulder.

"Wow."

"That's not all. No one has seen Sheriff Bob and his deputy all day. This whole thing is strange. Why does Kimball want to kill Elizabeth, and why me? I don't even know the man."

"Elizabeth needs to tell you the details, but it has to do with your grandfather's death about forty years ago."

"I don't understand any of this." Chloe walked down the hall. "I'm going to check on Elizabeth again."

"I'll drive you back to your hotel after we see Elizabeth."

"I wonder if she's awake. Do you think Willie B will stay the entire night?"

"It's very likely."

Chapter 22

The phone rang early Friday morning before Kimball finished his coffee. He placed his mug on the kitchen table and walked into the living room, picked up the phone, and answered in his usual rude voice. "What?"

"It's me. I got the sheriff to loosen up. The beef head talked when I held a gun to his skull."

"Go on," Kimball said as he walked over to the television and turned on the weather channel.

"Turns out your Sam Green isn't so squeaky clean. The sheriff had Green as a guest in his jail while he was in Wyoming. Green was trying to convince the sheriff of his innocence of another matter when he let it slip to the sheriff that he was there to persuade Chloe Parker to come to Mississippi. The sheriff said it had something to do with proving an old murder case in Green's hometown."

"I hope you are taking care of all this discreetly. My name better not come up in any of this. Do you understand me?"

"I was."

"Was? What does that mean?" Kimball asked.

"I didn't have any trouble out of the girl. I held a knife to her throat, and I think she peed herself 'cause she was all too happy to tell me what she knew." The associate chuckled. "Of course, she got me back with that crazy cow of hers."

"I hear a 'but' coming." Mitchell took the cordless phone with him into the kitchen and picked up his coffee mug.

"I had the sheriff under control. Okay? He was tied to a chair and spilling his guts about this dude he had arrested being some fancy lawyer from the Deep South. The sheriff was even laughing about holding him overnight. I was about to untie the sheriff when, out of nowhere, the deputy came in early. I mean, who does that? Nobody I know comes to the job early."

"What'd you do?" Kimball asked and sat his coffee mug on the counter.

"He—the deputy—jumped me. I had no choice. We got into a fight, and the next thing I knew, the deputy was falling to the floor. My knife struck him somehow. And the sheriff, well, he came at me when he saw the deputy fall. He picked the chair right off the floor and lunged at me. I know you said not to stir things up around here, but it happened."

"You idiot." Mitchell slammed his fist on the kitchen counter.

"Kimball, Mr. Mitchell. I'm sorry, but don't worry. I took care of the bodies, and they won't be found anytime soon."

"Is that supposed to make everything fine and dandy?" Mitchell threw his mug into the sink. The handle broke off the side and flew into the air missing Mitchell's head by an inch. He ignored it as it hit the kitchen floor and broke again. He walked around the kitchen island and went back into the living room.

"No, sir. I know I screwed up," the man said.

"You get down here to Mississippi before someone pins that on you. I've got a job for you anyway. Pack a few things, too, 'cause you might not be going back to Wyoming."

"Yes, sir."

"Catch the first flight out to Memphis. Give me a call when you arrive, and I'll pick you up if there's enough time before I go to the country club. If not, you can wait till my award ceremony is over, and I'll get you then." Kimball slammed the phone back onto the receiver.

Kimball had no plans to allow some little gal from Wyoming to mess up his life. He had worked too hard to create the façade of a rich rancher who cared about the poor. By accepting his latest public praise for Farmer of the Year, another piece of his cover would fall into place.

He sat on his leather couch and threw his feet onto the oak coffee table. He thought about the morning and all the mistakes that had been made recently. Why had he been so stupid? His father had told him many times that he was his own worst enemy. He scolded himself for going to the nursing home in broad daylight the day before. At least most of the police where still on his side, but he couldn't slip up too many times. If the wrong officer caught him, it would be hard to escape his fate.

He knew he would have to do the job right when it came time for the old bat to die. No halfway mess like his associate was pulling. Elizabeth's death would look accidental, and he would purge her from his life forever. Then he would take care of the girl.

Chapter 23

The Bishopville Police Department covered an entire city block. Chloe thought it had to be ten times bigger than the one in Snow Valley. The building set back a way from the main street, and a courtyard ran around the entire block. It appeared the city had spared no expense on the structure and landscaping. As they walked along the sidewalk, Chloe thought it looked more like a stroll through a city park than a police station.

"Things sure look nice around here," Chloe said. "Even the dew in the grass looks like it's been perfectly sprayed on."

"Well, we do have some offices around town that have their grass tinted."

"What?"

"You heard right." Sam looked at Chloe and grinned.

"You're joking."

Sam held the door and allowed Chloe to enter the building first.

She noticed the security measures surrounding the entrance of the building. It seemed the police were serious about keeping themselves safe.

Shortly after entering the building, Chloe and Sam walked into an interview room that was tiny compared to the rest of the rooms they had passed in the complex.

Two officers walked into the room directly behind them. The shorter, round-face guy asked how she was feeling and if she had thought any more about police protection.

The other officer took her statement and asked her to look through a few mug shots to see if she could identify her attacker.

An hour passed, then another thirty minutes. Finally, she turned the page, and there was the man that held her up against the wooden bathroom door. The anger in her voice caused her to speak louder than she really meant. "That's him. I'm one hundred percent sure." She pointed to a salt-and-pepper-haired man with small scars on his face.

"That's Kimball Mitchell," Sam said.

One officer asked if she was absolutely positive. Another one wrote something on his notepad. They were both very low-key about the entire thing.

Chloe didn't feel a sense of urgency in the place. She planned to ask Sam if this was the norm for law-enforcement officers in Bishopville. Sheriff Bob would have been out the door in a flash. Maybe these men just looked like they didn't care.

"Okay, we're done for now, Ms. Parker. Thank you for coming down to the station."

"That's it?" Chloe asked.

"Yes, ma'am," the taller of the two men replied. "We've got your statement, and we'll take it from here."

Sam stood and shook hands with both men. "Okay, well, thanks for your help. We'll get out of your way and let you get back to work."

Chloe stood. "Yeah. Thanks."

Within minutes, they were in Sam's Charger. He took the usual route back to Chloe's hotel. Chloe squinted in the morning sun and wished she'd brought her sunglasses along. She was glad Sam had offered to take her to the police department, but Chloe knew she might have been more vocal if he hadn't been there.

"Sam?" She asked.

"Yeah?"

"Are the police always so laid back around here? I really got the feeling they didn't seem to take this whole thing seriously."

"They're not too happy that you pointed out Kimball Mitchell. Like I said before, Elizabeth thinks he should have been in jail over thirty years ago, and the key was flushed down the toilet. But it's hard for some people to see him for what he really is."

"Are people that trusting here?"

"Mitchell is a deacon in the largest church in town, he's on the local school board, and he's a well-respected businessman. He knows how to work a public image."

"Does he have the Oscar in his living room?"

Sam drove the Charger to the front of the hotel, parked the car, and shut off the engine. "The year your grandmother's house was destroyed by a tornado, Kimball's father, Corbin Mitchell, put Elizabeth and your mom up in a little run-down trailer on his property. The local news made the Mitchell family out to be heroes to the poor and widowed. That began an image that didn't end with Corbin."

"You're kidding. Can't people see the real man?"

"They see what they want to see. Mitchell makes it appear he is giving away when really, in the end, he is taking."

"I need a weapon," Chloe said without hesitation. "It's not safe to be here without some kind of protection."

"I can get the cops over here anytime you want me to."

"From what I saw today, I'm not too impressed with the police. Don't bother."

"You know, you are welcome to stay at my place until you leave on Sunday."

Chloe turned and looked at Sam. He wasn't trying to seduce her. Sam's eyes told her he was concerned and wanted to protect her.

"Thanks, but I'm not as naïve as some people around here appear to be. And, Sam, come on. I know you gotta' have a couple of guns. Can't you just trust me to keep one till I go home?"

"I didn't invite you to Mississippi to end up in jail like I did in your hometown." Sam chuckled. "You don't have to only rely on a gun for protection. You've got me, and I really do have plenty of room. You won't even know I'm in the house if you don't want to know. Please at least think about it."

"Okay, but I think I'll be fine here. This hotel is really first class." Chloe opened the door and thanked him for going with her. She told him she would rent a car, and he wouldn't have to chauffeur her around the rest of her stay in Bishopville. Chloe planned to visit Elizabeth as soon as the hospital released her. She did not tell Sam she planned to find a gun in the meantime.

*****

One of Kimball's men on the Bishopville Police Department called and gave him a heads-up on Chloe's visit to BPD that morning. The cop told Kimball he had written down a fake description. He also warned Kimball that Chloe had picked out his mug shot from the DUI he had on file.

Before the cop hung up, he told Kimball he would expect some extra cash for his effort.

Kimball agreed.

Chapter **24**

The GPS on Chloe's rental had gotten her around town, but she wondered if it would find a dirt road in the middle of nowhere; at the least, that's the way Willie B described his plot of ground when Chloe spoke to him on the phone.

The next turn was off the pavement onto a gravel road. *This has to be the place.* She pulled the rental into the short driveway. The plank house had little or no paint and was weathered to the point of serious repair. There was a makeshift shop added to the end. It consisted of pallets stacked vertically one on top of the other. The roof was mostly tin. Rusty iron items, which looked as if they belonged in an old-farm museum, held up the walls of the shop.

On the large veranda sat a rocking chair and a small wooden table. Other than that, there was no furniture. Instead, the porch was littered with tomato plants and a variety of vegetables planted in pots.

The place was rustic but had a charm that she couldn't explain. She loved the galvanized containers that hung from the nails driven directly into the front of the house. Chloe hoped it was Willie B's place as she climbed the first step of the four-step stairs. The mailbox had been barely hanging on the post, and she hadn't seen a name or number to identify the residents anywhere.

Chloe knocked on the screen door and backed away in case someone other than Willie B opened the door.

The screen opened and a very large African American guy in his early twenties stepped out onto the porch.

"Uh-oh, I think I'm at the wrong address," Chloe said quickly. She turned to walk off the porch.

"Let me guess, you looking for Willie B?" The young man asked.

"Yes, yes, I am."

"You got the right place. Hold on. He's back here somewheres." The man stuck his head back in the door and yelled for Willie B. He let go of the screen and passed in front of Chloe. He walked to the edge of the porch and took a seat.

Chloe hoped he didn't hear her gulp as he walked by. His shirtless overalls showed his massive muscles. Chloe wondered what he did for a living but wasn't about to ask.

Willie B came to the door. "Well, I knew my nose was itchin' for some reason. I didn't figure you'd ever find us in the middle of nowhere?"

"You know I'm from Wyoming. I can hunt down anything, and I had my GPS."

Willie B laughed wholeheartedly. He asked if she wanted to come in for a while. Chloe refused and said the porch was fine.

She explained that for most of the year she was cold, and she had been thoroughly enjoying the warm air of Mississippi. She accepted Willie B's offer of sweet tea and watched him walk back in the house.

The young man yelled for Willie B to bring him a glass while he was at it.

Chloe looked out across a huge field directly in front of Willie B's place. "What do you grow here?" she asked, trying to make small talk.

"That, there's a cotton field," the man said.

"I'm Chloe, by the way." She reached her hand out and offered a handshake.

His huge, black hand swallowed hers. "Howdy, I'm Stump."

"Nice to meet you. Stump, was it?"

"Yeah, I know. I get that all the time," he said then grinned.

Willie B returned with the tea and passed it around. "Here, have a seat." He pointed to the rocking chair.

"No, you sit there. I'll sit here by Stump." She sat on the remaining end of the step.

"I see y'all met then," Willie B said.

"Yes, we have," Chloe said.

Stump grunted as he finished off his glass of tea.

"Listen, Willie B, about the events that happened yesterday at the nursing home. I want to thank you for staying the night with Elizabeth. I know hospitals are always uncomfortable."

"That man should have been stopped years ago. I'm sorry you had to ever meet him. Pure evil."

"I would agree. He told me I was next on his list. I believe he plans to kill me for some reason."

"I can't believe he hasn't already killed your grandmother," Willie B said as he rocked slowly in the rocking chair. "I think he didn't expect her to be as strong as she is. I bet he thinks of you the same way, and I can tell, you got a lot of Ms. Lizzie in you. He'll have a hard time gettin' rid of either of you."

"You're right, Willie B. I'm too stubborn to sit back and let someone try to kill me. That's why I'm here."

Willie B turned his glass up, finished off his tea, and sat it on the wooden table. "You want some more tea?"

"No, thanks," Chloe said as she placed her glass on the porch.

Stump spoke up. "I'll kill 'em if you want me's too."

"No, that's okay, Stump," Chloe said quickly. "I know you could do that in a heartbeat, but I can handle this. So I'm wondering if you have a weapon laying around that I could use for protection. I feel naked being down here without my gun." She thought about what she said and then blushed when Stump eyed her.

"Yeah, I've got a couple of guns," Willie B said. "But I ain't so sure 'bout handin' them out to you, little lady. I don't want you gettin' shot with one of my guns."

"Trust me. I know how to handle a weapon. Better than most men." She looked at Stump and said, "No offense."

"Yeah," Stump said.

"I'll have to think about this, Ms. Chloe. I don't know. Did you talk to Sam about this?"

"He's not the one being threatened," Chloe said.

"I just don't know. What would Ms. Lizzie think?"

"I promise to get it back to you early Sunday morning before I fly out. I won't say a word to anyone. It will be between the three of us."

Stump piped back in, "Go ahead, Grandpa. You know Mitchell is crazy."

Willie B got up and collected the tea glasses. "I'll be right back." He disappeared into the house.

Chloe figured that was the end of the conversation. She knew she didn't have time to wait for a purchased gun to come through. Sam had already said no, and now it looked like Willie B wasn't taking her seriously. Maybe she had read him wrong. She could try and persuade Sam to see things her way one more time.

The door opened, and Willie B was holding Stump's refilled tea glass and a Colt .45. "This is my only revolver. I've had it a long time. Bought it, oh, back around 1978. That's the year your grandfather died. Got me a rifle, too, that same year. This one is too much for you, though, little lady. I hate not to help you out, but you can't handle this."

"I'll make you a deal. You let me shoot at any target, and if I miss, I'll walk away. No feelings hurt. But if I make the shot, you'll let me use your .45 till I'm out of here. Deal?"

"Come on, Grandpa. See what she's got."

Willie B scratched his half-day-old beard. "I don't know. I doubt you can even hold this thing. But let's go around back, and I'll see what kind of target I've got for you."

Stump was the first one off the porch.

A small pond and several willow trees filled one side of the back-yard. An old fence was falling down and a partial henhouse stood in the corner. A huge garden rested on the other side of the property.

Willie B and Stump looked in every direction. Neither suggested anything.

95

Chloe noticed the remnants of an old scarecrow in the garden to the far side of the house. It had one hand left and part of an old straw hat covering its burlap face. Only one button clung to its eye socket. Most of the stuffing was long gone.

"Hey, what about that?" She pointed the gun barrel in the direction of the scarecrow.

Stump shook his head. "Man, that's too far away. You'll never hit it from here."

"I'll take out its last eye," Chloe said.

"Ms. Chloe, that's a button. You think you goin' hit that button from here?" Willie B asked.

"I know I can."

"Okay. Let's see it," Stump said.

Chloe stepped into the direct line of the scarecrow. She didn't hesitate. Within a split second, the scarecrow had a hole where its eye was once sewn in.

Willie B and Stump stared at the partial head of the straw man. Most of it was now missing.

"What did I tell you?" Chloe asked. She smiled bigger than she had in a long time.

Stump patted her on the shoulder. "Dang."

Chloe almost fell over. "Would you like for me to shoot anything else while I'm here?"

"Lunch," Stump said and chuckled. His generous grin revealed that most of his teeth were missing. A fact Chloe hadn't noticed before.

They all had a good laugh, and Chloe promised to use the weapon wisely. She swore not to tell a soul where she had gotten it or that she even had it.

As Chloe pulled out of the drive, she realized the weapon next to her made her feel like she was more in control of the situation. As she drove down the Mississippi back roads, a sense of peace settled in her soul. Chloe knew it wasn't just the .45 resting on her front seat that brought the feeling. It was more of an awareness of being where she belonged. But that was crazy.

Chapter 25

The drive to the country had been a productive one. Chloe had what she needed to protect Elizabeth and herself. She would leave the Colt in the glove compartment. At least it would be within reach if she needed it. She drove by a florist and picked up a bouquet of fresh daisies. They reminded her of the barbeque place where Sam and she had eaten together on her arrival. Chloe realized it was well past lunchtime, so she pulled into a fast-food restaurant and ordered takeout.

Fifteen minutes later, she walked into Elizabeth's peaceful room in the nursing home.

Her grandmother's eyes brightened when she saw Chloe coming through the doorway. "Oh goodness, I'm so glad you're here," Elizabeth said.

Chloe placed her lunch on the round table in the kitchenette. She looked around the small room. A beautiful wood carving hung over the table, and one straight-back chair sat near the wall. The kitchenette was the tiniest Chloe had ever seen. There was a small sink with a cupboard on each side. A tiny fridge rested under the countertop. A seating area was near Elizabeth's bed. Chloe walked around a small coffee table and over to her grandmother.

"How are you, Grandmother?" Chloe bent down and gave her a light hug.

"I'm doing fine, just fine. I couldn't get those awful people to discharge me early this morning. I wanted to be here for breakfast, but they made me wait and wait. Once you get in the hospital, you have to die to get out."

"We might not have enjoyed breakfast together but look what's on your tray. Your lunch is ready," Chloe said. "I have mine. So we can eat together now."

"Did you buy those daisies?" Elizabeth asked as she pointed to the vase Chloe was holding. "You didn't have to do that. I just loved the daylilies you brought me the night before last, but daisies are some of my favorites. My Morgan brought me daisies all the time."

"I'm glad I picked them then," Chloe said as she sat the vase of daisies on the coffee table.

"You shouldn't have spent so much on me. You might need your money to get back home on."

"My ticket is paid for, and you shouldn't worry about me. Besides, I have never been able to buy you flowers. So don't be surprised if I buy you more before I leave Sunday."

"Seeing you here in my room makes me so happy. I have so much to say," Elizabeth said.

"Let's eat. Then we will spend the rest of the day talking if you want to." Chloe pushed Elizabeth's food tray over to her, and they both prepared to eat lunch. She took a seat on the small couch, withdrew her hamburger, and took a bite. She looked up at Elizabeth who was saying grace over her meal. Chloe stopped chewing and placed the sandwich back in her lap on top of the take-out bag. She hadn't been raised to say grace but knew others were. So Chloe respected her grandmother and hoped Elizabeth wouldn't notice the bite of food in her mouth.

After they finished the meal, Chloe cleaned the area and pulled her chair over to Elizabeth's bedside. She took a folding chair nearest the large picture window and positioned it so the sun would be at her back.

"There is a pencil and a notebook I keep in the nightstand to write my thoughts on sometimes," Elizabeth said.

"Do you need it?" Chloe didn't know if she should say Elizabeth, Grandmother, or Grandma, or what.

"You might want to jot down some stuff from the old days. I didn't know if you were interested in the history of our family or not," Elizabeth said. She looked at Morgan's picture near the flowers.

Chloe caught the glance and rose to get the pencil and paper from the nightstand. She flipped the pages and saw Elizabeth's hand-written notes throughout the notebook. There were recipes and lists of all kinds; birthdays of people Chloe would never know, wedding dates, deaths, and many other things. She found a blank page about halfway through and folded the notebook back.

"I don't know where to begin. There's so much information I want to tell you. I don't know how much you want to know either, I guess."

"You tell me whatever you want to share 'cause I don't know anything except that my mom was born in Mississippi, my grandfather died years ago, and my mother was your only child."

"That will be a good place to start," Elizabeth broke in. "You see, I had two miscarriages before your mother was born. Morgan and I waited eight years for her. That year started out to be the best year of my life. But that happiness didn't last long. When little Anna turned three, your grandfather found out something that changed the course of all our lives, even yours."

"Really?" Chloe looked puzzled.

"We had plenty back then. Land, yes, lots of it. We raised cotton, timber, cattle, you name it. Your grandfather knew how to manage his affairs. We saw many years of increase before that dreadful year in the late seventies. It seemed like after that, life changed forever."

Chloe wrote down "late seventies" in the notebook. "What happened that year? What did your husband, I mean, my grandfather find out?"

"We'll get to that, dear. Can you bring me some more tea? My throat is so dry, and I want to talk."

"Sure, I'll be right back." Chloe walked down to the nurse's station and got another glass of tea for both of them. She spoke to a few residents that lined the halls in their wheelchairs as she returned to Elizabeth's room.

"Here you go." She handed Elizabeth the glass and took her seat.

Elizabeth took a sip and continued to talk. "Your mom was my little angel. All those other babies I didn't carry to full term are heaven's angels now, but God let me be with Anna for a little while before she left Mississippi."

"Why did she leave? Sounds like she was loved," Chloe said.

"There's a lot of the story that you don't know yet."

Chloe leaned back in her chair, crossed her long legs, and waited for more.

"Your grandfather learned something about Corbin Mitchell, our next-door neighbor, that year that eventually got Morgan killed. Your mom was a sick little girl, and we needed Morgan's strength and his wisdom. It was so cruel for the Mitchells to take him away from us."

"I know about losing someone. I wish I could have known my mom longer." Chloe took a sip of tea and then sat her glass on the dresser. "It's hard to lose someone you love."

"Your mom was sixteen the last time I ever saw her." Elizabeth's voice choked up. "We fought over things that were out of our control, and when the rodeo circuit left town, she hitched a ride with a cattle hauler all the way to Wyoming. I think she met your dad the day she arrived there."

"Why didn't you go after her? Make her come home?"

"I didn't know where she was."

"But you just said she was in Wyoming."

"Yes, but I didn't know that until a few years after she had left. Believe me, I thought of her every day. I called every family member I ever knew that lived outside of Bishopville. No one knew where she had gone. She just disappeared. I even accused Kimball of having something to do with her disappearance."

"How do you know she left with the rodeo circuit then?" Chloe picked up her tea glass and sipped as she listened to Elizabeth.

"She wrote me a letter and sent me a picture about five years after she had settled in Wyoming. The letter is in my Bible if you want to look at it. It's one of two that I have from her after she left home."

Chloe stood and placed her glass on the coffee table. She picked up the worn Bible and flipped through the pages until she came across the envelope.

"You're in the picture too. You were about six or seven in that photo," Elizabeth said.

"I am?" Chloe asked. She opened the envelope and found the one-page letter and photograph. She looked at the picture first and recognized it right away. Her family had gone to Yellowstone that weekend. Her dad took the photo while they were eating ice cream at the general store. Chloe wondered how she had forgotten about that weekend trip. It was a special time. She had turned seven, and out of the blue, her folks picked her up early from school. They surprised her with a camping trip to Yellowstone for her birthday.

"You recognize that picture, dear?" Elizabeth asked.

"Yes, it was taken on my seventh birthday. Do you mind if I read the letter?" Chloe asked.

"No, I don't mind. It's short, but every word was worth millions to me. It answered so many questions that I had carried. I knew my little girl was alive and well."

Chloe opened the letter carefully. For the second time within a week, she saw her mother's handwriting. She sat down on the end of Elizabeth's bed and took a deep breath. She didn't have any letters from her mom of her own, only some birthday cards. She looked at the words, and through blurred vision, she read the letter.

Dear Mom,

I have written you hundreds of times over the past eight years. More than anything, I allowed fear to keep me from mailing them. I didn't want the Mitchells to find me, and I didn't want them to know about the child.

I have kept her away from Mississippi and their evil clutches because I fear what could happen to her.

I know it doesn't matter so much now, but I wanted you to know that I left with the rodeo circuit that was in town that horrible weekend. As you know, I always loved the rodeo, and I figured I'd be happy in a place that had a rodeo every night of the summer. A cattle hauler was on his way to Cody, and I asked if I could go with him. I figured he couldn't hurt me any more than I had already been hurt. He was a perfect gentleman.

Today, I have a sweet husband. He truly loves me. The little girl in the photo is my daughter, Chloe. She turned seven the day this picture was taken. It is my hope that someday you will meet her.

I don't blame you for anything that happened. I know I said I did the last night we were together, but I don't. It wasn't your fault.

I love you, Mom. I hope we can be together someday. Until then I want to keep Chloe safe from the evil in Bishopville.

Love always,
Anna

Chloe dropped the letter to her legs. She was speechless. After a few minutes of silence, Chloe spoke up. "What did my mother mean in the letter, Elizabeth? What evil was she talking about?"

She hadn't noticed the soft snoring sounds coming from her grandmother. With the picture in her hand, she could easily see the resemblance in all three of them. Even at the age of seventy-eight and cancer ridden, Elizabeth still had the look of a well-kept lady. Except for the gray in her grandmother's hair, the texture and waviness were exactly like her mom's. Chloe rose from the bed and sat on the chair and reread the letter several times before replacing it in the Bible.

Chapter 26

The smell of the flowers in the courtyard made Chloe feel at home. Her mother's words hung in her head like darts hanging from a dartboard, halfway in and halfway out. She wished she knew what evil her mom spoke of and who had hurt her.

The fresh air felt good. Elizabeth's room had seemed a little too stuffy. Chloe was happy to see the two officers still posted at Elizabeth's door when she left the room. She pulled up the weather channel on her cell phone and checked Snow Valley's forecast. It read 52 ºF with winds of 40 mph. She decided she had made the right choice to come to the South. It was 93 ºF in the courtyard, and Chloe was loving the sun.

She called her dad first and checked in. She updated him on her meeting with Elizabeth. He made no apology for not keeping yet another promise. Chloe realized that the more she asked her father about her mother's past, the less he seemed to know about her. He didn't know anything as to why her mother had been so frightened that she never wanted to return to Mississippi. Mostly all he knew was Anna never wanted to talk about any life before she arrived in Wyoming.

She called Alice to clear her head.

"Hey, girl," Alice said. "Can I come to Mississippi and get warm? Winter just won't go away. It can't make up its mind if it's going or coming."

"Come on down. I'm sitting out in the hot sunshine. I'm actually sweating. If I had a bathing suit with me, I think I would be wearing it." Chloe looked around and noticed two elderly men sitting under a shade tree staring at her. "On second thought, I'm not on a beach."

"You don't want to send any of the residents into cardiac arrest." They both laughed.

"I spoke to my dad this morning. He told me Hank talked his son into coming up and helping you out for a while. Guess you're excited to hear that."

"You know it," Alice said. "I've seen him in town before. News around the diner has it that he's modeled for a western magazine a few years ago."

"Great, I can see it now. The cows will starve while you are making out. Don't forget you have a job to do."

"I know you're counting on me. I got this!"

"Did I ever tell you how my mom and dad meet?"

"No," Alice said.

"Dad told me she had been in Cody for just a few hours when he met her," Chloe replied.

"You're kidding."

"It was fate that they even met at all. He had lost his wallet in a truck-stop parking lot where he purchased fuel. She was at the station when he came back to look for it. Mom made him a deal that if she helped him find the wallet, he would let her come home with him and do odd jobs on his father's ranch until she could find a real job. When Dad agreed, she handed him the wallet. Mom had been hiding it in her back pocket the entire time."

"That's neat," Alice said. "It was their destiny."

"I think Dad found life easier by sort of checking out after Mom died. In the beginning, it was too hard for him to talk about her without getting emotional. He's always been so strong. Guess her death was more than he could handle."

"I guess," Alice said, "it probably didn't make it any easier since you looked so much like her."

"Yeah. Elizabeth says the same thing." Chloe took in a long breath. "I'm really worried about her. Not only does she have cancer, but there's a real loser in this town who can't seem to wait for her to die naturally. I think the entire police force is afraid to lock him up. I can't believe I'm about to say this, but we need Sheriff Bob down here," Chloe said.

"Oh, bad news about Sheriff Bob and the deputy. They still haven't turned up."

"Really? Keep me up to date."

"Will do. And, Chloe, please be careful down there. Do what you need to do and get home soon."

"I feel so peaceful here, even after the attack yesterday. I slept like a rock last night. I haven't done that in years."

Chloe hung up her cell. She wished she had packed shorts. Her jeans were sticking to her legs from the humidity, and as much as she loved her boots, they had to go.

Five minutes later, Chloe checked in on her grandmother and found her still sleeping. She decided to take a drive over to Sam's office to see if he was in. If he wasn't busy, maybe she could get another quick tour around the old Civil War town. She only had one more day in Bishopville, and didn't want to waste a minute.

Chapter 27

The antebellum homes were beautiful. They could have stood on their own grandeur, even in the middle of the high plains without all the gorgeous trees surrounding them. Chloe had seen pictures of the Southern mansions but never imaged how glorious they were.

The tree-lined streets were in full bloom, and flowers poured from the tops of huge planters that lined Main Street. Chloe watched as butterflies of all colors floated from one flowerpot to the next.

She enjoyed the four seasons of the Northwest, but the problem was one season was boss to the other three. Spring got the short end of the stick every year in Snow Valley, Wyoming.

Chloe was happy to take in the sensory overload when she realized that Sam had been staring at her while she was staring at nature. "Sorry, got lost in all the exquisite homes around me," she said as she pulled her brunette hair up into a twist. "It's easy to get lost in all this."

"I agree," Sam said.

For the first time, Chloe noticed Sam's nose crinkled when he smiled really big. "I see how you are. You say you're a lawyer, but you're really one of those good ole Southern flirts, huh?"

"No, I don't flirt."

"Oh really." She let her hair down and shifted her long legs in the front seat of his Charger. "Why don't you drive me by Elizabeth's old homeplace? I'd like to see where my mom grew up. It could take your mind off not flirting," Chloe said then grinned at her admirer.

"That's not such a good idea," Sam said. He placed both hands on the steering wheel.

"And why not? I would like to see as much as I can while I'm here. Who knows if I'll ever be back this way again?"

"Well, that would be a total bummer," Sam said. "But it's not a good idea to go to the homestead because Morgan and Elizabeth's land joins Corbin Mitchell's land.

"So?"

"So don't you remember being shot at and almost strangled to death by Kimball Mitchell? He still owns all that land, and he's been known to have guys ride the perimeter of his property on horseback with the sole purpose of looking for and shooting trespassers."

"I really want to see where my mother grew up. I've always wondered about her life. Besides, we don't have to go to the Mitchells' property."

"No, I don't think we should go."

"Oh, come on." Chloe leaned in a little closer to Sam. "It's not like we would be going in a tractor. Don't you believe in the power of this Charger? We can outrun any horse, right?" Chloe pleaded.

"I don't know," Sam said. He studied the steering wheel for a few minutes. "I guess we can go a little ways down the road, but—."

"Great." Chloe moved back to her side of the car, strapped, and buckled her seat belt. "I'm ready, let's go."

"Hold on," Sam said. "We'll go near the Pines Community, but we aren't going all the way to the Mitchells' ranch. And if I see his black Ford again, we are getting out of there."

"Okay, that's fine."

Sam drove out of town, and after a few twists and turns, he was on a gravel road not far from Willie B's place. Chloe didn't say anything about the trip she had made alone.

The area smelled of freshly plowed fields, and dust followed behind tractors far off in the distance. Clusters of massive trees blocked most of the sun as they drove back into a world that seemed to be guarded by pines protecting what lay beyond. Chloe marveled at the magnificent antebellum homes, minutes behind them, and the guarded farming country ahead. She wondered if Mississippians were as diverse as their land.

They passed through the thick forest. Then the road opened back into a clearing revealing another field off in the distance. Soon the road became lined with sparse pines that caused the sun to blink off and on like the turning lights of a disco ball.

"This community is known as the Pines Community," Sam said. He hadn't spoken much since they had turned off onto the gravel road.

"I can certainly see why they call it that. How much farther?"

"Actually, this is the area where your mom and family used to live. The Lee family has been in the Pines Community since I can recall." After a few more miles, Sam pulled his car to the edge of the gravel road. "Listen, I really don't want to go much farther down this road. Kimball Mitchell lives around this curve. There is a party honoring him at the country club tonight. It begins at seven thirty. We could meet him any minute heading into town."

"Chicken." Chloe opened the door and got out of the car.

Sam followed suit. "Seriously, you're going to call me names?" You don't know Mitchell. He is a dangerous person, and if he catches us out here this close to his property, well, there's no telling what he'll do."

"Come on. You said he was going to be in town tonight. I doubt he's even here. And I really want to put my feet on the road my mom used to call home."

Chloe ran down the road a little ways from the car. She turned and beckoned Sam to follow. Sam jogged up to her.

"Look, let's walk around the curve and take a peek at the ranch," Chloe said. "If we see anyone coming, we can run back to the car." Chloe's eyes danced with excitement.

"Okay, but we are not going far. Once we get around the curve, you will be able to see the Mitchells' ranch. After that, we are leaving. No questions asked. Okay?"

"Sure."

As they walked, the curve in the road straightened out again. Sam reached for her hand, and she didn't refuse. The sun was setting behind Kimball Mitchell's ranch. The buildings cast long shadows across the property. A two-story white house sat at the top of the hill. Oak trees followed the line of white fence that ran the full length of the driveway on both sides.

A couple hundred head of Black Angus cattle grazed on the hillsides. A small fishpond was off to the right where the ranch driveway broke away from the gravel road. Several horses lingered underneath the huge oaks that dotted the meadows.

Chloe strived to remember her mother. She closed her eyes and searched her memory for her mother's face, her smell, and her presence. Chloe thought of her as a small child running on the hillsides. Then she remembered Elizabeth lying in a nursing home bed, dying from cancer. What had her life been like before Morgan died? Chloe wanted to see the homestead place, but she knew Sam would never take her back there.

Sam grabbed her by the arm. "Look, there's Kimball's Ford leaving the main house. I told you he'd be leaving for town soon. Let's go."

They both ran back to the Charger. Sam started the engine. The car took the entire width of the road to turn. He made a couple of tries before he was able to turn completely around. Sam stepped on the gas and left a trail of dust behind them.

"That was way too close for comfort," Sam said as they exited the gravel road and entered the paved highway. "I knew better than to try this anyway."

"But wasn't it exciting?" Chloe asked. "Is the homestead place near the ranch?"

"No, it's . . . well, sort of. It's on the other side of the road. A little ways off the gravel and set back in the pines. And—" He looked at Chloe. "Don't ask. We're not going there."

Chloe sighed and leaned back in the car seat.

Chapter 28

Kimball Mitchell soaked in the praises of everyone at his award banquet. People raved about his ability to raise more bushels per acre of corn than anyone in the state. He was a very successful farmer and always had been. He loved listening to one person after the next brag about his power to drop a seed on concrete and watch as it sprouted. No one could grow crops like him, and he knew it.

He also knew the public would overlook his wrongdoings as long as he was of value to them. He played the banquet for all it was worth and even offered to hold a barbecue to benefit the local soup kitchen in his newest facilities at his ranch.

He had invited a few of his top-paid law-enforcement officers to join him at his table during the event. One detective had brought him up to speed on Chloe and her involvement with Sam Green. Another heavyset officer made the mistake of asking him for cash during the banquet. Kimball decided the unfortunate man would no longer be needed on his team. He would be assigned to the associate as soon as he reached Mississippi. Kimball noticed his watch. The associate hadn't called. He hadn't left a message on his phone either.

The party lasted till midnight, and Kimball drove home drunk as usual. When he pulled up to the ranch, he noticed a small car in the driveway. He exited his pickup with his weapon drawn. He silently walked toward the dark car.

A tall man stepped out of the car as Mitchell approached the back bumper.

Kimball assumed a position to shoot. "Are you crazy, man? I could have shot you," Kimball yelled.

"Sorry, Mr. Mitchell. I've been sitting here waiting for you. I didn't think about surprising you."

"I told you I would pick you up at the airport. Why didn't you call me?"

"I figured you had enough going on tonight with your party. I didn't want to pull you away, so I got my own car when the plane landed and drove on down. And I didn't get lost one time." The associate took a medium-size suitcase from the trunk. "Where do you want me?"

Mitchell pointed to the bunkhouse next to the barn. "You can sleep in there same as last time."

"Okay, that's fine," the associate said.

"I want you up early in the morning. I've got a job for you that involves a fat pig," Mitchell said as he stumbled his way into the house.

Chapter **29**

Rain poured down the face of Chloe's hotel window on Saturday morning. She had never seen it rain so hard. It sounded like bullets striking the panes, and it appeared to be white sheets coming in waves as they washed against the building's exterior. Chloe didn't have an umbrella and hadn't brought a raincoat. In fact, she didn't own a raincoat. She had several barn coats that were waterproof; she wondered if that counted.

Maybe if she waited for a few minutes, the rain would stop. It didn't. She decided if she wanted to visit Elizabeth, she would have to drive to the assisted-living home in the pouring rain. The front-desk clerk loaned Chloe an umbrella. By the time she arrived at the home, she had decided Mississippi had an ugly side too. Instead of Wyoming's wind, it was rain.

Chloe greeted the guards as she walked passed them. She gently pushed the door open. She wasn't sure if Elizabeth was awake, so she quietly stepped inside. Her grandmother was sitting up in bed watching the news.

"Morning, Grandmother." Chloe walked over and gave Elizabeth a light kiss on the forehead. She stood her borrowed umbrella in the empty garbage can and took a seat. She noticed her pants' legs were wet almost up to her calves.

"I'm so thankful you made it over here in this rainstorm. Weatherman said it is going to do this for at least the next two to three days. Let me turn this off." Elizabeth found the remote and turned off the television.

"Hope you got a good night's rest," Chloe said. She wanted to pull her boots off and roll up her jeans but wasn't sure if she should.

"Oh yes. I feel better than I have in weeks. Come on, sit down by me and let's talk."

"I'm soaked," Chloe said.

"Child, pull off those wet boots. There's a towel in the bathroom you can dry off with."

Chloe pulled the chair around by the bed and sat down on the edge. She pulled off her boots and leaned them against the bedpost. "I'm sorry we didn't have long to chat yesterday. I didn't want to wake you from your nap." She rolled both pants' legs up to her calves, went into the bathroom, and dried off.

"I seem to take too many naps these days. I can't help myself. I sit down or stretch out on this bed, and the next thing I know, I'm asleep." Elizabeth said as she pushed herself up a little higher on the pillow.

"That's okay, Grandmother. I understand. Guess what I did yesterday afternoon. I took Sam up on an offer to take a quick drive out to see the Pines Community. It is lovely out there."

"You did what?" Elizabeth sat up straighter.

"Oh, don't worry. We were fine. Sam showed me around Bishopville too."

"Chloe, Kimball Mitchell isn't someone to mess around with. Stay away from him. Don't you go back over there." Elizabeth reached for Chloe's hand.

She took her grandmother's hand and realized she shouldn't have said anything about the trip out of Bishopville.

"I want you to promise me you won't do anything like that again," Elizabeth said. "Sam's not a marksman. He can't protect you. If Kimball finds out—"

"It's okay. Really. We didn't do anything dangerous. We just took a drive out that way." Chloe tried to reassure Elizabeth. "Do you want some tea or anything?"

"No. I just don't want to see anything happen to you. You have to be smart as a fox around folks like Kimball."

"I understand. I won't do anything stupid while I'm here. Okay?" Chloe stood and walked to the window. The rain continued to fall. She had seen the fear in Elizabeth's eyes. What had this man done to her family? She wanted to change the subject. She turned and looked at her grandmother. Her face seemed pained and worried. "Hey, why don't we talk about Morgan some more? I know you enjoy talking about the good times," Chloe said as she walked back over near Elizabeth's bed.

"He was a man's man." Elizabeth wiped the corner of her eye with a well-used tissue. "He would have fit right in with those Wyoming men you live around." She looked at Chloe and smiled.

Chloe was glad to hear Elizabeth talking about something she loved.

"Morgan wasn't afraid of anything. No, sir. He couldn't back down from a fight. Too stubborn. Too Irish." Elizabeth's smile was replaced with a frown again. "He might still be alive if he'd never seen what Corbin Mitchell did that day."

Chloe sat up straighter. "What did he see, Grandmother?"

Elizabeth lay back on her pillow and looked toward the ceiling. A tear rolled down her cheek. "He saw Corbin's crew that day. They killed that poor man." Elizabeth wiped her face. "Morgan and Corbin had been rivals for years, and when Morgan saw Corbin shoot Cotton Joe—well, that was the nail in his own coffin."

"Cotton Joe?" Chloe asked.

"He was an employee of Corbin's. A scrawny black fellow that lived around bouts these parts his whole life. A hard-working old man. Rumors got out that he was stealing fuel from the ranch pumps, and Corbin was never one to check facts first."

"That's awful to kill someone over fuel."

The phone rang, and Chloe handed the receiver to her grandmother. "Yes," Elizabeth said. "Oh, wonderful. Thank you for rushing the job."

Chloe watched her grandmother as she propped the phone on her shoulder and massaged her ring finger with her right hand.

"I'll see who I can get to pick it up for me as soon as possible. Thank you so much. Goodbye." Elizabeth handed Chloe the receiver. "That was the jewelry store in the mall. My wedding band broke a few days ago. One of my friends found it in the cafeteria and returned it to me. I had Willie B take it to the mall and drop it off to be repaired, and it's ready."

"That's wonderful, Grandmother. Do you want me to pick it up for you?"

"Oh, sweetie, I would love it, but I want to spend every minute with you that I can."

"Of course. Me too, but I know you would like to have your ring back."

"Well, if you have a few extra minutes, maybe you could stop in and pick it up for me." Elizabeth smiled and rubbed her ring finger again. "I do miss it. I'll call my jeweler and let him know you are going to stop in."

"I would love to do that for you. Do you need anything right now?" Chloe asked.

"No, I was telling you why Corbin Mitchell killed Cotton Joe. There's a lot more to the story."

"I guess Grandpa Morgan reported it," Chloe said.

"That's what he did, honey. But in this part of the world, especially back then, if you had money, the police were known to lose evidence, or like in this case, not find any at all. They would trip over a dead body and say there was no evidence that a crime had even occurred."

"That's absurd."

"Corbin slipped them a wad of cash, and no investigation was ever done, no trial, nothing. I told Morgan to drop it, but he liked Cotton Joe. He felt sorry for his wife and four kids. Morgan said it was his duty to see to it that Corbin paid for what he had done to him."

"What happened after that?"

"Morgan did his own investigation. He went to the spot where he had seen Cotton Joe shot. He took our family video camera and recorded the area. There was a pool of blood and one shell casing lying on the ground near the blood. Morgan collected everything he could from the area. He brought the video and evidence home. Even had pictures developed that he had taken."

"One day, Morgan told me he had to go repair the fence on the back fifty acres. But before he left, we went out and dug a hole under the oak tree in the backyard. He had welded together this canister that looked like a time capsule he'd read about in a magazine. Morgan had placed all the evidence in plastic Ziploc bags and sealed them in the waterproof canister. I watched as he placed the container into a large trash bag and tied it up. He positioned the trash bag in the hole, and we covered it up. He told me he didn't want Mitchell to find the evidence, and that was the only way he knew to keep it safe."

"If he didn't trust the local police, why didn't he call the FBI?"

"Honey, things are different down here," Elizabeth said. "Morgan went to the chief of police and showed him the evidence, even the photographs he had taken of the shooting. But it didn't help. It only made things worse. That's why Morgan wanted to bury what he had. He knew the chief would tell Corbin Mitchell about the evidence, and that's exactly what happened."

"You mean, Corbin Mitchell found out what Morgan—Granddad—buried?" Chloe asked.

"There is always a willing body looking for a little money at the expense of others. Someone on the force told Corbin or Kimball that Morgan had some evidence. Fortunately, they never found the canister."

"I hope the police force has changed a lot since then."

"I try not to have a lot of dealings with them anymore."

"Tell me about the day Grandpa Morgan got killed."

"Morgan was so upset when he left that morning. So mad that we didn't even kiss goodbye. He had evidence against Corbin Mitchell other than just Cotton Joe's murder. He had lots of documentation he had kept over the years of the deceitful dealings of the Mitchell family. Morgan wanted something to be done, but he couldn't get any help from the authorities."

"That day is etched in my memory," Elizabeth said. "I remember not having breakfast done 'cause Anna had been sick the night before, and I slept late. I told him I would bring him some food as soon as I could. It wasn't long before I put Anna in the truck along with our lunch and drove down to the back pasture. I thought it would be fun to have a little picnic together. Maybe lift his spirit and mine. When I came to the fence line, Morgan wasn't there. I turned off the engine and waited for a few minutes. Then I heard it."

"Heard what, Grandmother?" Chloe leaned into the bed.

"A loud conversation between some men in a distance. The more I listened, the more I could make out the voices. I heard Morgan screaming at someone. So I left the food in the truck and took Anna with me. We walked toward the sound of the voices. I saw my Morgan and Kimball, Corbin's twenty-one-year-old son at the time, screaming at each other." Elizabeth reached for a Kleenex. She grew quiet for a while.

"What happened?" Chloe asked in a soft voice.

Elizabeth's eyes turned toward the window. The rain was still falling.

Chloe stood, walked over to her grandmother, and patted her arm. She asked if Elizabeth wanted to rest. Elizabeth assured her she wanted to talk.

"I saw Morgan get in Kimball's face. Kimball, always trying to please his father, pulled out a pistol and shot Morgan in the stomach. Morgan fell to the ground. I wanted to run to him, but I was holding Anna. I knew Kimball would have shot both of us."

"Oh, I'm so sorry." Chloe reached for a box of Kleenex and took a fresh one out for Elizabeth.

"Corbin had killed, raped, stolen, and you name it for as long as we knew him." Elizabeth continued. "But his son was worse than he'd ever been."

"Why hasn't he been locked up already?" Chloe walked to the windowsill and propped against it.

"Lawmen around these parts were afraid of him. Corbin would burn their houses down if they angered him for any reason. He would offer money first to get people to see things his way, and if they refused, he tortured them. It soon became easier to just sit back and take his cash."

"Where does he live now?" Chloe took her boots and pulled them back on. Her pants were still damp, but she didn't mind.

"He died a few years ago when his tractor flipped over on him and broke his neck. Kimball was Corbin's only heir, so he got everything."

The phone rang in Elizabeth's room, and Chloe answered to Sam's loud voice.

"I just saw Kimball's Ford in town. I know there are policemen at the nursing home today, and I've had men sent to your hotel room as well. So be looking for someone when you get back this afternoon."

"Protective custody. No, thanks. I don't need it."

"It's done. Be looking for a plainclothes officer. His name is John, and he's a good man."

"What? That is not going to happen, Sam," Chloe said. "I don't need a babysitter."

"You got one all the same."

"We will see about that. I don't know about here, but in Wyoming, we handle our own troubles." Chloe hung up the phone. *How dare Sam take it on himself to get me a babysitter?*

"What's going on, dear?" Elizabeth asked.

Chloe walked over to her grandmother and smiled. "A couple of new detectives are coming over to watch your room. It's your naptime and a perfect time for me to run to the mall and pick up your wedding ring for you. I'll be back before you know it. Now get yourself a good nap while I'm gone."

"There's so much more to tell you, but I'm so thankful my ring is ready."

"I'll be back soon." Chloe kissed her grandmother. She picked up the dry umbrella and went out into the hallway. A couple of men were standing at the nurse's station. Chloe passed them and walked out into the parking lot. The sun was shining, and the air seemed hotter than she remembered. She tucked the umbrella under her arm, strolled into the foyer, and walked out into the parking lot.

Chapter 30

"*Get up now,*" Kimball rested the cold barrel of his pistol on the associate's temple.

The associate opened his eyes, but he did not move. "Mr. Mitchell, did I oversleep?" he asked in a still voice.

"You could say that. I told you to be up early. I've had breakfast, read the paper, and killed a few squirrels. You're still lying here."

The associate's alarm clock rang loudly on the dresser. His heart almost stopped. "Can . . . I get up, sir?"

"I would advise it," Kimball said. He turned to walk to the bedroom door. I'll expect you to be sitting in the van parked out front in five minutes."

"Yes, sir. I'll be there." The associate dressed as quickly as he could and ran out the bunkhouse. The rain-soaked grassy hill soaked thru his socks as he tried to stop and pull on his boots. He opened the passenger door, climbed into the van. The sun was shining, and muggy air filled his lungs. He hated the South and wished he could go back to Wyoming. He didn't think he'd ever get the chance if the police found out he killed the sheriff and his deputy.

Kimball walked out of the main house wearing his white cowboy hat, starched jeans, and white shirt. He looked the part of a distinguished rancher and flaunted it when he could. He walked to the passenger side of the van, stopped at the door, and gave the associate a hard stare. "Get over. You're driving."

Within a few minutes, Kimball and his man were leaving the Pines Community and entering onto the main paved road. Kimball directed the man as they drove through town. They passed the mall and drove into a subdivision on the outskirts of the town limits. Kimball pointed out a house on the left-hand side of the road. The associate made a U-turn and parked on the opposite side of the street, a ways back from the house.

A patrol car was parked in the driveway of the two-story home. The associate noticed the bicycle leaning against the front of the car. Three small children ran back and forth kicking a soccer ball while a white-and-black dog barked and chased them.

"Looks like the happy little home," Kimball said. "Too bad the man had to get greedy. Can't stand greedy people. Won't tolerate them either."

"Is this the house you want to burn? The man's got kids," the associate said.

"So what does that have to do with anything? This will be a good lesson to all the other rookies on the force. It's time I remind them of who they are messing with."

"Boss, other people are home," the associate said. He looked around the neighborhood and saw a couple of guys mowing their lawns. "How are we going to do this in broad daylight, with kids in the front yard?"

"Watch and learn," Kimball said. "I'm going to call him and tell him if he wants his money, he needs to run down to the Baskin-Robbins on the other side of town. When he leaves, you are going in the back door, pull the plug on the stove, get the garage-door remote, and get the heck out of there. I'll take care of the rest."

"But what if his wife is in the house?"

"Do I need to tell you everything?" Mitchell asked. "Do whatever you want. Bring her or leave her, I don't care."

Kimball flipped his phone open and dialed the cop's home phone number. The wife answered, and Kimball asked to speak to the officer. He gave instructions to the guy and then hung up the phone.

Within minutes, the officer walked out his front door and told the kids to get in the car. All the kids and the dog beat the man to the vehicle. The officer moved the bicycle and jumped in the driver's seat. As the man drove away, Kimball ducked and picked up a huge wrench from under the passenger seat. He handed it to the associate and told him to make it quick.

"Do it the same as last time," Kimball said.

The associate got out of the van with the wrench and ran around the house to the back door. He pushed the patio door open and entered the dining room. He looked to his right and saw a tall woman washing dishes in the adjoining kitchen. Without hesitation, the associate ran behind her and struck her in the back of the head with the wrench. He pulled the stove forward enough to smash the pipe with the tool. Gas hissed as it immediately escaped the gas line.

The associate went to the back door. He saw the woman lying on the hardwood floor and a pool of blood around her head. He turned around and grabbed her by the feet and pulled her through the door. He worked as fast as he could in order to get out of the house. He dragged her body to the edge of the swimming pool and dropped her feet.

He ran back into the house and into the garage. Opened the car door, fumbled around until he found the garage-door opener, and then ran back through the house. He didn't want Kimball Mitchell waiting on him twice in one morning. So he hurried to the fence and ran out the backyard without closing the gate.

Kimball was finishing a cigar as the associate opened the van door and climbed in. "Took you long enough," Kimball said.

"I didn't think I was going to find the remote opener," the associate said. He tossed the device to Mitchell and leaned back in the seat. Neither said a word for a few minutes.

"How far to Baskin-Robbins?" the associate asked.

Kimball replied, "Ten to fifteen minutes one way, maybe more with the busy Saturday mall traffic."

"Are we going to sit here and wait for the officer to return?"

"Yes. Now back the van farther down the road. When this pig is roasted—" Kimball paused. "We'll have a little cleanup work to take care of. I'll drop you at the mall so you can hit a couple of stores. Use my credit card to get a decent alibi. I'll go to the carwash on the other side of town and peel off this expensive paint wrap. Can't have anyone identifying my van."

"You mean, this van isn't blue?" The associate looked at Mitchell in wonder.

"No, it's a peel-off paint." Kimball let his window down, took his index fingernail and dug at the blue color until it tore. He pulled a small section from the top of the door and stuck it in the associate's face. "Take a look at this. Anyone talking to the cops later will tell them a blue van was here, not gray."

"You think of everything, don't you, Kimball?" The associate shook his head.

Thirty minutes later, the patrol car came back in sight. The associate asked Mitchell to rethink what he was about to do. Kimball replied he couldn't allow one fat cop to get away with dictating how much he did or didn't get paid.

The garage-door remote control caused the spark needed to ignite the fumes inside the house. Kimball had what he wanted, and he never left the cover of the van. He threw the butt of his cigar into an empty pop bottle, and as the explosion went off, Kimball told the associate to drive.

The associate sped by the house. He refused to look at the burning patrol car.

Chapter 31

Chloe drove to the local library using the direction on her rental car's GPS. She hoped they would be open during the morning hours on Saturday. She wondered if the newspaper reported anything about the death of Cotton Joe back in the late seventies, and if so, could she find it?

The librarian led her to the archive room.

According to the article in the July edition of the *Bishopville Herald*'s 1978 paper, Corbin Mitchell was the only eyewitness to the death of Cotton Joe and claimed Morgan Lee of the Pines Community had shot Cotton Joe during a fit of anger. In a later edition, Corbin went on record to say that Morgan had turned the gun on himself after he had confessed that he couldn't live with what he had done.

Chloe realized the shame Elizabeth must have felt all the years since. Morgan had not only died as a killer but as a suicidal killer. There wasn't much of an investigation reported in the following articles. Chloe found only praise for the Mitchells. Most of the information made them out to be town heroes who had helped a grieving widow with a kid to get back on her feet. Another article mentioned Elizabeth as the widow of the killer.

She realized whatever the Mitchell family said went around Bishopville in the seventies. No one questioned them, and the only evidence law enforcement needed to pin the murder on Morgan was the word of a Mitchell.

Chloe gathered her things and looked at the clock. It was past lunchtime. She hoped Elizabeth would still be napping. She wanted to hurry and get back to her grandmother, but she would run to the jewelry store and grab her ring before she returned to the nursing home.

*****

Chloe parked her rental car in the nearest available space in front of the mall and went inside. She saw a sign for the jewelry store not far from the food court. She ordered a chicken sandwich, ate quickly, and then hurried into the store.

After a few minutes, she walked out carrying Elizabeth's wedding ring. A clothing store next to the jewelry department displayed a rack of new summer apparel near the entrance. Chloe combed the rack and decided on a black one-piece bathing suit. She went inside to pay. She spotted a white, lace cover-up and a pair of sandals on her way to the cash register. As she waited for the lady in front of her to finish paying, she found an assortment of ponytail holders and added them to her stack. Chloe thought about her cramped feet inside her boots. Her toes would need some polish if she wore the sandals. She remembered the cute shop next door to the clothing store and popped in long enough to buy a bottle of red polish. She paid and left the store.

On her way out of the mall, she saw a pretzel shop. She waited in the short line and wondered if Elizabeth liked pretzels or not. She decided to get two. They could enjoy them together while she visited one last time. She found she could hardly wait to get back to the nursing home and hear Elizabeth sum up the story of her grandfather. She knew there was a lot more to learn about Morgan and the Mitchells, but she didn't think it was possible to stay longer.

As Chloe waited in line, a large hand slipped around her waist. She hadn't seen Sam in the mall. She turned expecting to face him, but instead, she saw a man she thought she recognized but didn't know.

"Excuse me. Could you get your hands off me?" Chloe didn't mean it as a question. She stepped back and looked at the man's face again.

"What? Or you'll scream?" the man asked.

"Do I know you?" Chloe looked puzzled. She knew she'd seen his pimple-scarred face before, but she couldn't place him.

The man pulled his baseball cap farther down his brow and ducked his head. "I'm here to give you a fair warning, lady," the man said in a whisper. "Either you get out of town or you'll be buried here and spend the rest of forever in the Mississippi dirt."

"Excuse me?" The same odd sensation she'd had in her bedroom back in Wyoming washed over her. She had debated about changing her mind about the trip because of it. She wanted to throw up.

"It's simple, either you go back to Snow Valley alive or you'll be buried in the town your mother was born in."

"How do you know my mother? Who are you?" Chloe demanded.

"I'll give you time to think about it, but I won't be able to offer this option to you again. My employer doesn't know I'm talking to you, and if I'm told to kill you, I'll have no other choice. Do you understand?"

Chloe moved farther away from the man. "And who would tell you to kill me?"

"You don't have a lot of time to think about this. His order could come anytime." The man turned and walked out the mall entrance.

Chloe sat down at the nearest table and felt around in her large handbag. The revolver was still there. *Where did I see him before?*

Chloe walked to her car, but she was on full alert. A drizzle of rain continued to fall. She looked in every direction at the cars around her. Chloe noticed a gray van with tinted windows parked a few rows over from her. There were no other vehicles around it. She looked one last time around the entire area before she opened her car door. When she thought it was safe, she quickly unlocked the door and got inside then locked the doors immediately.

She took the gun from her purse and turned toward the back-seat holding the weapon with her finger on the trigger. To her relief, no one was there. Chloe heard a knock on the driver's window. She hesitated for a second and then slid the Colt behind her purse. She turned to see if the man from the mall had returned. A bald man dressed in a black suit held a badge to her window.

"Ms. Parker? Could you let your window down please?"

Chloe hesitated for a minute longer then let the window down. "Yes, officer. Can I help you?" She wondered if he had seen the weapon.

"It's Detective Jax, ma'am. I will be following you now that we've tracked your rental."

"I already told Sam I didn't need an escort. Thanks anyway, officer."

"I wanted to alert you to my presence, Ms. Parker," the officer said. "We don't want our visitors getting injured while they are in our state."

"Look, I'm not trying to be rude here, but I can take care of myself. You don't have to follow me around. Do you understand?"

"Yes, but my orders—"

Chloe raised her voice. "I don't care what your orders are. Sam isn't my father or my husband. Okay? So it doesn't matter what he says. What matters is what I say. So leave me alone." She began to let the window back up.

"I don't take orders from Sam Green if that's who you are refer-ring to. I'll be behind you if you need anything." The officer nodded and said, "Ms. Parker, you have a good day."

Chloe shook her head and put the window up. She decided she would give Sam a call when she got back to her hotel. She'd had enough of his butting in. She had almost reached her hotel when she met a couple of ambulances heading in the opposite direction. She could hear more sirens blaring in the distance. She looked in her rear-view mirror again but didn't see the detective's unmarked car.

Chapter 32

The associate swayed back and forth on the porch swing looking at his carefully stacked display of empty beer cans. It was two in the afternoon, and the rain couldn't make up its mind if it wanted to quit or not. For now, it had stopped. Steam rose from the earth much like a sauna after water is poured over rocks.

"I can't take this humidity, boss," the associate said. He took the last can from the cooler, downed it in one long drink, and placed the empty can at the top of his pyramid. Kimball Mitchell stepped off the porch at that same moment, and the cans toppled over.

"Are you kidding me," the associate said under his breath.

Kimball turned and looked at the man. "What?"

"Nothing." He dropped to his knees and began restacking the cans. "You know, you never told me why you hated that old woman and her granddaughter so much," the associate said.

"I don't have to tell you anything. You work for me. Remember?" Kimball looked up at the cloudy sky. The day had been successful, and it was still early afternoon. He was sure the police department was scrambling around trying to find evidence of who killed one of their own. He hated Bishopville's continual growth. New officers were always in and out of town faster than ever before. He was finding it harder each year to stay on top of the rookies. He thought back to what seemed like yesterday. There were only a few men to pay off; now he didn't even know a lot of the guys on the force. His longtime friend and chief of police had to retire due to a bad heart, opening the door for a new force. This smart-mouth, younger generation had the nerve to ask him for more money. Mitchell couldn't tolerate people ordering him around; no one asked him for more money and lived to brag about it.

The smell of freshly plowed earth filled the air, and Kimball drew in a long breath. His crops were his favorite things, and fall was his favorite season. He looked forward to the harvest after a long hot summer. Each cornstalk was a small money tree. He knew his greed had won him Farmer of the Year. He didn't care so much about the title, but he did revel in the cash flow from the bumper crops.

"Look, if you don't want to tell me, it's okay," the associate said while finishing the pyramid, "but if you expect me to help you kill anyone else, I'd like to know what they did to deserve death." He felt an urge to throw up. He stretched out across the porch with his head hanging off facing the ground. His foot kicked the pyramid stacked neatly against the wall of the house and down it came again.

Kimball walked over and sat on the edge of the porch. "You've worked for me a long time. When I first met you back fourteen or fifteen years ago, I hired you to run Anna Lee off the road. And now, you're questioning my motives."

"I didn't mean anything by it, Mr. Mitchell. I must be drunk," the associate said. He was silent for a few minutes. "I remember the wreck. I looked in the car to make sure the woman was dead. But she must have been thrown through the windshield and down into the ravine. I never did find her body. I was shocked to see a little girl crumpled up in the back floorboard. Still don't know how she survived the crash."

"Well, she did," Kimball said. He took his cowboy hat off and wiped the sweat from his forehead with his bandana then replaced the hat.

The associate sat up on the porch and hung his legs off the side.

"I've let her live all these years because I've held her over Elizabeth's head. I was right in getting rid of Anna. She had already gotten in touch with the old bat and told her about the kid before

I had a chance to tell her myself. If I had waited any longer, one of them would have bankrupted me from blackmail."

"I don't understand, boss. What could Elizabeth get out of you?" The associate stood and walked over to the nearest tree to relieve himself.

"She could claim anything," Kimball said. "Always wanted this farm back in her possession from the day she sold it to my dad. Now, she has the little brat here in Mississippi. With the old bat being this near death, there is no telling what she'll pull."

"What can she do, she's an old woman," the associate said. He returned to his seat on the edge of the porch.

"She knows more about me than I'd rather get into right now. For all I know, Elizabeth has called that gal down here to set up some scheme to blackmail me. She just won't let the past go."

"Let what go? Besides, you really think she could think up some scheme at her age? She's almost dead for crying out loud." The associate laughed. "You should have killed her years ago."

Kimball walked over to the nearest brush pile and returned with a stick about three inches in diameter. He held it like a baseball bat and swung the stick into the associate's legs that were hanging toward the ground.

The associate screamed out in pain. "What did you do that for?"

"You don't think I haven't tried to kill her? I'm sick of people second-guessing me and telling me what I should and shouldn't do. I've had it." Kimball swung at the man again. The associate lifted his knees to the porch and curled into a fetal position.

"I'm sorry. I didn't mean anything."

Mitchell struck the man across the hip with the stick. He swung to hit him again. The associate looked at him through eyes of fear. "Please." He held both palms toward Mitchell. "I'm begging—"

Mitchell flung the stick across the yard. He slowed his breathing. "Protecting my money is all the reason I need to get rid of someone. No telling what the two of them have cooked up. She'll be accusing me of God knows what if they stay together. She'll try to turn me in for murder if she gets half a chance."

"Does the old woman know anything that she could really use?" the associate asked, stopping a groan as soon as he made the sound. He drew his body across the porch and leaned his back against the wall of the house near his turned over beer cans. He rubbed his right hip and left knee to ease the pain.

"None of your business." Kimball walked over to the cooler. It was empty. "Did you drink the last beer?"

The associate looked at the toppled pyramid. "Yeah, boss. You want me to make another beer run?"

"No, forget it. I have to clear my head. I need to think of a way to get rid of my problem and make it look like an accident. I want you to get up and go find the boys. Make yourself useful. I'm not paying you to vacation in Mississippi. I'm sure there's some plowing or cattle work you can do."

The associate struggled to stand straight.

"I'm going over to the new facilities. The Morton building is almost done. The men are putting the finishing touches on this weekend. I need it ready as soon as possible," Kimball said.

Chapter 33

A *plain-clothed* officer sat in the hallway near Chloe's room. She started to tell him to leave but decided she didn't really mind the guy sitting there as long as he left her alone. Chloe walked into the hotel room and placed the .45 in the closet safe.

The message light on the hotel phone was flashing. She listened to Sam's voice telling her he decided to send someone over to her room even if she had refused the help. She hung up the receiver without listening to the rest of the message and turned on the television while she tried on the new bathing suit.

She noticed the news correspondent didn't have the Southern drawl she had been hearing since she'd stepped off the plane in Memphis. She decided the reporter had to be a transplant from another part of the United States.

The news was being broadcasted live from a residential area where a two-story home had been burnt to the ground. Firemen were scattered around the surrounding properties carrying water hoses. The report stated an explosion had all but leveled the home. Firefighters were afraid the heat from the fire would spawn other fires on the rooftops of surrounding homes and were working ferociously to put them out at first sight.

The television station cut to a second reporter who stated that authorities said it was possible fumes had seeped from a gas leak inside the house. A small spark could have ignited it.

Law-enforcement officers were stunned to learn it was the home of one of their own and a full-scale investigation was underway. A total of four had died in the explosion, and another was in critical condition. Prayers for the officer's family were requested. "More information would be forthcoming," the reporter said and switched back to the station.

As Chloe tried on her new bathing suit, she recalled Elizabeth's words: "Kimball's father would torch the homes of any law-enforcement officers who dared to arrest him." She wondered if Kimball had been responsible for the explosion.

She removed the bathing suit, dressed in her jeans and T-shirt, and then picked up her phone to dial Alice's number.

"Hello," Alice said.

"Boy, do I need to talk," Chloe answered.

"What's up?"

"You remember the loser I told you about earlier? Well, I think he did something almost unspeakable."

A few minutes later, Chloe had summed up the entire day's events. She even told Alice about the man in the mall but regretted it later.

"Do you really believe the person who set those fires was your grandmother's neighbor?" Alice asked.

"Yes, without a doubt. He should have been arrested for the attack on Elizabeth and me, but the police didn't touch him."

"Unreal. I have some unbelievable news too. The update on Sheriff Bob and the deputy is bad, really bad."

"What is it?" Chloe asked.

"A horn hunter found their bodies this morning. He was up in the Big Sandy area hunting for elk antlers and found a human arm instead. The hunter investigated further and discovered two partial bodies in a wooded area near the Old Smith Bridge."

"The Old Smith Bridge? That's almost one hundred miles from Snow Valley."

"Yeah, and law enforcement might never have known it was the sheriff and his deputy if the killer had been smart enough to remove their uniforms. He even left their badges attached. I mean, even without the bodies intact, the identification was simple," Alice said.

"Do they have any suspects?"

"They haven't said much. It's an open investigation, but I'm keeping my ears open. If I find out anything, I'll let you know."

"Please do," Chloe said.

"I went into town yesterday to pick up Hank's son at the airport. We ran in the diner to get some lunch, and I saw Doc. I told him to talk to you after you get home about helping out. He's still very busy."

"How is everything else in town?" Chloe asked.

"I didn't want to tell you, but with the different law-enforcement officers in town, my boss is going crazy. He wants me to come back to work ASAP. I wished I hadn't stepped foot into the diner after I saw how busy it was."

"Why didn't you tell me? At least I'll be flying out tomorrow and should be there by dark. I don't want you to get fired because of me."

"It's okay. I told my boss I'd see him Monday morning," Alice said. "Right now, it's kind of scary with everything that has happened lately. I mean, first, I'm almost kidnapped or killed, and then the sheriff and the deputy are killed by some nutjob. I don't know about you, but I'm watching my back more carefully. I have one of my pistols with me at all times now. I also got my new bottle of bear spray in my saddlebag. I see him again, I'll hurt him," Alice said.

"Don't forget, that's not hair spray. You'll be up a creek if it gets in your eyes."

"Cute, Chloe."

"Hey, just saying. And speaking of pistols, I was able to get my hands on a .45 from the old man I met at the nursing home. He's a sweetheart who happens to keep a couple of guns around. He's got a grandson our age that's as big as a refrigerator."

"Okay, now he's who you need to hang out with while you're there."

Chloe and Alice said their goodbyes. Chloe decided not to return Sam's call; instead, she decided to go visit Elizabeth. It was early afternoon, and she could spend the rest of the day with her.

Before she left the hotel room, Chloe decided to call her dad to see if he was going to make it to the ranch that night as planned. If he could get home early enough, Chloe thought Alice could go to the diner to help out. She picked up her cell and dialed his number.

A few minutes later, Chloe left her room with a frown on her face. *Why can't that man help out just a little bit? Do I really have to do it all?* She noticed the policeman leaning back in his chair reading a fishing magazine.

"You might as well go home. I told the other officer I didn't want protection. So you're dismissed too." Chloe walked down the hall to the elevator.

The man tossed his magazine to the floor and walked toward the elevator behind Chloe. She pressed the elevator button and waited.

The officer spoke, "I'm only here because—"

"Because of Sam Green. I know." Chloe interrupted. The elevator door opened, and they stepped in. She heard the officer speak into his mic and knew she might as well live with the shadow for a while.

The officer followed her to the small rental car and motioned toward a black car near hers. She noticed the bald detective sitting in a car parked a row over. The officer opened the door for her and said, "Be safe, Ms. Parker, and have a nice day." She threw her hands up and got in her car. Chloe drove through Bishopville to the nursing home. The detective in the black car matched every move she made.

Chapter 34

Elizabeth was sitting up in her bed eating a very early dinner when Chloe walked into her room. "It's great to see you enjoying your meal. Is it dinnertime already?"

"We eat around three every afternoon, and if we want a snack, they bring that later. Most of us are asleep when you, young'uns, are eating," Elizabeth said and wiped her mouth.

"You sure look like you are feeling good," Chloe said as she leaned over and gave Elizabeth a hug. "Look what I have." She handed Elizabeth her shinny wedding rings.

"My rings!" Elizabeth took them and slid the rings on her finger and commented on the beauty of the diamonds. She turned her hand and checked the soundness of the work. "They are as pretty as the day we married, and Morgan placed them on my finger."

"I'm so happy I could pick them up for you. I know you will rest better having them back on your finger."

"Oh, child, I rested just fine without them. But, I am glad they are where they belong for now. I want you to have them when I am gone. They are yours if you want them."

"Wow. Uh, are you sure?" Chloe asked.

"I'm sure. You're my only granddaughter, and they belong to you."

"I don't know what to say, but—thank you. They are truly beautiful." She lifted Elizabeth's hand and admired the rings once again. "I'm happy I was able to get away from the ranch and come to

Mississippi and meet you." She placed her grandmother's hand back on her gown and turned to find her bag.

"I'm happy too. In fact, I don't remember the last time I felt so good. It must be because you are here," Elizabeth said.

"You might not believe it, but the same is true for me as well. I've slept like a baby since I've been in Mississippi."

"Were you not resting in Wyoming?" Elizabeth asked.

"Sometimes I have too much on my mind to really rest. There's a lot of responsibility in running a ranch, and at my age, I always wonder if I'm doing it right." Chloe took the bag of pretzels out of her large purse and placed them on the table. They were flattened, but she knew they would taste the same. "I know you had dinner, but I love these things. I can't go to the mall without buying one, so I bought two this time. I wasn't sure if you liked them but figured I'd eat it if you didn't. I don't get them very often. Our mall is over two hours away from our ranch."

"I adore pretzels," Elizabeth said.

Chloe handed her one wrapped in a napkin and offered her a bowl of sauce. Elizabeth took the pretzel but turned down the cheese sauce. Chloe was happy to see she had something in common with her grandmother. She sat at the foot of Elizabeth's bed, and they ate in silence for a few minutes.

"After my mom died, my dad was my best friend for a long time," Chloe said. "But he started to withdraw more each year. I know my mom's death was really hard on both of us. But sometimes I think it was harder on him. He doesn't talk a lot anymore. Mostly, he gives horse clinics around the country. He's in Montana now, and it looks like that's where he is going to stay." Chloe took another bite of her pretzel and washed it down with a hot pop she had in her bag.

"Oh my. I'm sorry, sweetie."

"It's okay. He taught me a lot during my younger years, so I know more about ranching than most people my age, but sometimes it would be nice to have a little help. His clinics have taken off. I don't think he ever dreamed he would be so successful."

Elizabeth finished her pretzel before Chloe, wiped her mouth, and asked for a glass of ice water. Chloe left the room and went to the nurses' station for a couple glasses of ice.

The nurse handed her the glasses and said she would be down to help Elizabeth into her wheelchair in a short while. Chloe thanked her and then returned to Elizabeth's room with the glasses.

Chloe filled one glass with water at Elizabeth's tiny sink and poured her hot pop into the other one. She handed Elizabeth the water glass and took a seat near the bed. "The nurse told me to tell you she'd be down in a few minutes." Chloe sipped on her pop and was thankful for the ice. "I went to the library earlier today. I wanted to check the newspaper archives to see if there was any more information about Cotton Joe's death," Chloe said.

"What did you find?"

"It was reported like you said. Morgan Lee was accused of taking the life of the poor farmhand and then committed suicide."

"Yes, that's the way every paper within fifty miles reported it."

"Can you tell me the rest of what happened after my grandfather died?"

"I'd love to tell you the rest of the story. I know you have to fly back tomorrow morning, and I wish you didn't have to leave so soon. Thursday was a waste. That sorry man stole yet another day from us. But I'm trying not to think about all the plundered years gone by."

"I know, me too," Chloe said. "I would've loved to have known about you years ago. I really could have used a motherly figure in my life, and you were here all along." She finished off the pop in her glass and sat it on the coffee table. "Would you like for me to open the window so we can enjoy the scenery and fragrance from here?"

"Yes, that's fine," Elizabeth said. "It gets too cold in this room anyway."

Chloe stood and walked to the window. She moved the curtains back. Light poured into the room. The oak trees' branches kept time with the wind's speed as they swayed back and forth. Warm air flowed into the room.

"Looks like another storm is coming," Elizabeth said.

"Oh, it's only the wind." Chloe turned to take a seat near the window. "It blows all the time where I'm from." She smiled at Elizabeth and realized how fond she had become of her.

The nurse tapped lightly on the door before pushing it open. Within a few minutes, Elizabeth was sitting on one side of the small kitchen table, and Chloe took a seat on the other side. She wondered if Elizabeth was still taking chemo. She looked so fragile and tiny in the huge wheelchair.

"Where did we leave off before you left this morning?" Elizabeth asked.

"You were telling me you saw Kimball shoot Morgan. I mean, Granddad."

"Oh yes. There have been three devastating days in my life. The day Morgan died, the day your mother left home, and the day I found out she had died. On each of those days, I know my own heart stopped for a while. I looked for you so long, and I almost gave up a few times. When Sam found out I had cancer, he promised me he would never stop looking for you."

"He's loyal, if nothing else."

"Once he latches onto something, well, that's it. He'll die before he lets go," Elizabeth said.

Chapter 35

The building crew was ready to leave by the end of the day on Saturday. Mitchell didn't mind paying them overtime. He had plans. A crew hanging around to tidy up the lawn was out of the question.

He positioned himself so he could see the full length of the massive building. Kimball pressed his shoulders back and held his head high as he strolled through his newest addition to his ranch. It was a two-story, one hundred yards long by fifty yards wide, state-of-the-art ranching facility.

A full veterinary office equipped with the ability to operate on-site had been situated at the west entrance of the building. There was an area set aside near there for a complete calving operation. The east side was a combination of a sales arena and offices. A kitchen adjacent to the office area was large enough for Kimball to offer a meal to everyone in the Pines Community. The building was fit for any event Kimball desired to host. But first, he would christen his new building with the blood of his longtime adversary.

He had spent a fortune on the facility. He expected an even higher return. With his latest farming award, he would be able to draw the attention of different individuals to put on clinics and even rent the building for summer training services, maybe even to the university. Everything would be perfect if his idiot associate didn't mess things up; he would be celebrating by morning.

Kimball walked outside the building and saw the associate sitting in a tractor with the cab door open talking to one of his hired men. Kimball strolled over to the tractor. "Is this all the two of you have to do?" he asked.

The hired man excused himself, and the associate climbed down from the tractor.

"If you think this is nice, wait till you see inside my newest addition," Mitchell said. He turned and walked to the office door. The associate followed. Mitchell showed off the entire downstairs with the enthusiasm of a teenager with a new ride.

They walked to the kitchen, and the associate stopped. "This could be in any restaurant."

Kimball noticed the associate admiring the wide selection in the freezer.

"Go ahead. Get a snack. It's dinnertime."

"Yes, sir. Thank you." The associate made himself a ham-and-cheese sandwich, and Kimball turned down his offer to make him one.

Kimball took one of the twelve barstools and leaned against the countertop. "There are six bedrooms upstairs." He beamed. "Pick the one you want tonight. There's a game room and an entertainment center on the north side of the building. I want you here all night and not running around town," Mitchell said. He walked to the huge fridge and took out a bottle of water, opened it, and began to sip. "I need you up and in this kitchen early in the morning. I'll be over around 5:30 a.m. We have to get everything together for tomorrow. The old bat will never expect us coming back a second time. No one will."

After the associate finished his sandwich, Kimball took him to the veterinary office. "What do you see here, man?"

"I see a top-notch facility. I mean, you could do surgery in here if you had to."

"That's right. I spent a ton of money, and you almost messed it up for me," Kimball said. He placed his hand on the back of the associate's head, and before the man could realize what was happening, Kimball slammed his head into one of the stainless-steel countertops.

The associate grabbed his head and stumbled backward. "What'd I do this time?" He gave Mitchell a stare filled with tears.

"You idiot. They found the sheriff's and the deputy's bodies in Wyoming. I thought you said you had buried them." Kimball grabbed the man by the shirt collar. "You think you're the only person on my payroll in Wyoming? If the murder of those two cops get pinned on you, it could lead back to me. I can't have that now, can I?" Kimball pushed the man backward.

"I can't believe they found them this quick. I took them a long way from Snow Valley," the associate said as blood poured down into his mouth.

"I prepared this facility so I could continue artificially inseminating my cattle. In order to AI my heifers, I have to have semen straws. Right?" He glared at the associate.

The associate walked over to the wash bay and found a cloth, soaked it in cold water, and placed it under his bloody nose. He leaned against the wall and stared at Kimball.

"Would you like to say something to me?" Kimball asked. He waited a minute and then continued. "I didn't think so. You had to go and kill Bob, didn't you?"

"Bob?" the associate asked.

"Why couldn't you have roughed him up a little? You better hope you don't get caught. Bob was an old hunting pal of mine. In fact, I met him before you. He's the one who gave me your name."

"You mean, you knew the sheriff?" the associate asked. He found a tall stool, sat down, and leaned his head back to stop the bleeding.

"Yes, I knew him. For your information, all those Black Angus cattle you saw as you drove up the ranch road, every one of them is the result of an artificially inseminated cow. How am I going to keep making a profit if the man who secured straws for me, at no cost, is dead?" Kimball's head tilted sideways. "Can you explain that?"

"I had no idea," the associate whispered.

Chapter 36

Chloe excused herself and walked down to the vending machine to get another pop. She realized she hadn't returned Sam's phone call and didn't want to be rude even if she was upset with him. She dialed his number and waited for his reply.

Within a few minutes, they made plans for Sam to pick her up after her grandmother had gone to sleep for the night. Sam offered to call the cops off as long as she was with him. She agreed, thinking to herself, as long as she had Willie B's gun in her purse.

When Chloe walked back into the room, Elizabeth commented on how much she loved Chloe's smile. Chloe thanked her, walked over to the window, and leaned against the windowsill. A light breeze blew in across her back. She sipped her drink and decided to ask the question that had been bugging her. "I've wondered why you didn't turn Mitchell in yourself since you were an eyewitness to Morgan's death?" Chloe asked.

"I went to the chief of police the same day Morgan died. But Corbin had already gotten word to him. He knew I was on my way. He's retired now, but he was of no help to me," Elizabeth said. She rolled her wheelchair over to the sitting area near the couch. "When I returned home, Corbin and Kimball were waiting for me on my front steps. I got slapped around a good bit, but that wasn't the worst of it. Anna was running around in the yard. She was only three at the time. Kimball grabbed your mom by the feet and hung her upside down in front of me. He was laughing like a crazy person." Elizabeth shook her head. "He threatened to slam her against the utility pole."

"No way," Chloe said.

"I didn't know what was going to happen. Corbin promised me if I went to the cops again, he would kill Anna. I knew he would do it, so I let it go for a while. The first three years after Morgan's death were the worst years of my life. I had so much hatred built up in me. I couldn't stand myself."

"I can see why."

"I shared with a friend how miserable I was, and she told me about Jesus. She said he would take away the hate and replace it with his love. But I found it hard to believe in that kind of peace."

"Me too," Chloe said.

"At the end of those three years, I was awakened one morning to Anna pulling at my sleeve. She told me her heart hurt. I took her to the local doctor. Ended up, she had to have surgery because she had a hole in her heart. I didn't have any money. Morgan had been our provider, and I didn't know where to turn. My friend kept telling me that Jesus would provide. But Anna was getting sicker by the day."

"What happened?" Chloe asked.

"I did what I had to do. I went to Corbin and accepted an offer on our land. He had tried to purchase our farm right after Morgan's death, but I hated his family so much. I couldn't even look at him. I thought I might do something I would regret if I was around him."

"I know what you mean." Chloe sat on the couch in front of her grandmother and crossed her legs under her.

"My stubbornness and hatred almost caused us to starve to death. When I realized Anna would have to have the surgery, I took the little tad of money Corbin offered and gave him our land deed. Every square foot of it, gone. The money was barely enough to cover the hospital expense."

"No." Chloe shook her head.

"Yes, and I would do it again because it saved your mother. Corbin promised to let me live on the land in our homestead house as long as I wanted to, but then the tornado hit in the eighties. A seventy-year-old oak smashed into the wooden-frame house and destroyed it. That's when I moved into Corbin's house trailer. I think he thought he would keep me close enough to keep his eye on me. I regretted moving into his trailer many, many times over."

"Couldn't you go somewhere else?"

"No, for once I moved in, Corbin made sure I never had any money to move out again. He took what he wanted from me, literally. Finally, after years of abuse, I ended up going to church with my friend. She never stopped praying for me. I gave my life to God. I was finally able to forgive and let go of all the resentment I'd carried over the years. I learned the peace I once believed didn't exist really did."

An attendant tapped on Elizabeth's door and asked if she wanted an afternoon snack. Elizabeth told her she was ready to lie down again, and she would like some ice cream. The man helped Elizabeth back in bed and told her he'd bring her a snack.

When the attendant left, Chloe asked, "Why does Mitchell want the two of us dead? I mean, all this happened years ago, and I doubt the cops would listen now if they didn't believe you back then."

"Oh, my dear, there is still more you don't know. You see, Corbin or Kimball would stop by on a regular basis back then. It was their house trailer, and I had no privacy. Either they raided my garden for fresh vegetables, tore down my clothes from the clothesline, or Kimball would chase your mom all over the yard with a snake. Corbin said he had to keep me straight. He didn't want me to forget I wasn't ever to go to the police."

Chloe picked up a small pillow and hugged it. She wished she had been around back then. She would have given both of them a piece of her mind.

"But I finally got them one day," Elizabeth said. "Corbin and Kimball stopped by while Anna was still in school, and I was hanging out a fresh load of clothes. Corbin demanded I go in and fix them both lunch. I had been growing stronger in the Word, my faith, and my own person. I had even bought myself a tape recorder. I did," Elizabeth said and then smiled. "And on this one day, when they stopped by, I happened to have the small recorder sitting on the bar in my kitchen."

"They took off their barnyard boots and crashed on my couch while I fixed sandwiches. When I walked by the recorder, I found the courage to press the record button. They never knew what I had done. During the meal, they talked about their good fortune of having a free maid around the place to take care of their needs. Kimball blurted out he was glad he had shot Morgan."

"Out of the blue?" Chloe rose up slightly from the couch.

"Yes, and he went on to say the day his father had shot Cotton Joe and pinned it on Morgan was a red-letter day. Kimball always was a little loudmouth. Anyway, they both laughed, but I'll get the last laugh. I still have the tape today. And I still have all the evidence Morgan buried on his last morning on earth. And, I can still testify to what I saw, as long as I have breath."

"I wish you could have gotten it in the hands of the right authorities," Chloe said.

"I tried to one year. The year your mother died in the car crash. I never had proof, but I know Kimball was responsible for the accident. Your mother had written me a couple of times. Kimball found out and was going to stop it one way or the other." Elizabeth propped herself up more in the bed. "After you turned ten, I never heard another word from your mom. I hired a private investigator and gave him one of the photos of you and Anna, but he took my money and left town."

"What makes you think Kimball had something to do with my mom's accident?"

"Kimball began going out west years ago on fall-hunting trips. Still goes every year, as far as I know. The first year he went was three years before your mother's death. The year of your tenth birthday, he stayed an extra-long time. I remember thinking I was glad for the peaceful break that fall.

"Surely, Kimball didn't cause my mom's death." Chloe shook her head.

"I believe he did. It was too coincidental. When Kimball returned, he was extra unbearable. I figured it was his way of making up for lost time. Now, I understand he was gloating over his victory. It wasn't long until he brought a newspaper to me. A front-page article showed pictures of a terrible accident which took the life of a young woman who had died in Montana. He was making a mockery out of Anna's death."

"You know she died in Wyoming now, don't you?" Chloe asked. My mom's car rolled five times the night she crashed. Police said she must have been thrown from the car. They never found her body. My dad told me he thought the wildlife must have found her before the wreck was discovered the next day."

"Mitchell lied to me in order to throw me off from ever finding you. Somehow, as awful as the news was, I knew you were still out there, but I didn't know where. So even though it was one of the worst days of my life, it gave me hope that I could find you."

"If he is responsible for my mom's death, he'll pay. Where is the tape today?" Chloe asked. She stood and walked around the room. "This has to be reported to someone with the power to do something about it."

"Chloe, listen to me." Elizabeth reached out and took Chloe's arm as she walked by her bed. "I don't have long to live. If I die before the evidence is found, Morgan's name will forever be tarnished."

"I wish there was something I could do," Chloe cut in.

"There's no time, dear, you have to leave in the morning." Elizabeth let go of Chloe's arm, and Chloe sat on the edge of her bed. "Willie B has the directions written down in his notebook. He knows the land, and his grandson, Stump, is a big ole boy. He'll be here to help Willie B find the canister, if anything happens to me."

"I should be the one helping, not someone in the neighborhood," Chloe said.

"No one's been around the old homestead in years. There used to be snakes all along the creek bed. It's a dangerous overgrown place by now. But Stump can handle it. He's a little older than you and has tons of energy, which Willie B and I don't have anymore. He eats fried snake all the time according to Willie B," Elizabeth said.

She snarled her nose. "He won't be afraid to get in there and find the canister. I just hope and pray it isn't rusted out."

"Is the tape in the canister too?"

"No, I have the tape here. I am so glad I didn't leave it in the house trailer. It would have gone up in smoke like everything else."

Chloe looked at her watch. "I wish we had longer to visit. I know you should have been asleep a while ago. I am considering asking my dad if I can change my flight and extend my visit a little longer, but I'm sure he will say no. I'm lucky I got to come at all."

"I wish you could stay, but I don't want you here to look for some old evidence which might not even be there anymore. I'd love to have more time to get to know each other," Elizabeth said.

"I know. I would love that too."

"This has been a shabby reunion compared to the one ahead."

"What do you mean?" Chloe asked.

Elizabeth padded her vein-ridden hand on the edge of her twin bed. "Come closer, dear. I know you'll be leaving soon, but I can't let you leave Mississippi unless I tell you one more thing."

Chloe turned toward her grandmother, and Elizabeth took her by the hand. For a moment, Chloe remembered the soft touch from her mother's hands when she was a little girl trying to go back to sleep after a terrible nightmare.

"I see something in you I once saw in my own heart," Elizabeth said. "It's hard to lose someone we love, especially when their body is never found, and we can't properly mourn them. It's even harder to lose someone so young and full of life. Your mother was special. She didn't have an easy walk across this earth."

"I know. Her life was too short."

"That's not exactly what I mean. What I have to tell you will be hard for you to hear, but you need to learn it from me. Anna fled Mississippi because she had been—raped."

Chloe let go of her grandmother's hand and stood by the bed. "Did you say my mother was raped? Wha . . . When was she raped? By whom?"

Elizabeth rose up in her bed slightly. "I'm sorry, dear. I hated to tell you, but you needed to know because—"

"No," Chloe said. "No." She turned and walked to the window-sill again and then looked back at Elizabeth. "Who raped her? Was it someone you knew? Who? How old was she?"

"She was a teenager. Her life was a series of one horrific event after the next."

"Was the man arrested?"

"My dear, I know this isn't easy to comprehend. It was a long time ago, and someday the man will be punished for what he did."

"What do you mean 'someday'?"

"There was no such thing as DNA testing back then. It would have been her word against his, and Anna was too weak to fight him. You're not like her in that respect. Still, I know your heart. This isn't the end. Justice will be served."

"No wonder she never wanted to come back here."

"Sweetie, she did want to come home, but she wanted to protect you more."

"Why did she need to protect me?"

A light tap came across Elizabeth's door. A male nurse stuck his head in. "It's getting late, miss. Your grandmother should have been asleep a while ago. Can you continue your visit tomorrow?"

"It's okay, James," Elizabeth said. "We'll wrap it up and say our goodbyes real soon."

"All right. Do you need anything else?"

"No, thank you. We'll be turning off the lights soon." Elizabeth waved *night* as the man closed the door behind him.

"I can't believe all this." Chloe turned and looked out into the darkness. "I don't know what to think."

"In all your mother went through, she never became bitter. We are different."

"I don't even know what you mean by bitter, but I know anger." Chloe looked back at her grandmother.

"If you come back in the morning, I'll share the final piece of your mother's tale with you. But I want to pray with you before then because I want your heart to be ready to accept what I have to tell you."

"I'm too upset to pray. I don't even know how to pray. Just tell me."

"Death comes to us all, but the good news is we don't have to live full of hatred and anger. Those who have gone on—" Elizabeth stopped. "Well, we don't have to carry on over them like people who have no hope."

Chloe wasn't sure how to react. She was so torn up inside. She wanted to cry, pull away, and hug her grandmother, all at the same time. She stood there frozen staring at the floor in disbelief. She longed to feel something other than the anger and coldness she'd carried deep inside since she had awakened almost frozen to death in the back floorboard of her mother's car, crying out for a mother who would never answer.

But she didn't know anything about praying to Elizabeth's God. She wondered if it was possible for him to heal her aching heart. She walked back to her grandmother's bed, knelt beside her, and rested her head against her arm.

Chapter 37

*S*am *pulled up* to Chloe's hotel at 9:00 p.m. Chloe came out of the building wearing her favorite white, cotton tunic with a thin camisole underneath. She wore a pair of Capri leggings and the new sandals she had picked up at the mall. Chloe could have been walking on air; gravity couldn't hold her spirit down. The thinner clothes and sandals had nothing to do with the freedom in her soul.

Sam stated she looked more beautiful every time he saw her. Chloe knew her heart was clean from the inside out. Before coming to Mississippi, a hike in the mountains or a horseback ride in the backcountry always left her full of energy. But today, those things weren't necessary. She had found a new source of freedom, thanks to her grandmother's prayers and wisdom.

Sam took her to his favorite Italian place, and Chloe loved it from the first bite. They had almost finished eating when Chloe's cell rang. She recognized the number and told Sam it was Alice, and she would call her back. When dessert came, Alice called again. Chloe decided she had better answer.

"Okay, first of all, it's not my fault," Alice blurted out after Chloe said hello.

A sickening feeling came over Chloe. She thought about the ranch then the expensive heifer. "What isn't your fault?" Chloe was almost afraid to ask.

"It's Hank. Late this afternoon, he fell off the grain bin and broke his pelvis."

"Oh no. Is he okay?" Chloe asked. Sam reached across the table and took Chloe's hand.

"He's in the hospital. His son is staying with him until they get him comfortable. I guess Hank will be in the hospital for a while."

"Where are you?" Chloe asked.

"I made it back to the ranch a few minutes ago. Please don't be upset. It's going to be okay. Your dad is coming in tomorrow, and we'll be fine until you get here," Alice said in a reassuring tone.

"Dad's not going to be there tomorrow."

"Really, wait." Alice left Chloe hanging and then returned. "He left a message on the answering machine sometime today, man."

"It's okay, Alice. Everything will be okay. Hank's son can do the feeding tomorrow, and you exercise the horses. I'll be there in the afternoon. Don't stress."

Sam squeezed Chloe's hand as he listened to the conversation. Chloe realized she was at peace. She relaxed and told Alice to stay in touch. Chloe informed Sam of all that had happened after she hung up. They finished their dessert and were about to leave when Alice called again.

"Yes, Alice," Chloe said.

"I almost forgot to tell you about the new development. A video clip taken from the police station has been playing all day on the news. Law-enforcement officers believe it shows the man who is responsible for killing the sheriff and his deputy."

"Send me a link. I'd like to get a look at the guy."

"I'll do that."

"Thanks," Chloe said. "Sam and I are dining out. Can I call you when I get back to my hotel room?" Alice agreed and apologized for calling during their meal.

Chloe and Sam enjoyed the rest of the night together. He drove her back through the antebellum area, and they sat out on the grass in the square located in the middle of town. Chloe loved the warm nights. They lay on the blanket Sam had been thoughtful enough to bring along and watched the fireflies and stars. She was thankful Elizabeth had been wrong about the storm moving in but right about everything else.

Before the night was over, Sam kissed her for the first time. She laughed to herself as she thought of him saying it was all her fault. He claimed if she hadn't been so beautiful, he could have resisted a little longer.

*****

Chloe debated if she should call Alice back. It was after one AM when Sam dropped her at the hotel and said good night. He promised to take her to the airport and would be by around seven thirty to pick her up.

She slipped into her nightshirt, climbed into bed, and checked her email. Alice's email was near the top of her inbox. She opened the attachment and saw a picture, which caused her to look twice. It was the man from the mall. Chloe couldn't believe her eyes.

The link was from the local news in the Snow Valley area. Chloe watched the video clip taken from the surveillance camera in sheriff's department in Wyoming a second time. She recognized the interior of the building right away. *Who is this man? What is he doing in Mississippi? Why had he killed the sheriff? And, why is he threating to kill me?*

Chloe decided to call Alice whose voice gave way that she was mostly asleep when she answered the phone.

"Alice, this guy in the video clip is the same guy who confronted me in the mall. I know him from somewhere but not a clue where."

"Yeah, I thought the same thing. That's odd. Word around the café is he's the veterinarian's assistant from over in Cody who quit the other day, but I find it hard to believe."

"That's it. That's where I know him from," Chloe sat up in bed. "I knew I had seen him somewhere in Wyoming. He helped me unload a sick horse a few years ago when Doc was out of town, and I used the vet's office in Cody.

"Why would he want Sheriff Bob dead? And what is he doing in Mississippi?" Alice asked.

153

Chloe sat on the edge of her bed. "Listen, Alice. I'm beginning to think this man has ties to my grandmother's neighbor. At any rate, I'll show this to Sam in the morning, and he'll know what to do."

"Yeah, how was the date, by the way?"

"It was wonderful. He's so funny. We went to the square in Bishopville and lay out on the grass. I laughed so hard. I haven't felt like this since before my mom died."

"I'm really glad," Alice said and then yawned. "You'll have to tell me all about it when you get home, but I'm going back to bed now. As you know, chores can't be put off in the morning."

"Yeah, sorry for calling so late. Before you go, I wanted to ask about Hank," Chloe said.

"He's going to be okay, but it'll be a while before he can come back to work."

"I'm so thankful his son is there to fill in. Sorry, I had to put all this on you," Chloe said. "I'll make it up to you somehow." They said their good nights, and Chloe laid her head on her pillow, but she did not close her eyes. Her mind shifted from Wyoming to Mississippi, from Kimball Mitchell to her mother, from her loyalty to her father to her newfound loyalty to her grandmother, and surprisingly, Sam.

Chapter 38

Kimball *followed the* gray van into town right after sunrise on Sunday morning. He had warned his associate to do as he was told this time, or he wouldn't need a job if he screwed up again. Kimball spent half the previous night trying to figure out how to grab the old bat. She had better be outside like Rodger said, or he would have to rethink the entire abduction.

The van turned into the nursing-home drive and backed into the nearest empty space by the courtyard. Kimball pulled to the side of the road outside the line of view of the patrol car parked near the home's entrance. He didn't want them to spot his pickup until he was ready to be seen. Kimball studied his watch until a full five minutes passed. He figured that would be enough time for his associate to exit the van, open the back door, and walk through the oversized pergola which connected the courtyard to the main building.

Kimball stepped on the gas and set his hand on the horn at the same time. The pickup wheeled into the parking lot of the nursing home with the horn blaring. Both law-enforcement officers were standing in the entrance, drinking their morning coffee. Kimball saw them turn toward him. Each officer threw their cup in the air, reached for their weapon, and squatted near one of the huge, white columns. Kimball ran the pickup over a small flower bed. He turned the steering wheel, and his pickup clipped the edge of the patrol car. Kimball attempted to watch the courtyard and the van while he was driving, but he was moving too fast and couldn't see if the associate had been able to grab her or not. He would have to risk it.

He turned to leave the parking lot, and both policemen jumped into the damaged patrol car. Kimball knew he would have to drive fast to outrun them, but he would love every minute, even if they did catch him.

He had instructed his associate on what to do with the old bat in case a rookie cop arrested him. But Kimball doubted he would be arrested, and if he was, he had several thousand dollars in the glove compartment as his get-out-of-jail-free card. He would not be locked up. Not on this important day.

The patrol car followed him down the main street. Kimball grabbed an opened beer can and took a big swallow. Then he poured some of the beer down his shirt and into the floor of the pickup. He tossed the can into the floorboard, and it fell among the collection from the associate's latest binge.

Kimball decided to pull over before the officers called in for backup. He knew a few thousand dollars could only be spread so far. He had planned to use his usual "I'm too drunk to know better" excuse and then offer them money. He looked in his rearview mirror to see if the van had pulled out of the nursing home yet, but the flashing lights blocked his view. Kimball would have to wait till he reached the ranch to see if his plan had worked.

Chapter 39

Willie B had intended to meet Chloe in Elizabeth's room so he could get his revolver back before she flew out. He wanted to have the carving done before Chloe left town, but it hadn't turned out exactly like he wanted it to. He decided he would mail it to Chloe after she returned home.

As Willie B neared the assisted-living home, he saw dozens of patrol cars lining the parking lot in front of the building. He immediately worried they were there because of Elizabeth. Lights flashed in every direction as law-enforcement personnel covered the property.

The local news station's van was positioned in the middle of the paved lot. A patrol officer was directing traffic and motioned for Willie B to continue driving forward. He drove past the home and entered a gas station where he parked. He got out of his pickup and walked back.

Within a few minutes, he was standing next to the entrance. "Officer, please, over here."

An officer walked over to Willie B. "Move on, sir."

"But, officer, my friend lives here. I need to know if she is okay."

"I'm sorry. I can't give out any information at this time. You'll have to move on, sir."

On his walk back to his pickup, Willie B dialed Elizabeth's room number four times. He didn't get an answer. He called Sam the second he reached his pickup. Sam promised to let him know as soon as he found out any news on the events happening at the home.

Chapter 40

The Morton building's south side had an extra-large garage door for eighteen-wheelers to pull through. Several horse stalls lined the wall. A circular pen was located on the east wall near the sales arena. Dust blew up as the associate drove the gray van to the edge of the concrete floor. He stepped out of the van and opened the double back doors.

Elizabeth lay still on the floor. She hadn't moved since he held the washcloth seeped in chloroform to her face. The white attendant uniform he wore had caused no alarm. She didn't even yell when he slid the cloth over her face from behind.

As the associate rolled Elizabeth over to get his arm under her body, her head banged the side of the van. The associate heard the loud sound. He checked to see if her head was bleeding. It wasn't. He moved his large arms under her body and lifted her from the van floor. She didn't weigh as much as two sacks of horse feed. He threw her over his shoulder and hauled her up the steps to the top floor. Kimball had been very specific as to the room he wanted her placed in, and he didn't need Kimball on him anymore.

*****

Kimball pulled into the Morton Building minutes later. He couldn't help but smile at the sight of the open van doors. He knew she was finally under his control without anyone to protect her.

As he walked through the office door, and by the kitchen, he noticed the associate sitting on a stool eating a large tuna sandwich. A bag of chips had been dumped on the bar and a one-liter Pepsi sat next to the chips.

"Don't worry, she's in the right room, and she'll be coming around soon." He sat his sandwich on the countertop and spun the barstool to face Kimball. He smiled from the pleasure of knowing nothing had gone wrong this time.

Kimball spoke, "I paid off a couple of newbies. It cost me extra to keep them from arresting me. Had to swing by the ATM and get more money than I had on me." He walked over to the fridge and took out a pop. "When was the last time you checked on her?"

"About fifteen minutes ago. The associate returned to his snack."

Kimball walked over the cabinets lined along the office wall. He removed a small first-aid kit, found the tiny vial of smelling salts, and walked over to the associate. "Go check her again. If she's not awake, wake her." He handed him the vial.

Chapter 41

S*am knew he* had to call Chloe. His fingers unwillingly dialed her cell number.

"Good morning, I was thinking about calling you," Chloe said.

"I'm coming over early, okay."

"Okay, I've almost finished packing my suitcase."

"I'll see you in about ten minutes." He closed his phone and finished dressing. Sam dreaded to tell Chloe the news. He wasn't sure how she would take it. He grabbed a blue polo shirt and slid it on and then reached for the pair of jeans he had tossed across the recliner the night before. He dressed, hurried to his car, and pulled out onto the road toward Chloe's hotel.

His cell rang as he drove through a red light. A friend on the force told Sam an eyewitness had not identified the abductor as Kimball Mitchell. A much younger guy than Mitchell had been seen picking Elizabeth up, placing her over his shoulders, and then throwing her in the back of a gray panel van.

Sam pulled into the hotel's check-in area. He jumped out of the car and ran into the lobby. He didn't wait for the elevator to open; instead, he took the nearest stairs and ran the two flights to Chloe's floor. He slowed his breathing before knocking on her door.

*****

A single suitcase sat next to the door along with Chloe's bag. She was brushing her hair when the knock came. Chloe tossed her hair back and fluffed it with her hand. She threw her brush in the bag, walked to the door, and looked to see if it was Sam. She noticed his blond hair was falling down into his eyes. She knew he always wore it flipped back. She opened the door and right away knew something was wrong.

"Did Elizabeth die?" Chloe asked in a shaky voice. She fell into Sam's arms.

He held her a minute and then gently pushed her back. "Tell me what's wrong," Chloe said.

"She didn't die." Sam hesitated. "She's been abducted."

Sam helped her to the edge of the bed. "What are you saying?"

"Someone came in the courtyard and took her early this morning. The residents are saying it wasn't Kimball Mitchell but someone younger."

"No, this can't be true." Chloe cried. She put her face into her hands.

"I was told two patrol officers chased Mitchell out of the home's parking lot about the same time this happened."

"Could he have paid someone to do it?" Chloe asked.

"I really don't know what's going on right now. Willie B had gone to visit her when he saw all the patrol cars at the home, and then he called me." Sam sat next to her on the bed and placed his arm around her. "It will be all right. We'll find her."

Chloe sat motionless for a few minutes. Then she remembered she had to catch a plane for home in a few hours. "What am I going to do? Hank is injured. Alice needs to get back to work, and I have a male model feeding my cattle. And to top it off, a father who is too busy to notice. What a mess."

"You know I'm here for you. I'm taking you to my place. Mitchell is still out there, and I don't believe for a minute he isn't the one responsible for Elizabeth's kidnapping. No arguing. If you decide to stay, you can stay with me. At least, I'll know you're safe."

"I will have to call Alice."

"Let's go. I'll run you by my house then I'll go to the assisted-living home and find out as much as I can."

"I had rather go with you. Elizabeth needs both of us. We have to find her."

"And we will, but you need to decide if you are staying here or leaving. It will give you time to make some calls."

"Okay, I'll go to your place. I'll call you as soon as I know what I'm going to do about home. I can't go with Elizabeth missing. Who knows what Mitchell is planning."

Sam stood and picked up Chloe's suitcase near the door. "Are you ready to go?"

"No, give me a minute to check the closet." Chloe went by and lifted her purse off the floor. She walked to the closet and opened the safe, placed Willie B's weapon in her bag, and closed the closet door. "I'm ready."

Sam drove straight to his house and let Chloe in the front door. He gave her the alarm code and told her not to open the door for anyone. He promised to be back as soon as possible. Sam kissed Chloe goodbye, and within minutes, he was on the road again.

Chapter 42

*C*hloe *locked the* door and dialed Alice's cell number. She walked around the house drawing all the curtains closed while she waited on Alice to answer. She fought to hold the tears back.

Alice didn't have time to say more than hello.

"You are not going to believe what happened. My grandmother was abducted from the nursing home." Chloe couldn't hold back the tears any longer. She found a box of tissue and wiped her eyes.

"What?" Alice replied. "Chloe, are you there? Are you serious?"

Chloe raised the phone back to her face. "I don't know what to do. I have to stay here. I can't leave with Elizabeth missing. She might need me. I know Kimball Mitchell had something to do with her disappearance."

"Slow down, take a deep breath. You're not making a lot of sense," Alice said.

Chloe sat down on the couch and forced herself to relax. "Elizabeth told me to stop in this morning to say goodbye." She dropped her head into her hand. "I can't believe this."

"She'll be okay. The police will find her," Alice said in a reassuring tone.

"I don't have any faith in that at all," Chloe said. "My grandmother showed me how to pray last night, but now I can't remember any of it."

"Just try to believe that she is going to be okay. You have to believe," Alice said.

Chloe stood and walked to one of the front windows. She lifted the edge of the curtain and looked up and down the street. "I don't know if I can ask this, but is it possible you could stay at the ranch for a few more days? I don't want you to lose your job, but I can't leave now. I just can't." Chloe dropped the curtain and walked over to an oversized ottoman and took a seat. "I'd never forgive myself if I left and Elizabeth dies at the hands of that man. I know there has to be something I can do to save her."

"I don't know what you can do to help her, but I have been happier these past four days than I have in the last four years. I know I am rusty, but I can handle this job. Everything is going to be just fine on this end."

"I would be glad to have you stay as long as you like," Chloe said.

"Trust me, okay? And don't think about this ranch anymore. You go help Sam and take care of yourself and Elizabeth."

"All right. Please don't be like the rest of my employees and run off while I'm here." Chloe tried to smile.

"No way. I love it too much."

"I have to call the airline and change my ticket."

"Don't worry. We will be fine here," Alice said.

"I'll stay until Elizabeth is found. It's time I let my father know how I really feel. I'll call him later today and let him know what is going on. I'll even tell him that you are the newest employee at the ranch. If any of you need anything, let me know. And tell Hank's son I'm thankful he is there. He can stay as long as he's able."

Chloe hung up and dialed the familiar numbers of her dad's cell. Their normal conversations never lasted long, but this time she would get his attention.

As she listened to the phone ringing on the other end of the receiver, Chloe remembered her rental car parked at the hotel.

Chapter 43

Sam called and told Chloe he had met with the assisted-living home's director. She had promised to do whatever it took to bring Elizabeth home. No ransom demands had been made, and the FBI in Oxford had been notified. Sam was working with some friends from the Bishopville City PD and the County Sheriff's Department to do what could be done locally. A task force had been formed. Sam told Chloe to stay put. He would be back as soon as he could. Before he said goodbye, he told her to expect a plainclothes officer to be patrolling the neighborhood and mostly his home.

*****

Chloe decided to call the hotel's concierge to arrange to bring her back to the hotel so she could get her rental car. Within thirty minutes, a gentleman arrived in the hotel's minivan and took her back for her car.

Chloe made sure Willie B's gun was in her bag. Once she got in the rental, she locked the doors and headed back to Sam's place. As she pulled up to the house, she noticed a gray van parked a couple of houses down the street. Chloe realized she didn't have a remote control for the garage door. She knew she would have to unlock the front door to get back into the house. She took the revolver out of the bag and stared at it. She knew she would have no problem using it if necessary.

The front doorsteps were a mere five yards in front of Chloe. The associate came from the side of Sam's house at full speed. She raised the weapon with her finger on the trigger. The associate took her to the ground causing the gun to go off. As she fell, the gun flew out of her hand. The associate was on top of her.

"You listen." The associate's hot breath went across her face. "Kimball wants a trade. The old bat for all evidence she has against him. You have one, and I mean only one, chance to save that old granny of yours. We'll be in touch." The associate raised his body off hers and ran down the road toward the gray van.

Chloe picked herself up off the ground and ran for the weapon. She got a couple of shots into the back glass of the van as it pulled away. Chloe ran toward the road and shot once more. The van veered slightly and then continued at full speed out of the subdivision. She dropped to her knees.

Seconds later, a local patrol car approached Sam's house from the opposite direction. The officer switched on his lights and got out of the car. A few neighbors had wandered out of their houses.

Chloe shuddered as the officer touched her shoulder. He was talking to her, but she wasn't sure what he was saying. He took the .45 from her hands, helped her up to a standing position, and then walked her toward Sam's house.

The officer told her to stay put at the front entrance and allow him to check the house. She waited by the door but watched her surroundings. A few minutes later the officer returned and told her it was all clear. Chloe went into the house alone while the policeman walked to the other patrol car.

Chloe watched from the front window as the two men talked for a while. The second car left, and the original officer walked back toward the house. Chloe moved to the kitchen bar. Her hands trembled as she lifted a glass of water to her lips. She could hear the officer on the phone making promises to Sam.

"Is he on his way?" she asked as the young officer hung up.

"Yes, ma'am. He will be here shortly. I'm not going to leave until he gets here."

Chloe dropped her head into her hands. She wanted to pray and managed to whisper, "Help us. Please."

She had walked to the front window five times to see if Sam had arrived before the door finally opened. Sam threw his keys on the foyer table and hurried over to Chloe.

"Are you okay?" he asked. They embraced.

"Yes. I'm okay."

"Are you crazy?" Sam pushed her back far enough to see her face. "You could have been killed. I told you not to open the door."

"I know," Chloe said. They both took a seat on the couch. Her hands had stopped shaking, but she had a huge headache. "I wish I could have gotten a better shot. I can't believe I missed him," she said. Sam placed his arm around her shoulders.

"Did you see the man?" Sam asked.

"Yes and—" Chloe looked at her phone. "I even have a picture of him. Well, it's a video clip." She played the short clip Alice had sent her. She told them the man in the video was the one who had attacked her on the front lawn and the mall.

"Send this to me and Officer Ryan."

Chloe quickly forwarded the link to the two men.

"Tell me what happened," Sam said.

"He told me I had a chance to save Elizabeth. One chance. I have to find all the evidence Elizabeth has and get it to Kimball Mitchell. He didn't tell me any details, only that he would be in touch."

"This ties the guy to Kimball Mitchell," the officer said. "Do you know anything about the evidence he asked for?"

"Yes, I have a cassette tape Elizabeth gave me to take back to Wyoming for safekeeping. It's in my bag."

The officer asked for the tape. Chloe stood and went to the kitchen table. Her purse was lying open. She pulled the old cassette out and handed it to Sam who handed it to the policeman.

As the officer slid the cassette into his pocket, Chloe remembered every negative word that had been spoken against the Bishopville Police Department. She thought of the detectives they had spoken to after Kimball had attacked Elizabeth and her and how Kimball was never even brought in for questioning. She was glad she had converted the cassette to an MP3 on her Mac. Elizabeth had entrusted the cassette to her, and she had freely given the only hard copy to a possible enemy.

"Can I have that back please?" Chloe asked.

"I need to turn this in as evidence," the officer said.

"But I'm going to need it to trade for Elizabeth's life."

"Don't you worry, we will handle any transfers. Is there any other evidence in your possession?"

Chloe thought about the how frail Elizabeth was. She knew she had to save her if at all possible, and she knew the cops couldn't be trusted to do their part. She answered accordingly to what she had been asked. "No, sir. None."

"Are you sure this is all of it?" the man asked again.

"Chloe," Sam said, "Officer Smith is a longtime friend of mine. You can trust him."

"I'm telling you, that's what Elizabeth gave me while I was visiting her. I don't have anything else. Do I need to say it again?" Chloe looked at the officer wishing she'd never said anything about evidence.

"No, you don't," Sam said. He walked with the officer to the door.

Chloe heard them chatting at the doorway. The man told Sam he would be in touch with the detectives in Wyoming regarding the suspect in the video clip. The policeman left, and Sam locked the door behind him and set the alarm.

"He will be sending other patrol cars around every so often. We'll be fine," Sam said.

"I'm not worried. Three times I have been attacked by either Kimball or his man. There won't be a fourth." Chloe stood quickly. "Oh crap, he took my weapon too. That was Willie B's gun." She walked over to Sam and grabbed him by both arms. "You have to get it back."

"I'm sure it will be logged in as evidence, temporarily. You did fire a weapon inside the city limits. There's an ordinance against discharging firearms in the city. He'll have to make a report, and the gun will most likely be returned to Willie B."

"Most likely, won't be," Chloe said sarcastically. She turned and went into the kitchen, and Sam followed her.

Sam opened the fridge and took out a yogurt. "Would you like one?" he asked.

"Yes, please," Chloe said. "You have to get Willie B's gun back, Sam."

"When did you get that cannon from Willie B anyway?" Sam asked. "You are full of surprises, aren't you?"

"He loaned it to me two days ago on Friday. Do you have any weapons at all?"

"Yes, I do. And they are locked in my gun safe where I'll leave them until I need one. So don't ask again. And let's back up a little. Friday, we went to the police department—"

"And—" Chloe shoved a bite of yogurt into her mouth and swallowed. "As you can see, they can't be trusted. So I found my own protection. I could have been killed today."

Sam walked over to the counter where she was standing. He put his arms around her and kissed her forehead. Chloe offered him a bite of yogurt, and he accepted. "I'm glad nothing happened to you," Sam said. "I'm not looking forward to you leaving, just so you know."

Chloe slipped away from Sam's arms and walked to the trash. She tossed the empty cup into the container and placed the spoon in the dishwasher. "I'm glad I was able to work it out with Alice so I can be here a little longer. My dad isn't too happy with me right now, but I have to start living my life at some point."

"I'm glad you are still here. In more ways than one," Sam said.

"Yes, well, Elizabeth is my main focus right now."

"Of course. Mine too," Sam said.

Chloe was already thinking about the other evidence buried under the oak tree. She wanted to tell Sam her plans to go after it; she wanted his help, but she knew he would never agree to it. She would get the evidence and save her grandmother's life, with or without Sam or the police for that matter.

Chapter 44

Elizabeth woke up in a strange room. A pain shot through her head. She turned to see where she was. She reached up and felt a bump on the side of her head. Elizabeth closed her eyes again; she wanted to go back to sleep. The uneasiness in her stomach and the pain in her head weren't going to make that easy.

She smelled bacon cooking in the distance. She looked around the unfamiliar room. The only furnishing in the entire space was a wall-mounted television, a small two-drawer end table, and the twin bed she lay in. People were talking on the television, but Elizabeth couldn't make out what they were saying. She leaned her head back against the pillow and tried to avoid touching the knot.

Elizabeth sought to focus her eyes and her brain. She noticed the digital numbers on the TV screen. She forced herself to think about the time. The last thing she could remember was sitting out in the courtyard waiting for the early morning praise-and-worship group to show up.

She thought about the numbers in front of her, and she began to realize it was almost 8:00 a.m. She wondered if Chloe had caught her morning flight. Surely, she came to the nursing home to say goodbye.

At first, Elizabeth hoped Chloe was on the plane back to Wyoming, but then she thought about just how far Kimball's arms reached. Chloe would never be safe as long as Kimball Mitchell was alive.

The door opened, and a tall man walked in with a tray of food. "Got your breakfast, Granny," the associate said. "Boss told me to bring some smelling salts, but I thought I'd wake you with the smell of food. After all, it could be your last meal."

Elizabeth sat up a little in the bed. "Who are you, and why am I here? And for that matter where—"

"Whoa, hold your panties, Granny. Too many questions at one time." The associate placed her food tray on her lap. "I think you'll enjoy this meal. I made it myself." He lifted the cover, and the smell of bacon was irresistible.

"I'm not hungry," Elizabeth said.

"Now, Granny. I know you are, so eat up. Besides, I won't have time to run back and forth to check on you. I was told to offer you something."

"Who told you that?"

"Eat. I'll be back in fifteen minutes to get the tray." The associate left the room.

She looked at the bacon and eggs and decided she might as well eat a bite or two. Fifteen minutes later, the associate came back.

He moved the tray and placed it on the end table. He opened a closet door and stepped inside. When he returned, he was pushing a brand-new wheelchair. "You want to try out your new wheels, Granny?"

Elizabeth turned her head toward the door and decided not to answer.

"Okay, here's the deal," he said. "You are in a special room. Actually it was built with you in mind. It's soundproof, has handicap access to the bathroom, and no windows, as you might have noticed." The associate walked around her bed and looked at her. "I will return every few hours until we get what we want. You can either sit in your wheelchair or stay in the bed. It is up to you, but once you pick, I won't be back for a while, and no one will hear you if you scream until your toenails pop off. Got it?"

"Yes, I have it." Elizabeth stared at the man. She tried to memorize every detail she could while he stood in front of her.

"So you staying in bed all day or getting in the wheelchair, Granny?"

Elizabeth told him to help her into the chair. The associate did and then left the room. She was alone to explore. He was right. There was nothing to explore. She found the remote on a tray which had been attached to the bottom of the television. Elizabeth changed the channel until she found the weather. She realized it was still Sunday and then turned the television off. But it was so quiet that she decided to turn it back on.

Chapter 45

*M*onday *morning, Chloe* stood in the kitchen waiting for the coffee maker to switch off. She pulled her robe together at her chest and sat at the bar. Chloe wasn't really listening to the television until she heard Elizabeth's name. She stood and walked quickly over to Sam who was sitting on the couch going through his briefcase. A young female reporter looked somewhat cheerful as she reported the news.

"A task force has been formed to locate a local resident of the Gentle Breeze Assisted-Living Home here in Bishopville. State and local law enforcement have combined their efforts to locate the missing seventy-eight-year-old who was abducted early yesterday morning. An eyewitness said Elizabeth Lee, from the Pines Community, had only been a resident of the home for two months and was taken from the courtyard while participating in an early Sunday morning worship service. The FBI field office in Oxford has offered assistance to the task force and is on standby. In a related incident, the Wyoming Division of Criminal Investigation has a detective consulting on the case. Officials believe there is a connection between a suspect wanted for questioning in the recent murders of law enforcement officers in Wyoming and the kidnapping of the missing elderly woman from the Gentle Breeze nursing home. There will be more updates as they become available. If you have any information regarding this case, officials are asking for your help. Please call the number at the bottom of your screen."

Chloe turned her eyes to the pergola leading into the court-yard in the background behind the redhead reporter. She could not believe she had been sitting in the very courtyard enjoying the warm air and her grandmother's presence a couple of days before, and now Elizabeth was missing. She felt Sam's arm reach around her shoulder.

"It's going to be okay," Sam said. "I know most of the guys on the task force. They are part of the recent additions the new commissioner has brought in. We don't have to worry about these guys being in Mitchell's pocket."

"What about the ones you don't know? I want my grandmother to be okay. She's so old. I don't think she can handle a lot of abuse from Kimball Mitchell." Chloe leaned into Sam's arm.

"Elizabeth's tougher than you think. I've known her a long time, and she isn't one to roll over and die." Sam looked into Chloe's tearful eyes. "If she was, this illness would have taken her out a long time ago."

"You're right. I can tell she's a strong woman, but Mitchell is stronger."

"We'll find her," Sam said. He drew Chloe closer to him. "Before I leave this morning, you have to promise me you won't get any bright ideas about leaving the house until I get back. I have some business to take care of, and I'll be home soon." Sam rose from the couch and lifted Chloe to her feet. "I'll find out the latest updates on Elizabeth's case while I'm at the police precinct. Officer Smith is going to release the .45 into my care, and then I'll get it to Willie B next time I see him."

Chloe promised but only halfway meant it.

Sam gave her a kiss and after making her promise three more times. He left for work.

An hour later, she was going insane waiting for Sam to return. She checked the time on her cell and realized Alice was probably taking her breakfast break. She sat in the middle of Sam's huge couch and dialed Alice. Chloe asked about Hank first and then filled Alice in on the details from the day before.

"I'm so sorry, Chloe," Alice said.

"Nothing seems to be happening. The local law enforcement notified the FBI, but I don't think they are even involved yet," Chloe said.

"At least they are close by and can pitch in quickly."

"My grandma told me there is evidence buried near her homestead which will expose the crimes of the Mitchell family. But now, when and if I do find it, I'll have to turn it over to Kimball, or he will kill her."

"What are you going to do? And no matter what you do, don't go out looking for the information alone. Can you get Sam or someone to go with you?" Alice asked.

"Sam would be of very little help in the woods. I don't think his Italian leathers would work too well in the swamp and snake-infested backland."

"Don't go by yourself, Chloe, you hear me," Alice begged. "I know you are too stubborn to ask for help, but don't do this alone."

"If I don't think I can handle it, I'll get help."

"Please listen to me. I want you back in one piece."

Chloe promised, said goodbye, and hung up. She dialed Sam's number, but it went straight to voicemail. She walked around the house and wondered if she could possibly find Elizabeth in the backwoods of Bishopville. When she decided she didn't have a clue where to start looking, her mind turned to the canister. Chloe remembered Elizabeth telling her Willie B had the directions to the location of the evidence. She gathered her things and planned to spend the rest of the day looking for the old homestead on Kimball's land. It couldn't be hard to find; after all, she was an expert hunter. Finding an old house in some pine thicket would be a lot easier than a cave in the side of a Wyoming mountain.

Chloe dumped the contents of her bag onto the guest bed and then went on a scavenger hunt for items she might need. She took a roll of toilet paper and bug spray from the bathroom, and she grabbed a towel, rolled it up, and tucked it under her arm.

In the kitchen, she found some fruit, a couple of granola bars, and a few water bottles. She pushed the stuff into her bag, but everything didn't fit. She wandered into the utility room and found Sam's bike hanging from the ceiling and a backpack hanging on a hook beneath it. Chloe emptied the backpack and took it to the kitchen.

Within a few minutes, she had everything tucked inside and was ready to hit the road in her rental.

Chloe decided to visit Willie B, get the directions she needed, and then make her way out into the Pines Community to find the old homestead. If Sam got tied up with authorities and his work, he wouldn't be back for a while. She didn't bother leaving a note.

Chapter 46

Chloe didn't need the GPS as she drove out of town. She went straight to Willie B's home. She thought about how well he knew the area and could guide her in the right direction, but he was too old. She knew she could hunt with the best of men, yet she wondered about her sense of direction in a pine thicket of Mississippi. It would be different from the mountainsides. In Wyoming, she could climb to the top of a mountainside and see for miles around her. As she neared Willie B's home, the trees pressed in on both sides of the gravel road, begrudging the space the gravel occupied.

When she pulled into Willie B's driveway, she was encouraged to see Stump sitting on the porch steps of the old plank house.

Chloe parked, got out of her car, and walked to the house. The early morning wind had a friendly, warm breeze as she stood on the porch.

"Hello, Ms. Chloe," Stump said and threw his massive hand up in the air.

"Morning, Stump, how are you?"

"I'm good. Heard 'bout Ms. Lizzie. Hope she's okay," Stump said.

"Yeah, me too." She placed her hands in her blue-jean pockets and looked toward the screen door. She peered into the house, but it was dark beyond the light of the doorway.

"Did you come to bring Grandpa's revolver back? Are you leavin' today?"

"No, I came to visit Willie B, if he's home."

"Yeah, he's around. Hold on. I'll get him for you. He's down to the chicken coop repairin' a tore-up fence. Somethin's been gettin' his chickens, and that makes him madder than anything." Stump rose and walked around the side of the house.

Chloe trailed him. "I'll follow you if it's okay."

"Sure." Stump motioned for her. "Grandpa's down there bangin' on everything, acts like it's all about the chickens, but he's been pacing the floor and cleaning all morning. I finally got him out of the house when I told him another chicken was gone."

"We're all on edge," Chloe said.

"Yeah, Grandpa's worried sick."

They walked around a huge fig tree beside the house. The barn was located down a small hill and to the southwest of the old plank home. Chloe could see a fence which ran along the hillside and then out to the little barn. She couldn't see Willie B until they walked around the side of a rusty tin wall. The chicken coop ran along the south side of the barn. The coop, like the barn, looked handmade and pieced together many times throughout the years.

Willie B was pulling the broken wires back together and nailing them to different locations on the bottom boards which ran along the coop.

"Morning, Willie B," Chloe said as she leaned toward him and give him a slight hug. "I don't know what to say."

"I don't know either, child. I've been 'bout to go crazy. Thought I'd come out here and work on this old coop to take my mind off things." Willie B slid his hammer into his overalls and turned to walk toward the house with Chloe. She gave him her arm, and they climbed the slope slowly. "Stump and some others been handin' out those sheets of paper with Ms. Lizzie's picture on it. I think they got 'em hangin' in every store in town by now."

"Thank you, Stump," Chloe said. "Sam told me about it. I would have helped, but I was confined to the house. I'm supposed to be there now, but I got tired of sitting around doing nothing."

"You goin' stay a little longer in Mississippi?" Willie B asked. "Sam told me someone attacked you at his house. He said a cop took my .45 away from you." Willie B stopped walking.

"Are you okay?" Chloe asked. She was surprised at how fast the man had gotten out of breath.

"Yes, I just have to stop and wait for my body to catch up with my want to."

"I understand," Chloe said. "I'm sorry about not being able to give your gun back to you myself." Chloe looked at Willie B. "I hate to ask, but I'm going to need your help again."

They rounded the fig tree and the ground leveled off. Willie B partially straightened his back and patted Chloe on the arm. "Thanks for the support. It's gettin' harder to get down to the old coop and back."

"No problem," Chloe said as they continued to walk toward the porch.

"I ain't got but one more gun. Hope that ain't the kind of help you need. I gots to keep it here to get rid of whatever's attackin' my hens." Willie B turned to Stump. "But Stump has his huntin' rifle."

Stump frowned.

"That's wonderful, but I need your help with something else," Chloe said.

Stump walked over to his grandfather. "I'll work on that coop while y'all sit awhile."

Willie B handed Stump the hammer.

Chloe watched as Willie B struggled to straighten his back more.

"I was down there longer than I thought and can't get goin' again, and I left my walkin' cane," Willie B said as he turned toward the coop.

"Where is it?" Stump asked.

"I left it over by the barn door."

"I'll get it," Stump said and ran down the hill. Within a minute, Stump returned and handed his grandfather the homemade cane.

Chloe wished Willie B was able to help her find the old homestead, but she would have to go alone or take Stump.

Chapter 47

For the first time since Chloe had heard of her family in Bishopville, a moment of doubt struck her as hard as the hammer Stump used to drive the nails into the barn. She wondered if she would ever find one tiny canister in the thick pines in which she'd never stepped foot in. She wondered if her keen sense of direction would work in the Deep South. And she wondered if Elizabeth was still alive.

Willie B took a seat in the rocking chair on his porch. "You want me to get you somethin' to drink?" Willie B asked.

"No, I'm fine. I wanted to visit with you about Elizabeth's situation." Chloe moved to the edge of the porch and took a seat. She crossed her legs and leaned against the wooden pole holding the roof above the old porch.

"I figured that was what you were here fer."

"Elizabeth told me she gave you the directions to a canister. If I can find it, I might be able to save my grandmother's life."

"Yes, she gave me the directions, but I'm bound to an oath not to give them to you unless you agree to let Stump go with you."

"What?" Chloe asked.

"Ms. Lizzie saw the same strong will in you that was in Morgan. So when she had me write down the directions, she made me promise I would not tell you the location until you promised to let Stump help you."

"I don't need Stump."

"Oh yeah?" Stump said as he came around the corner of the house. "What you gonna do in them woods by yourself?"

"I can take care of myself."

"Little lady, I reckon that'd be true in Wyoming, but you ain't in Wyoming no more," Willie B said.

"All I want to do is go to the homestead, find the canister, and get the information to Kimball Mitchell before it's too late to save my grandmother. There's no telling what he'll do to her."

"Well, I'll give you them directions when you agree to let Stump help," Willie B said. He rocked his chair back and forth.

Chloe knew she had no choice. "Fine. Stump can go."

"Okay, we in business then." Willie B slapped his leg with his right hand. "Stump, go in the house and get us all some tea and bring out my old pocket notebook on my nightstand. We all gots to be careful, but we'll get our Ms. Lizzie back."

"Yes, sir." Stump lumbered across the porch and ducked his head as he went into the old house. The screen door closed behind him.

Chloe shifted around and let her legs hang off the front porch. "We don't have many homes in Snow Valley with a porch like this."

"I don't guess I'd want to live there then. I spend most of my days enjoyin' the breeze as it drifts across here," Willie B said.

"I hate to bother Stump with this. I'm capable of digging around an old house until I find the canister."

"Yes, ma'am, I's sure you are. But them woods ain't been lived in for a long time now. It's overgrown with vines and snakes. Not to even talk about Kimball Mitchell. If he finds you down there messin' around, he won't even ask questions. He'll kill you and throw your body in the lake behind the house with the rest of the corpses that rest there."

Stump came back out of the house with three glasses of tea. The notebook was stuck in his sleeveless shirt pocket. "Ms. Chloe, I know you don't like sweet tea, but it's all we had made up."

"It's okay. I'm getting used to it." Chloe took the plastic tumbler and turned it up. For a while, the three chatted about Elizabeth and the chances of finding her. Chloe sensed a peace around her. Even with Elizabeth's life hanging in the balance, she knew everything was going to be okay.

"I agree I might need some help with those dreaded snakes. We only have rattlers in Snow Valley, and my family's ranch is too high in elevation for them, so I don't have a lot of experience in dealing with those creatures." She placed her empty tea glass on the floor of the porch and stood up. "Now, Stump, if we come across a grizzly or mountain lion, I'll handle them, but I heard you eat fried snake, so you take care of all the things that crawl. Deal?"

"That's a deal," Stump said. He rose to his feet and shook her hand.

Chloe noticed he was more massive than she had ever realized. He could handle the grizzlies and the lions. "You ready to go?" she asked.

"It's still early. Guess I'm as ready as I'll be later on," Stump said.

Willie B removed one sheet of paper from his notepad and handed it to Chloe. "I made a copy of this map and put it on my dresser in case anything happens to me while y'all are gone. But I won't be able to come lookin' for y'all if you don't return before nightfall. I can't be out there stumblin' around in them woods no more. So don't get separated from each other. And, Stump, you take care of her."

"I won't let nothin' happen to her, Grandpa. I promise." Stump turned to walk toward the pickup.

Chloe reminded Stump to get some water and any tools he might need to take with them. She thought about Sam and how upset he would be if he came home early. She thought about calling him but changed her mind. He would only try to talk her out of it.

"Oh yeah, I better get us a couple of shovels," Stump said as he ran back down the hill to the barn and disappeared behind the wooden door for the second time. A few chickens flew out of the old barn, and Chloe could hear banging and metal reverberating all the way up the hill.

Willie B spoke up, "I know he is a little short on a full trough, but he is stronger than four mules. Give him a chance, and you'll be happy to have him around."

Chloe had sought to work on a poker face but had never seemed to master the art of covering her true feelings in her expressions. She realized she must have been frowning. "I'm sorry. I know he is a fine man. I'm used to getting my things and jumping right in. Waiting or patience isn't one of my strengths," Chloe said.

"He's a good boy, and you can count on him."

"I'm sure," Chloe said.

"I'll go in and fix y'all a jug of water to take. And I'd better fix something for Stump and you to snack on too."

"There's no need. I brought snacks if we get hungry."

"Little lady, I'm sure as little as you are, if he saw your snacks, he'd just get mad. I'll be right back." Willie B struggled to get up from his chair, leaned his weight onto his cane, and then walked into the house.

Chloe was ready to get going, and now she was waiting on two men. For a second, she remembered she was the one holding the directions. It couldn't be too hard to find. She could leave, but she wouldn't do Willie B like that.

She took the note from her jean pocket and opened it. The hand drawing showed an old house in the middle of the folded paper. A squiggly line must have represented a stream of water. She noticed a star marked on one side of the house under what appeared to be a grove of trees. What she didn't see was a road in and out of the pines.

Stump returned with a handful of items and threw all of them into the back of Willie B's old truck. "Guess I'm driving," he said.

Willie B came to the front door carrying a large cotton sack. "Here, boy, put this in the truck too. You'll get hungry. Ms. Chloe, I went over the directions with Stump as soon as I found out Ms. Lizzie was missing. Stump knows the area. So stay with him."

"I will. Don't worry."

Chapter 48

"*Hello, are you* in there, old bat?" Kimball snapped his fingers. "Wake up." He twisted a handful of gray hair in his large fingers and lifted Elizabeth's head off the back of her wheelchair.

Elizabeth groaned. Her eyes flickered.

"Wake up. No whining." Kimball let go of her head.

Elizabeth's neck bounced left and right against the canvas backing of the chair. The knot touched the metal edge of the wheelchair, and she yelled out in pain. She opened her eyes. "I . . . I guess I must have fallen asleep again. How long have I been here? I remember someone helping me into this chair, but I don't recall when that was," Elizabeth said.

Kimball knelt in front of her. "This is Monday. Time for us to get down to business."

"Monday?" Elizabeth asked as she looked around the room. She was hoping it was only a nightmare, but she realized she was indeed inside Mitchell's property and under his control.

"Yep, that's right. You've been sleeping like a baby." Kimball rose and walked around her wheelchair. "You stink old bat. Guess I'll have my man push you in the shower and hose you down. Can't promise he won't try to drown you though."

"You don't have to do this, Kimball. You know I have learned over the years to let sleeping dogs lie." Elizabeth strained to get comfortable in the wheelchair.

"Well, that's all well and good," Kimball said as he sat on the edge of the twin bed. "But I can't say I really believe you. You had to get your granddaughter involved, didn't you? Huh? What'd you do, tell her to blackmail me for something? Beg for money?"

Elizabeth looked at Kimball but didn't answer him.

"I'm going to ask you a few questions, and if you do a good job of telling me what I want to know, we'll talk about getting you back to the old folks' home and your friends," Kimball said.

"We both know you're lying," Elizabeth said.

He grabbed the wheelchair's handles and pulled her in front of him.

Elizabeth raised her head and looked him in the eye.

"Whether you go back to the home or not, doesn't really matter now, does it?"

"No, I guess it doesn't anymore." A single tear rolled down Elizabeth's cheek.

"Good. Then let's get started. The sooner you answer my questions, the sooner you'll have lunch."

Chapter 49

Stump drove the pickup off the gravel road and down a forgotten dirt path which led into a pasture.

Chloe's eyes followed the only visible fence line she could see until it veered off in another direction. The trees didn't waste any time taking up the open space. She could understand how the neighborhood was dubbed the Pines Community.

She was glad the pines would cover them. Stump had to park the old truck somewhere out of Kimball Mitchell's sight.

"This is the road your Grandpa Morgan and your grandmother used as their driveway to the old house place, but Kimball doesn't use it much," Stump said. "There's another road that trails off from his ranch and comes down on the other side of the property, and he uses it. I saw 'em haul timber out on this road a few times over the years, but that's about all they use it for anymore."

"How far in the woods is the homestead?" Chloe asked.

"Oh, it ain't too far back in there. Maybe a couple of miles." Stump dropped the pickup into a lower gear. The front tire hit a hole, and Chloe's head touched the ceiling of the truck. Stump looked at Chloe. "You okay?"

"I'm fine. I'm tougher than I look, so don't worry about me."

"We have to stop pretty soon and walk in the rest of the way," Stump said.

"Why can't we follow the dirt driveway back there? I don't mind bumpy roads."

"Well, there's a creek that runs just before you get to the house. Morgan built a small wooden bridge across it, but ain't nobody done any work back this way in a long time. I went ahuntin' up here last winter. Old bridge ain't safe anymore. I'd hate for the pickup to fall through. With all the heavy rains lately, the creek is going to be full anyway. We might not be able to cross."

"Oh, we'll cross. We can't let a swollen creek stop us," Chloe said.

As they drove deeper into the woods, the sun had less and less space to enter, and Chloe noticed the change in temperature right away. Pines of all sizes crowed each other for what sunshine did make it through. Many trees were bent over and crossed those beneath them.

Stump explained how ice would collect on branches and bend the trees downward. He explained the weight was so brutal on the younger ones that they never recovered. They were doomed to live a slanted life. He told her some had to get out of the way so others could grow. He pulled the truck around a thicket and parked the nose facing inward. "Well, time for a little walk."

Chloe gathered an ax and the rifle while Stump collected his food and a couple of shovels.

"The house is just over this hill," Stump said. He threw his snack sack over his shoulder and walked to the base of the hill with Chloe behind him.

Brush covered the hillside. Chloe couldn't even see the ground beneath the thick vines and weeds. She looked for an opening to walk through, but every branch seemed to intertwine with another. "How are we going to get through this mess?"

"Hold on," Stump said. He turned and walked back to the pickup. When he returned he was holding a machete. "Glad I remembered to bring this guy along." He took the machete and whacked at the brush. The limbs reluctantly dropped their hold. "You follow after me, but don't get too close."

"Do you want me to carry some of those tools?" Chloe asked.

"Nah, I got this. But here, you take the food." Stump handed her the cotton bag his grandfather had packed.

The weight caught her off guard. She tipped forward and almost fell into Stump.

"You all right, Ms. Chloe?"

"Yes. Here, tie this to my backpack." She handed the sack back to Stump and turned around for him to connect the sack to her backpack. "Were you thinking we would be out here long?"

"Couple of hours maybe," Stump said as he continued to whack at the brush and vines.

Chloe wondered about the task of climbing the small hill covered in some type of vine she'd never seen before with branches so close she couldn't see how a rabbit could get through them.

Stump took the lead and swung the machete wildly into the thick growth. After a few minutes of climbing and stopping and climbing and stopping, Chloe knew there had to be a better way. "Hey, Stump. Hold up a minute."

Stump turned around. Sweat poured from every pore on his face. His sleeveless shirt was soaked. He held the machete at his side and stood still. "Yes'em. You all right?"

"Look, I know I've never been here before, and you know the area better than I do, but do you think it would be easier to follow the road around to the house than climb this overgrown hill?"

"Well, we could go by the road, but you remember that creek. You got to cross it if you go by the road. This way, you ain't got to."

"Is the creek worse than this?" Chloe looked up the hill. She knew it would take hours before they reached the top at this rate. She didn't mind the workout, but she didn't have any desire to be in the thick of the woods any longer than she had to be. She thought about Sam coming in for lunch and her not being at his house.

"Like I told you, I ain't been down that way since last huntin' season. But I already know that old bridge ain't goin' hold up the truck's weight. A lot of them boards are plain rotten."

"If we go this way, we won't reach the house until dark."

"That's all right. I brought a lantern. Oh shoot, Ms. Chloe. I left it in the back of the pickup."

"Stump, we aren't going to be here that long. Don't bother with a lantern."

He threw the machete into the ground, dropped the other tools, and was on his way to the pickup before she finished half her sentence.

She picked up the tools and followed him.

"Look, Stump," Chloe said when she reached the side of the old truck, "let's leave the pickup here and walk down the old path. I think we will be okay. We'll cross the creek on foot, and it will save us a lot of work cutting through that jungle of a mess."

"Okay, Ms. Chloe, but I tell you now. I-I can't swim." Stump looked embarrassed. "If that creek is up too far, I ain't crossing it."

"We will be okay, and I know it will be a lot faster than the alternative." Chloe looked back at the overgrown hillside and shook her head. With all the chopping Stump had done, she couldn't make out the trail he was cutting.

Stump took the ax, machete, and the two shovels from Chloe. She carried the rifle in one hand and lugged his snacks on her back. Stump marched his way to the old pathway without complaining, but Chloe knew he wasn't happy.

The walk down the grass-covered road went a lot faster than the vine slaying Stump had in mind. Within a few minutes, they arrived at the old bridge. Chloe could tell it was crudely made. There were no rails, and nothing about it looked safe. But she wasn't going to say so.

It had served its purpose in its glory days, but those were long gone. She was excited to see the old homestead place. For a moment, she could sense her mother running through the woods as a small child. Maybe she'd find a tire swing at the house.

"I told you, this creek would be up," Stump said as he stopped at the water's edge. "I ain't crossin' this old rotten bridge."

"It will be okay, Stump. Look we'll walk right on the edge of the bridge. It's the largest beam, and it will hold us."

"I ain't walkin' on no beam. I ain't no twirly girl. Besides, you can't even see the whole beam. Don't you see that water on some of them boards? Nope, no way."

"Look, Stump, you can follow me. Look at your snack sack on my back, and don't look at the water."

"I can't do it, Ms. Chloe. I just can't."

"Stump. I need your help. You told your grandfather you wouldn't let anything happen to me. Remember?"

"Let's go back, and I'll chop faster. We can climb the hill in a little bit."

"No, Stump. We need to hurry. Now come on, and let's get this done." Chloe stepped on the edge of the wooden bridge and began her trek over the aged wood. The overpass moaned as she walked across it. She watched every step she took and prayed she didn't see one of the venomous snakes everyone had told her about. Chloe hoped Stump was behind her. She reached the other side within a few minutes and turned to check on Stump's progress. He hadn't moved an inch. He was on the other side of the bridge holding two shovels in one hand and the ax and machete in the other.

"Stump, what are you doing? Come on."

"I tried, Ms. Chloe. I really did, but I can't swim. The water's too high, and I know . . . I can't do it."

Chloe raised her voice. "Stump, get yourself over here. I need your help."

Stump hesitated then placed one foot on the bridge and froze. He looked down at the water moving over the wooden bridge and then back to Chloe. "I . . . I ain't doin' this." He backed off the bridge.

"What is wrong? You are so strong. You can do this. It's no more than a few steps," Chloe pleaded.

"I almost drown when I was just a tadpole. I ain't never been in the water since then, and I ain't going to start now. I'll go back and climb the hill. You go on, and I'll meet you there later." He turned and walked back down the path.

"No, Stump. It will take you too long."

"I don't care. I ain't crossin' no rotten bridge."

"Stump. Get back over here." Chloe shouted toward Stump's back.

"Nope." He turned and looked at Chloe. "The old house is up the road a little ways." He pointed to the right with the hand holding the machete. "I'll be there in a while. Just watch where you step, and you'll be fine without me." He let the machete fall to his side then turned and walked away.

Chloe shook her head. She knew she had to reach the old house and find the canister. She turned and headed down the pathway toward the homestead. She hoped the house was near, but all she could see was an overgrown arc in the trees in front of her.

Chapter 50

Sam drove his Charger into Willie B's driveway. He had been completely swamped at his office and then visited the precinct to collect Willie B's gun and get an update from his friend on Elizabeth's task force.

He had made up his mind to tell Willie B he had to promise never to give Chloe a gun again. He didn't want to hurt the old man's feelings, but he knew Chloe could be persuasive when she wanted to be.

Sam could smell fresh mustard greens and corn bread cooking as he climbed the steps of Willie B's porch. He knocked on the door and waited. The .45 rested in a brown paper bag at his side.

Willie B swung the screen door opened. "Come on in, Sam. I'm 'bout to take up some greens if you'd like to sit down to a plate."

"No, thank you. I would love some, but I'll eat with Chloe when I get home."

"You're welcome if you want 'em," Willie B said. He walked into the kitchen, and Sam followed him.

Sam placed the bag on the round kitchen table. "Willie B, I brought your gun back. Thank goodness, Chloe didn't kill someone with it, but she sure attempted to. Please don't give this to her again," Sam said.

"I'm sorry, Sam, I got tag teamed by her and Stump the other day and gave it to her. But she knows how to handle a weapon, now that's fer sure." Willie B dipped himself a plate of greens over a square of corn bread he had placed in the middle of his plate. "You sure you won't have some? Pork seasoned and hot. If Stump were here, you wouldn't get a bite. Better be glad he is gone with Chloe."

"What?" Sam was about to take a seat at the table but stood again. "Chloe is at my house. What do you mean 'gone with Chloe'? Where?"

"She didn't tell you? She came by this morning."

"This morning. Are you kidding me? I told her to stay put." Sam wanted to pound the table but controlled himself.

"Well, she came by and asked Stump to take her back there to the old homestead place to find the canister Elizabeth told her about."

"And you let him take her? Willie B, you have to be kidding me." Sam walked around the small kitchen table. "She—they could be shot by one of Kimball Mitchell's men for trespassing."

"I figured you knew about it." Willie B sat his food on the table and poured himself a tall glass of milk. "You want a glass?"

"No, thank you, and no, I didn't know." Sam leaned against the fridge. "What time did they leave?"

"Oh, it was real early, not long after breakfast. I reckon it was around eight o'clock. She pulled her car around back before she left. She was tryin' to keep Mitchell from seein' it."

"That's good. I didn't see it when I pulled up. I don't know why she didn't tell me what she was planning."

"She's tryin' to help find her grandmother, so don't be too upset. Besides, Stump's with her," Willie B said. He ate slowly. "Do you want me to call Stump and tell him to bring her back to the house?"

"No, I'll call her cell and tell her myself," Sam said. He excused himself and walked out onto the front porch and dialed Chloe's number.

The phone rang several times, but there was no answer. Sam looked for Stump's number on his cell phone and dialed it. As the phone rang, Sam paced the porch. Finally Sam heard Stump's voice.

"Hello, Sam. I just happened to hear my phone ringin'," Stump said. "Almost missed you."

"Stump, get Chloe and get back over here to your grandfather's house. Now."

"Well, sir, that's goin' to take me a little while. I haven't made it to the old house yet, but I'm almost there."

"Let me speak to Chloe."

"She went down the road. She ain't with me right now."

"What do you mean she went down the road? Is she by herself in those woods?" Sam tried to control his temper. He pounded his fist on the porch post.

"I went up a hill, but she took the road. I can see the old shack from where I am, but I'm a little ways away from her."

"Stump, you better not let anything happen to her. She doesn't know those woods. I'm going to be at your grandfather's waiting for you. You better be here within the next thirty minutes, and I mean it," Sam said.

"I'll do my best, but I can't promise on that one. It might take me that long to finish cuttin' my way through this tangled brush, but I'll hurry."

Sam started to say something else but realized Stump had hung up the phone already. He walked back into Willie B's house and into the kitchen.

"What'd you find out, son?" Willie B asked as he placed his empty plate in the sink.

"They split up. She is alone."

Willie B sat a rounded off mound of greens and corn bread in front of Sam. "Eat. It'll make you feel better. You gotta have a little faith in the people around you, Sam."

Sam looked at the plate of food. He wanted to go get Chloe, but he knew his car wouldn't make it far down the wet road. He thought about calling a friend on the force who owned a four-wheel-drive truck to come help him. Soon, he realized his hand had been taking the greens to his mouth, and they were half-eaten.

Chapter 51

The associate opened the door holding a food tray, and Kimball stepped in behind him. Elizabeth looked up from her wheelchair. She had slumped to the bottom and had no strength to lift herself up again.

"You look like you might be hungry this time around," Mitchell said. "It's been a long time since the half piece of bacon you ate yesterday morning."

"Could you please help me up. I'm hurting," Elizabeth said.

Mitchell pointed to the associate and waved his finger toward the bed. "Get her back in bed."

The man sat the food tray on the end table, lifted Elizabeth out of the wheelchair, and placed her on the bed. He tossed the thin cover over her bony legs, placed the tray on her lap, and removed the plastic covering.

"Eat up, old bat," Mitchell said. "I don't want you to die on me yet. You haven't told me much since yesterday."

"I don't think I have the strength to eat," Elizabeth said as she looked at the tray. The bowl of tomato soup and the grilled-cheese sandwich looked good, but she was exhausted.

"I said eat. I have to know what you and that kid have been planning against me."

Elizabeth picked up the spoon. She got a small amount of soup to her mouth after spilling most of it. The red soup ran down her neck and onto her duster collar. It was good, so she took a second bite.

"You like it, huh, Granny? I'm a fine chef," the associate said.

"Get on out of here and get some work done," Kimball said. "You can come back and get this tray after a while." The associate opened the door and left the room.

Elizabeth ate a few more bites and stopped. She was so drowsy. "I haven't had any medication since Saturday night. That's been almost forty-eight hours ago. I have to have my pills. You know I have heart trouble. I need my medication and—" She coughed and almost lost her breath. "Food on a regular schedule. I can't go on like this."

"I brought you food, so eat. I'll see about the medication later. You might not need it if you don't give me what I want." Mitchell sat in the wheelchair and rolled over to the edge of her bed.

"You killed my Morgan. You had my daughter killed, and you've tried to kill Chloe and me. And for what? Greed, land, money, or plain envy?" Elizabeth asked. "We both know Morgan could out farm you two to one. Yes, you've had success, but Morgan had God on his side. You've never had a crop as big as the ones Morgan produced, and you never will." Elizabeth placed the spoon on the tray. "His blood is still crying out on that land for justice, and as long as it does, you won't ever have peace."

"You better watch your mouth, old bat."

"You're going to kill me anyway. That's all you've been reduced to is a murderer. Whatever good you could have done on this earth will forever be tarnished by your own greed. Your father was right about you."

Kimball pushed the wheelchair backward as he stood up. He picked up the food tray and threw it against the wall. Tomato soup splashed across the drywall; the bowl twirled on the floor, and the sandwich landed under the tray. The glass of milk hit the door and bounced onto the floor.

"I told you to watch your mouth, old bat," Kimball said.

Elizabeth got louder and held herself up in the bed as high as she could. "You didn't have to kill Morgan. He was a good man." She coughed again. "You took him and my daughter from me and left me to live on this earth without them. I had bitterness and hatred in my heart toward you for many years. You thought you had ruined my life. But now, I feel sorry for you. You're the one in misery, not me."

"We'll see about that. Killing people comes as easy for me as farming does, and I have no problem getting rid of one little gal from Wyoming."

"I don't worry about your threats anymore, Kimball. I used to. I was a coward for too many years," Elizabeth said. She coughed a few times and cleared her throat. "I should have demanded years ago that someone help me put you away. I had to live without my family because of you. I could have enjoyed Chloe's presence instead of worrying that you would kill one of us. You took years and memories away from me that I can never get back, but you can't take my future. God holds that, and you can't steal it away," Elizabeth said.

"God?" Kimball slammed his fist into the wall. "I don't believe in God. Look at you. You shouldn't either. Here you are in my house, in my bed, and at my will. I could snap your neck. If your God were so great, you wouldn't be dying from cancer. You stupid, old bat." Kimball paced around the room.

"You're the one who better watch it, Kimball." Elizabeth followed him with her eyes. "God is going to see you punished for all you've done."

"Huh, that's funny. Look who's threatening who." He leaned against the bathroom door.

"You should confess your sins."

"To you? Yeah, right, so you could record them and turn me into the law," Kimball said as he moved closer to her.

"No, I've already got you on tape confessing to murder, and I'm no longer worried about your threats."

"I knew it. You devious, old bat," Kimball said as he reached for the wheelchair. He sat down, rolled up to the bed, and gritted his teeth. "That's what I want. I want what you have against me so that little gal can't use it when you die. Do you understand me?"

"I'll never tell you where anything is. I'm not afraid of you anymore," Elizabeth said. She coughed, and then she coughed so hard it took a while to stop. She noticed the glass on the floor and wished she had something to drink. She labored to catch her breath. "I'm not giving you anything. You'd use your blood money to pay the judge off anyway, but you can't pay God off," she said.

The door opened, and the associate walked in. "Whoa, what happened here?" He walked around the tray and the milk glass.

"Go get a mop and clean this mess up," Kimball barked. "And when you're done, I have another job for you." Kimball stood, walked to the edge of the bed, and bent so that his face was directly in front of Elizabeth's. "You'll be sorry you didn't give me what I wanted, old bat." He held himself up and turned to walk out the door.

The associate picked up the tray, the bowl, and the glass. "I'll be back to clean this up. Do you want any more food?" he asked Elizabeth.

"No." She leaned her head back on her pillow and closed her eyes. She knew it wouldn't be long before it would be over.

Chapter 52

Chloe held the rifle against her side as she walked alone in the gentle breeze. Even with the undergrowth of smaller trees and vines, the place had a charm about it. Chloe could hear birds singing in the tops of the hardwoods. Some songs she didn't recognize. She had planned to be in and out of the woods as fast as she could.

In Wyoming, if the moon was bright enough, she could see all around the barn even at midnight, but she didn't think the canopy of the oak trees would allow much light into the forest at night.

She made the bend in the road and noticed an outline of an old house ahead. It appeared to be swallowed by a massive oak tree that had fallen across the middle of the home.

An owl took flight as Chloe walked in the vicinity of a huge tree near the old home. It startled her at first, but she managed not to jump. The path was gone now, and knee-high grass covered the entire area. Chloe remembered the warnings about snakes in the Pines Community. She chose her steps carefully as she approached the house. Chloe pushed aside the thoughts of judging the place and tried to remember this was her mom's home in the early years of her life. She thought about the letter her mom had written and the pain she must have experienced before she left. She wondered if her mother had been raped in the old house or somewhere else. She wondered who had been so cruel.

The oak tree appeared to be as big as the house beneath it. Almost all the bark had fallen away, and the wood had turned a dark grayish color. Huge lumps of dry dirt clung to the exposed root system as if they were clinging to a broken necklace. The smaller limbs had long since broken away from the larger branches that remained. Some of the stripped branches protruded upward toward the sky while others had been driven into the ground by the force of the fall. Long, green vines had almost taken the back of the house and were running along the tree trunk.

As Chloe drew near to the house, she looked in through the broken glass of a side window. A threadbare, torn curtain beckoned her as it blew inside the house with the stir of the wind. Chloe looked around the forgotten rooms. She was careful not to touch the broken glass, which remained in the window casing.

The tree had landed in the center of the old house, and the broken wooden floor had crumpled underneath the weight. Animal droppings were all over the furniture that remained in the home. A large fur patch of an animal long since deceased lay against one wall. Chloe wondered if a coyote might have drug it back that way. Small rodent bones were scattered throughout the area. Vines grew upward from the cracks in the floor and rose toward the light which streamed in from the split in the roof. Chloe could see dusty broken dishes on the shelves of cabinets whose doors hung open from the jolt.

She pictured Elizabeth teaching Anna how to cook. She strived to imagine the sound of the two of them laughing and playing in the kitchen together. Her eyes searched the floor for anything that might have belonged to her mom. But mostly she saw dust from years of neglect and exposure.

Chloe took careful steps over the undergrowth of dead branches which cluttered the ground. She was thankful she had been carrying the weapon when Stump went the other way.

She leaned the hunting rifle against the old porch and then removed the backpack that had grown heavy. She untied Stump's snacks and fumbled around for a bottle of water. She knelt on one knee and attempted to relax her back as she drank.

She reached into her jean pocket and withdrew the hand-drawn map. She studied Willie B's drawing of the layout of the property.

She found the porch and then turned the map to align with where she stood. A small x marking the burial spot was located about fifteen feet from the west side of the house. A circle of stones had been drawn around the x.

Her eyes scanned the ground for any stones on the property. But the grass was so tall and so thick she couldn't see anything that looked like a stone. Chloe lifted herself from the soil and walked around the area.

She let one foot push the grass to the side as she covered what she thought was the front yard. Chloe's boot hit something. She moved the grass to the side and realized it was a small white washbasin.

The few sunny spots in the yard became dark. Chloe looked at the sky. Clouds had rolled in while she was walking around the house. The western sky had become dark and heavy. Chloe knew if the rains returned, she wouldn't be able to get back across the bridge, but she refused to leave so soon. She heard a rustling sound coming from in front of her. She walked over to the porch, grabbed the rifle, and pointed in the direction of the sound.

"Hey, don't shoot me. It's Stump. I don't want to look like that scarecrow." He walked out from behind a large pine tree carrying his tools.

"Stump, don't ever sneak up on someone who has a weapon."

"Okay, Ms. Chloe." He threw his hands in the air then lowered them. "I'll not do it again. Right now, I gotta get me some of that water. I'm 'bout to die from thirst. Next time, I'll carry the snack bag." Stump dropped the ax, shovels, and machete to the ground and reached for the bag. He drank his mason jug of tea in less than a minute.

Chloe noticed his massive muscles and how the sweat beaded up on his bare arms. She hadn't realized the sweat running down her own back until she looked at Stump's soaked shirt. She waited until Stump had finished off his second jug of water before she spoke again.

Stump put the jug down and wiped his mouth with the back of his arm. "Man, that hit the spot."

"There's so much undergrowth here. I don't know why I was worried about Kimball seeing us on his property. You can't see anything in these trees," Chloe said. "At least, the clouds are making it cooler."

"It's gonna rain again and in a little bit too," Stump said as he found a banana in his sack.

"There wasn't any mention of rain in the forecast."

"Well, that don't mean nothing. Them old educated boys don't know the weather. I'm glad I got that hill cut open. We'll have to go that way if it rains before we find the canister." Stump lifted his banana and finished it in two bites.

"What's important right now is we find the circle of stones on this map," Chloe said. She began to walk around in the grass carefully continuing to look for the rocks.

"Okay, let me see what you got there," Stump said and then threw the banana peeling on the ground. He took the map.

"Where do you think they are?" Chloe asked.

"I think you are on the wrong side of the house, Ms. Chloe. We need to go around on the back of this old shack. I can't really figure out this map, but Grandpa told me where the burial spot was."

"I tried to line the porch up with the drawing," Chloe said. She took the paper and turned it the way she thought it should be in comparison to the house.

"We'll see. That's where you needed me. This old house had a front and back porch. You're on the wrong side of the house."

The first raindrop hit the old tin roof then another.

"I told you it was going to rain," Stump said looking up at the sky. "We better get out of here. We can come back tomorrow. Besides, Sam called, and he's mad. He said he wanted me to get you back to Grandpa's as soon as I could."

"I really wanted to find this today, Stump. Sam will keep." Chloe continued to walk around in the grass. "It will probably stop raining in a few minutes anyway."

"This is Mississippi, little lady. When it starts rainin' here, it can last for a couple of days."

Lightning struck in the far distance. Stump collected the tools he had tossed aside. "I'm out. You better be behind me. Storms can move in fast."

Chapter 53

S*am walked out* into the stifling air. The sky had changed completely in the forty-five minutes he had waited on Chloe and Stump. He paced the front porch and watched as the storm moved across the area. He knew his car would never make it down the dirt road to the old homestead, but he was getting ready to try it anyway.

"Willie B," he called.

"Yeah." Willie B put the kitchen towel down, walked into the living room and then out onto the porch. "I saw them heavy storm clouds movin' in from the west as I was dryin' the dishes. Try not to worry, Sam. Stump won't let nothin' happen to Ms. Chloe."

"I know he won't, but they are on Kimball's land, and who knows where Kimball is. Have you got anything I could drive down the logging road? My car won't make it."

"I got my old tractor in the barn. But it moves slower than a handicapped turtle," Willie B said.

"If they are gone much longer, I might have to use it." Sam walked to the edge of the porch and watched the heavy threatening clouds moving toward them.

"My tractor ain't one of those new jobs like Mitchell's got. It's old, and it ain't got no cab. You'd get soaked if you drive it in this storm or struck by lightning."

"I've got a friend with a four-wheel-drive pickup. I will give him a call and see if he can come over here."

*****

Stump was already on his way into the thicket. Chloe quickly collected her backpack and zipped it shut, draped her arms through it, and picked up the rifle. It took several fast-paced steps to catch up with Stump.

"Are you sure this speed is necessary?" She shifted the backpack as she reached his side. "It's a little rainstorm."

Stump turned and looked at her for a second. "There ain't no such thing as a little rainstorm in Mississippi." He turned and started walking again. "Besides, can't you feel the electricity in the air? We gots to hurry," Stump said.

"This means I can't get the canister. Elizabeth could be at the point of death. I don't know how much time Mitchell is going to give me." Chloe had to walk fast to keep up with Stump. "Now, we'll have to come back in these woods tomorrow."

"You better hope this rain don't go all night. It gets marshy back in here. Old trucks can't pull in red clay mud. We'd have to walk halfway from Grandpa's house to the homestead if it rains all night. The ground is already soft from the rains we got the other day."

"Whatever it takes, I have no choice. I must find the canister," Chloe said.

"I'm with you. Just not today," Stump said. Lightning strikes danced across the sky, and the wind blew hard enough to blow the pine treetops over. Huge raindrops bombarded them as Stump led the way to the path he had cut through the tangled mess.

The grass on the hillside had become slippery from the rain. Chloe had climbed to the top of several mountain peaks but none like this. The grass blades under her feet gave no support and glided her foot downward. She was used to dry rocky ground which her feet could grip into as she climbed.

The thick pine needles stung her arms and face as she fought her way up the hill through the trees.

Carrying the rifle in one hand, Chloe pulled herself up the slope using the pine limbs. Sap clung to her fingers. The rain had turned into pea-size hail, and the winds had picked up to the point that Chloe became concerned a tornado might be in the area. Hail pelted the top of her head. Chloe stopped under an oak tree to take cover from being battered by the elements, and then she thought of the house below her. She knelt to the ground and found the towel in her bag. She folded it the best she could in the wind and draped it over her head. She moved farther up the hill and watched for Stump.

She had almost reached the top when the hail stopped. She could barely see Stump from where she stood at the top of the incline. He was a good ways ahead of her and had already made it to the base of the hillside. Sharp edges lined the narrow passage he had cut.

As Chloe neared the bottom of the hill, mud gave way from underneath her, and she slipped back into one of the sharp stubs. Dropping the rifle, she fell into the tangled mess of branches.

For a moment, she was afraid to move. She couldn't tell how far the wedge had rammed into her side. If it was too deep, she knew she could bleed to death.

Chloe reached her hand around and felt the area where the freshly cut stub had gone in. She brought her bloody hand back around and knew the wound was deep enough she should be concerned. She clutched at the wound to stop the bleeding. Her shirt lay open as blood mixed with her white skin and jeans in the falling rain.

"Stump," Chloe yelled. But he never heard her over the sound of the thunder and wind. Rain pelted her face as she lifted herself skyward. She could see Stump putting his tools in the back of the truck. She yelled louder, "Stump! Help!" He never turned around.

Chloe lifted the rifle off the ground and shot into the air.

Stump came running toward her.

Chloe dropped the gun to the ground. The trees began to spin, and everything turned an odd shade of grayish-white.

*****

Either the truck's wheels spinning or the sound of Stump slamming his fist into the steering wheel woke Chloe. She was sitting in the old truck, and the towel from Sam's bathroom had been tied around her waist. It was soaked in blood and water.

"Stump, what . . . what's going on?"

"You passed out on me, that's what. I got to get you to the hospital. Sam is goin' kill me when he finds out you are hurt. These slick tires aren't making it easy to get out of here. Do you think you can manage to steer this thing if I get out and push us backward?"

"I think so. Let me get my bearings." Chloe held up as straight as she dared, but her side tore open again, and she yelled out in pain. "I don't think I can move."

"If we don't get you some help, you could bleed to death," he said. "Then I know Sam will kill me."

"I don't know if I can slide over there. I'm thinking I'll open this gap more."

Rain beat on the windshield. Chloe tried her cell, but the bars were no longer there. They both sat motionless unsure of what to do next.

Chapter 54

*S*am's friend drove the four-wheel-drive pickup out of Willie B's drive and up the road toward Mitchell's property. Willie B sat on the porch looking to the northeast toward the old homestead. He said another silent prayer and hoped Chloe and Stump had found the evidence before the storm hit.

He tried to remember the last time he had been back in that part of the Pines Community. *Had it been once or twice since the year of the tornado?* The Lee Ranch was the nicest ranch in the Pines Community until Morgan died. Willie B remembered how often the Bishopville Timber Company was around Morgan's place, always hauling out pines and hardwoods. Without Morgan and with little Anna being so sickly, Elizabeth didn't have a fair shot at keeping the place. Mitchell swept in like a lion and took it all.

Willie B pictured the old place in his mind. He hoped the last thirty-something years had rotted the tree enough for Chloe and Stump to dig the evidence out from under it. Elizabeth was counting on it now more than ever before.

*****

The worst of the storm had moved out, but it was still raining. Thunder was to the east of the Pines Community, and Stump could see the dimmed flashes of lightning as it moved farther away from the ranch.

Stump decided to walk back to the gravel road and had made it to the gate when he saw a pickup coming toward him. It began to slow down. Stump didn't recognize the pickup. He had left the rifle with Chloe in case she needed it but was glad the machete was in his hand. As the pickup drew closer to Stump, he could see Sam sitting in the passenger seat and a bearded guy he didn't know sat behind the steering wheel.

Sam opened the passenger door and jumped out of the pickup. "Where is Chloe?" Sam moved his arm over his eyes and blinked from the falling rain. He drew his collar up closer.

Stump pointed back toward the homestead and spoke loudly, "She fell, and she was bleeding. I think we got it stopped before I left the truck. I was afraid to move her, so I left her there."

"Get in," Sam shouted. He opened the cab door and climbed into the passenger seat. Stump scaled the bed of the pickup as quickly as he could and crouched down. His large hands gripped the pickup bed to keep from being tossed around as the driver drove like a madman down the slippery road.

When they reached the old truck, Sam was out of the pickup in a flash and almost slipped in the mud. He ran toward the vehicle. Stump followed. Chloe was conscious and drinking from a water bottle when they reached her. Sam opened the passenger side of the older pickup and found blood on the seat and door panel.

"Chloe," Sam said, "are you all right?"

"I'm okay, more mad at myself than anything. Lot of help I've been to Elizabeth. Might as well be in Wyoming."

"Stop it. Let's get you out of here. Be still, and let me take a look at what we've got before I move you."

"It not bad, a gash, really."

Sam lifted the towel Stump had wrapped around Chloe's waist. The wound was fairly deep, and it was still bleeding.

"Okay, it doesn't look life-threatening. I'm going to slide you out of there, and we'll get you to the emergency room." Sam picked Chloe up and carried her back to his friend's vehicle. Stump grabbed the rifle Chloe had propped against the clutch of the old pickup and ran to catch Sam.

Sam placed Chloe in Stump's arms and then climbed back into the four-wheel drive's front seat. Stump lifted Chloe up to Sam and then jumped into the bed of the pickup again.

The driver spun out in the mud, and Stump got a face full of wet Mississippi clay. The rain washed most of it off by the time they reached the gravel road again.

The driver stopped the pickup and allowed enough time for Stump to jump out over the tailgate.

As soon as Stump's feet hit the gravel, the driver sped off. Stump ducked to dodge the flying gravel. He turned south and walked toward Willie B's house.

Chapter 55

Kimball *ordered the* associate to go to the nursing home and find the tape Elizabeth had mentioned, and then he stormed out of the office. The associate found his attendant uniform, dressed, and walked over to the barn.

An old blue Volkswagen was parked near the barn door with the keys hanging in the ignition. The associate opened the door and folded himself to get into the tiny car. Within minutes, he had entered the downtown Bishopville's busy four-lane highways.

The town was buzzing with law enforcement, so he sat as low in the seat as he could, but with his six-foot-four frame, that wasn't far. He pulled the baseball cap down to his ears and checked his speed. Then he noticed the Volkswagen's gas gauge was almost on empty. He cursed Mitchell for sending him in such a small vehicle. He turned into a fuel station and began to pump his gas.

He took out his credit card to pay at the pump but then decided cash would be better. He went into the station to pay the clerk and turned to leave. The local newsstand was located by the front door. The associate's Wyoming driver license's picture was plastered all over the front page. For a moment, he froze. Then he realized how much he had changed since the photo was taken. The associate was thankful his hair was much shorter now, and he had gotten rid of the hippie look he had been so fond of.

He walked around the convenience store until he found a makeup aisle. He picked out black mascara, paid the cashier, being sure to keep the baseball cap pulled low, and left the store. A few blocks from the nursing home, he pulled the Volkswagen into an alley and penciled in a thin mustache. The associate took a look at his disguise and hoped between his sunglasses, baseball cap, shorter haircut, white nursing uniform, and his penciled in mustache, that no one would link him to the photo in the newspaper.

Kimball had warned him not to mention his name if he was stopped for any reason. But he wondered why he couldn't reap the same benefits as Kimball from the cops.

When the associate drove into the nursing home's parking lot, he spotted one patrol car at the front entrance. He knew he would have to slip in from another access. He went around the building to the kitchen loading area, got out of the car, and waited for an employee to exit the building.

The associate didn't smoke but noticed the large five-gallon bucket filled with sand and at least fifty cigarettes of all sizes sticking out from the dirt. The door opened, and he grabbed one of the longer cigarette butts and pretended he was putting it out in the sand. The associate grabbed the door before it closed behind the large black lady leaving the kitchen. Once inside, he looked at his watch and realized he'd been waiting a full thirty minutes.

Picking up a large box of paper towels, he continued through the halls in the direction of Elizabeth's room. He walked directly behind the officer who was flirting with the two female desk personnel. No one even noticed him.

Within minutes, he was inside the room. He placed the box on the floor near the door and went straight to Elizabeth's closet. He threw clothing, piece by piece, out onto the carpet. Then he looked at the shelf above the rod. It held a couple of boxes and an old suitcase. He threw them onto the bed. The associate unzipped the suitcase first and dumped everything out. He shifted through the odds and ends of vintage clothing. There was nothing. He opened both shoeboxes and found they each contained old pictures.

The associate walked over to the end table near the bed. He pulled open the top drawer and dumped it onto the other half of the bed. He picked up the Bible and flipped through the pages. The picture of Chloe as a young girl fell to the floor. He tossed the Bible on top of it.

The second drawer held paper, pencils, some books, and an extra box of Kleenex. The associate stepped back away from the small table and glanced around the room. He noticed the small kitchenette. Within minutes, he pulled every dish from the shelves. Still nothing.

He couldn't go back to the ranch without anything. He saw Elizabeth's old leather purse lying on the floor behind her bed and dumped everything onto the carpet. The associate got on his knees and used his hands to push the items around. He saw a cassette tape in a clear box. This has to be it. He shoved the cassette into the front pocket on his V-neck shirt and was about to stand when he heard laughter coming from the hallway. The door to Elizabeth's room had been slightly pushed opened.

The associate dared not to look at the person standing in the doorway. He stayed low and bolted from behind the bed. He hit them low like a football player taking out his opponent and made a mad dash through the halls and back through the kitchen. He hit the exit door even harder.

Seconds later, he was driving away from the home in the Volkswagen. He heard sirens in the distance, but he cut across a few back roads and made his way out of town.

When he was able to relax, he took the baseball cap off and placed it on the passenger seat. The associate noticed the cassette player in the Volkswagen and decided to slip the tape in to see exactly what he had. He hoped he could hear some juicy tidbit to hold against Kimball. The associate took the tape from the clear box and placed it into the cassette player. He turned up the volume and smiled.

Finally Mitchell would get off his case for a while. The associate thought he might even be able to turn the tables on Kimball if the tape had enough information on it. He would sell him out to the FBI in a heartbeat.

The tape started, and for a moment, the associate was confused. He was trying to hear Kimball's voice confessing to the killing of

Morgan; instead, a bass voice poured over the speakers. The sound of an African American Southern preacher blasted his ears. The cadence of the gentleman's voice did nothing for him. He fast-forwarded the tape and pushed play again. Still the same voice boomed from the speakers. He fast-forwarded once more to the end. Yet the same voice continued to preach hell and brimstone, ruining his chances of being able to blackmail Mitchell.

The associate ejected the tape, let down the window, and threw the cassette onto the street. He thought about stopping the car, backing up, and running over the plastic piece of junk again. The associate knew he couldn't go back to the nursing home and look anymore. He cleared his head and tried to think like an old woman with something to hide. *Where would she put it if not in her own home? Sam's house or maybe the old man she hung around.* He decided to take a drive to the suburbs and pay Sam a visit.

Chapter 56

Chloe leaned on Sam's arm as she sat up on the examination table. The bald, middle-aged doctor had cleaned her wound and stitched her up.

"I'm glad I don't have to stay overnight. Let's get out of here while we can," Chloe said. "I know you don't plan on letting me out of your sight, but really, I'm fine."

"I guess I'm going to have to lock you in instead of locking others out. You scared me half to death."

"Look at your shoes," she said trying to change the subject.

Sam looked down and smirked. "It's okay. I needed new ones anyway." Red clay mud stuck to the leather. His khaki pants were splashed with mud all the way to his knees, and Chloe's blood had stained his white, starched shirt.

"You are a mess," Chloe said and smiled at Sam. "I can't believe you haven't noticed already. I'll get you a new pair of shoes before I leave as my thanks for coming to my rescue."

"I'm glad you are okay. I don't know how that stub missed a vital organ. There sure wasn't a love handle it could have pierced," Sam said with a grin. He walked over and gave her a slight hug. "I can't believe you went out to the old homestead without saying anything." Sam stepped back and took a seat on the only chair in the room.

Chloe propped up on the edge of the examination table and groaned slightly. "I wanted to tell you. I really did. But I knew you wouldn't approve. I know you are a little overprotective."

"I feel responsible for you, that's all."

"Elizabeth is in danger, and I have to help her the only way I can. Do you understand? I wasn't trying to slip around behind your back. I have to do something to get Kimball to turn her loose. I don't know if the task force is even trying."

"Most of the time they are working, and you don't even know what they are doing. The detective from the Wyoming Division of Criminal Investigation has confirmed the man in the video clip is a resident of Wyoming. His name is Winston Cook. He was the veterinarian assistant in Cody, Wyoming, like you thought he was. The news clip doesn't show everything. Word is Cook beat the two men senseless and then shot them."

"I wondered how he's connected to Mitchell. Do you think they could have met on one of Kimball's hunting trips?"

"I'm sure that's exactly what happened. You could have been killed," Sam said. "Do you understand?" Sam reached and took Chloe by the hand.

"Yes, but Elizabeth is weak, and she can't hold out long at the hands of someone like Kimball Mitchell."

A light tap came across the door, and an attendant pushed a wheelchair into the examination room. Sam helped Chloe stand, get into the seat, and then pushed her down the hall. The attendant followed.

Sam left Chloe with the attendant at the exit door and went to get his car. Within a few minutes, he arrived at the curb in his Charger. He got out of his car and came around to the wheelchair. Sam reached under Chloe and lifted her out of the chair. She draped her arms around his neck and ducked her head as he loaded her into the car.

"How did you get your car here?"

"After my friend dropped us at the ER, he did me another solid and took a couple of guys back to Willie B's. One drove the Charger here and the other took the rental to my place." Sam turned the engine over. "Home?"

"Gladly," Chloe said.

*****

The associate parked the Volkswagen four houses down from Sam's house. He walked across the street and along the sidewalk until he neared the home he had spotted Chloe going into the day before.

A patrol car came around the curve in front of Sam's house, and the associate saw it. He ran for cover behind a small playhouse in the yard next to Sam's.

When the patrol car was out of sight, he came from behind the playhouse and walked into Sam's backyard. He made his way around the outdoor patio furniture and barbeque grill until he came to the sliding glass door.

The associate placed his hand on the handle and attempted to slide it. It was locked. He took his Leatherman tool from his jean pocket, pulled out the flat-head screwdriver, and jammed it between the two doors. The sensitive alarm system sounded at the slightest separation of the two doors.

Startled by the ringing alarm, the associate let the Leatherman fall to the patio. He ran around the house, down the sidewalk, and jumped into the Volkswagen. Slumping down in the seat, he started the engine. He turned into a nearby driveway, backed up, and left the area as quickly as he dared to drive. The associate hoped he wouldn't meet a patrol car before he could get out of the neighborhood.

His cell went off about the time he made it to the intersection. He answered to the angry voice of Kimball Mitchell.

"Yeah, boss," he said.

"I thought you would be back by now. Are you in the mall shopping again? Get to the ranch. One of my ranch hands discovered a pickup on the far south pasture. You better be at the ranch in less than fifteen minutes." The phone went dead.

Chapter 57

"*You better be* careful. That tractor is slow as molasses with a touch of concrete mixed in. If Mitchell gets after you, you won't be able to get away from him," Willie B said. "You 'member that, son."

"I know, but right now, your pickup's sitting out in the open like a huge dartboard. If Kimball's men see it, he'll be up here pounding on your door. I'll have to go get it tonight."

"I don't think you better take Chloe back down there. Sam's pretty upset with us. He ain't goin' let Chloe out of his sight now," Willie B said.

"Yeah, he's done took a likin' to that one," Stump said. "But Ms. Chloe's got a mind of her own. She ain't one of them city gals who don't want to break a nail. She'll give Sam a run."

"It's gettin' dark," Willie B said, "and you better hurry. You know that old tractor's lights haven't worked in years."

Stump took his cell phone out of his pants pocket and flipped it open. "My cell's dead. All this water probably killed it." He stood up from the table and tossed the phone onto the kitchen counter. "Maybe I won't need it. You'll know where I am."

"I wish I knew where Ms. Lizzie was. Lord, I reckon I do," Willie B said.

"I know Grandpa. Me too. If Mitchell hurts her, I'll kill him for you." Stump grabbed his raincoat hanging near the front door. "I'm taking this in case it rains again." A few minutes later, he stepped out on the porch wearing the raincoat over his bare arms. He reached down and grabbed the rifle. "I'll be back, Grandpa, as soon as I can."

"You be careful, son," Willie B said as he walked to the front screen.

Stump stepped off the porch and went to the barn. The tractor refused to start, so he kicked the tire, hit the steering wheel, and cursed it a few times. The engine purred after Stump picked up his rifle and threatened to shoot it.

It took thirty minutes for Stump to reach the ranch road again. The storm had left the air muggier than before, and Stump had removed his raincoat not far from his driveway. When he reached the old pickup, he backed up to the front bumper. He climbed down out of the tractor, found the chain, and tied it to the old truck.

It took a while. The tractor was slow but had the pulling power of an elephant. The truck came out of the clay mud as Stump zig-zagged the steering wheel left then right. Willie B's old truck was covered in red clay. The tires were almost twice the size they normally were. Stump knew he couldn't leave the pickup overnight in Mitchell's field. He had to tow it home, but he had no one to drive it for him. He wished he had gotten his grandfather to come with him.

Stump figured the only way to handle the situation was to unhook the tractor from the pickup and drive the pickup home. He'd have to walk back later for the tractor. Within a few minutes, he had hidden the tractor behind a cluster of trees and was behind the steering wheel of Willie B's pickup. He shifted the transmission to the lowest gear. He would do his best not to get stuck again.

Chapter 58

S*am wasted no* time in getting home after he received the call from the alarm company. He told Chloe to wait in the car until he came back out of the house. His front door was standing open, and detectives were coming and going from the home. A couple of friends from the force were parked in his drive and walked over to greet him when he stepped out of his Charger.

The tallest officer spoke first, "We looked around, and it appears the suspect didn't enter the home, but we wanted to make sure it was safe before you entered the residence."

Sam spoke to the officers nearest him, "Did anyone in the neighborhood see anything?"

"No one has come forward yet, but one of the first officers on the scene found a Leatherman tool on your patio near the sliding-glass door. We'll be testing it for prints later," the policeman said.

"Are you sure he didn't get in?" Sam asked as he walked into the front door and looked around the house.

"We don't believe so," the tall officer said.

"Nothing was disturbed. The intruder must have been scared off," the officer said as he checked his cell phone. "We'll be in and around the neighborhood if you need us, Sam. Just let us know."

Within a few minutes, Sam had escorted the police out of the house and helped Chloe in from the car. The house was quiet, and they were alone again. Sam helped Chloe to bed, and then he went through the house checking windows and doors. He prepared their dinner and prayed for a quiet night. He whispered a prayer for Elizabeth and hoped that she was okay.

Chapter 59

Willie B came to the screen door and saw Mitchell standing on his porch with a man he didn't know but had seen on the news as a possible suspect in Elizabeth's kidnapping. He didn't open the door. "Mr. Mitchell, wh . . . what can I help you with?"

Mitchell pushed the screen into Willie B's body, and the old man fell backward to the floor. Kimball forced his way into the house. The associate stood by the door and waited outside.

Willie B wasn't sure if he should try to get up or stay still. "Mr. Mitchell, what can I help you with?" Willie B asked again.

"You got yourself one stubborn old lady friend, don't you?" Kimball asked as he knelt by Willie B. "She's not giving me what I need, so I thought I'd come pay you a visit."

Willie B leaned against the bottom of the couch. "I don't know what you're talkin' about."

"Don't tell me that," Mitchell said. He rose to his feet and walked around the living room of the small house. "I have been patient with the old bat, but I'm afraid I am completely out of patience."

Willie B struggled to pull his weight off the floor and managed to sit on the edge of the couch.

Kimball walked over to a small card table near the television and stopped. Willie B's collections of wood carving tools were hanging in order from the smallest to largest on a homemade tool holder. Kimball ran his finger along the wooden hanger until he came to a tool shaped like a crescent moon. He removed it from the hanger and tested the blade by running his finger gently across the edge.

"Mr. Mitchell," Willie B said, "is Elizabeth still alive?"

"You better be worried about yourself." Kimball walked over to Willie B and sat on the couch next to him. "Interesting set of tools you got here." He rolled the handle of the tool between his index finger and his thumb.

"I do wood carvin's for people, sir." Willie B pointed to a piece of wood he had carved into the shape of a basket. "I sell them sometimes if I need extra money."

"Well, now, aren't you the entrepreneur."

"Gives me somethin' to do on long winter nights."

"Yes, I guess it does." Mitchell drove the crescent blade into Willie B's cloth couch and drug it back toward his side. "I want to know where the old bat hid a tape recording of me," Mitchell said through his clenched teeth.

Willie B drew his legs closer in. "I don't know about no tape, Mr. Mitchell. Ms. Lizzie never told me 'bout one."

The associate banged on the screen's doorframe. "Hey, boss, you better get out here. There's an old pickup turning in the driveway."

Kimball stood and walked to the doorway. Willie B stood and looked out the living room window. He was happy to see Stump and his old pickup pulling into the driveway.

Stump threw the pickup door open and got out. "Who are you?" Stump yelled at the associate.

"Uh . . . hi, there, uh, I'm a Bible salesman. You want to buy one?" The associate walked slowly down the front steps and smiled at Stump who had made his way to the house. "I've got a sample in the pickup. Be right back," the associate said as he walked a couple of steps past Stump.

"No, I don't think so. I know you. You're that fellow whose picture has been on the news. Ain't you?"

Kimball turned to Willie B. "This isn't over. I'll catch you another time." Mitchell placed the tool in his shirt pocket, went into the kitchen, and out the back door.

Willie B heard the door slam. He moved quickly to the front screen and yelled at Stump. But Stump couldn't hear him. He had the associate pinned to the ground and was hitting him across the face with his fist.

"You don't mess with my friends," Stump said.

Willie B stepped out onto the porch and saw Mitchell coming around the side of the house. He slipped into the pickup and cranked the engine.

"Stump," Willie B yelled.

Stump looked up and saw the Ford backing around in his driveway. The associate managed to free himself from Stump's grip. He scrambled to the truck and jumped in the passenger side as the Ford made its final turn. Mitchell floored the gas, and the truck took off down the gravel road.

Stump ran up the steps and grabbed Willie B's shoulders. "Are you okay, Grandpa?"

"Yes, I reckon so. Just shook up a little."

Stump ran into the house and returned with the landline phone. He dialed 911 and reported the incident to the operator. "They gonna send someone over here, Grandpa. At least I showed that man a thing or two. I should follow them and see if they have Ms. Lizzie at Mitchell's house."

"No, Stump, you can't." Willie B took a seat in the rocking chair. His hands trembled as he tried to relax. "We'll tell the police when they get here 'bout the man on the television hanging out with Kimball Mitchell. I reckon this will give them a reason to go to Mitchell's house. I just hope it's not too late for Ms. Lizzie."

Stump rubbed his knuckles and sat down on the edge of the porch. "If I hadn't got here when I did, I hate to think what those men would have done to you. I'm so glad I came back in the pickup instead of the old tractor."

Chapter 60

Mitchell's cell phone rang as he pulled into the gravel road. One of his payee's from the force was on the other end. Less than a minute later, Mitchell snapped the phone closed.

"We got cops on our tails now. I blame you for every bit of the trouble. I told you killing the sheriff in Wyoming was a stupid move," Kimball said. "I knew it would lead to problems eventually." He slammed his fist into the steering wheel and cursed the associate. "I wish I had never hired you. If I can't shake the heat, you'll go down first."

The associate rubbed his jaw. "I'm glad that ox didn't kill me back there." He found a rag in the door panel and pressed it to his nose to stop the bleeding. "I feel like I've been kicked in the face by that crazed cow again."

"Are you going to cry? Did you hear what I said?" Kimball stared at the associate. "Now the police are after us all because you had to mention my name in front of that gal. I told you to never say anything about me."

"What can I do about it now?" the associate asked.

"Stay out of sight, for one thing. Do you remember where the hunting cabin on the ranch is located, and how to get there?"

"I think so. It's been a while, but I think I can find it," the associate said.

"When we reach the ranch, you take the four-wheeler in the barn and go to the cabin. And don't you dare come back to the ranch until I let you know it is all clear."

"Yes, sir."

"If I need you, I'll send a ranch hand for you."

"Okay, works for me," the associate said. He pulled down the truck's visor, removed the rag from his nose, and looked in the mirror.

Kimball hit a pothole in the road and almost lost control of the Ford. The associate grabbed the dashboard with one hand and strived to hold his nose with the other. The pickup swerved back and forth until Mitchell got control. He turned into the ranch road and drove as fast as he could to the Morton building. Mitchell pulled in front of the barn and slammed on the breaks. The associate jumped out of the truck and ran toward the barn door.

Within seconds, the associate drove a four-by-four out of the barn and passed Mitchell who was scrambling to get inside the Morton building's office door.

*****

The associate gave the off-road vehicle all the gas he could as he drove away from the ranch, down the driveway across the gravel road and then turned onto a ranch road. Within seconds, he was in the middle of the pine thicket. The sun was resting on the horizon as he made his way into the deepest part of the woods. He could hear sirens echoing as they entered the Pines Community. He was glad he had made a clean getaway.

Water stood in the low areas on the road, but the associate drove through the middle of the puddles and never slowed down. He came to a fork in the road, stopped, and looked left then right. The associate couldn't remember which way to turn. There were no markings of any kind to give him a clue, so he took the left. He thought he was going in the right direction until he came upon a large lake situated in a shallow section of the property. The associate wheeled the four-wheeler around and gunned it back toward the fork; he took the opposite direction and sped over the hills and hollows until he spotted the cabin off in the distance in front of him. He slowed the four-by-four and looked west toward the ranch. Lights flashed in the distance as dusk settled in. He turned toward the cabin and noticed an old shack not far to the south. He remembered Kimball telling him the Lee's once called the area home.

The associate drove as fast as he dared in the approaching darkness until he reached the hunting cabin. He rushed up the front steps across the porch and inside the cabin.

The associate made his way in the dark through the living room trying to remember the layout of the cabin. He went through the kitchen and then exited the house through the back porch. He located the generator near the back steps and started it.

When he re-entered the kitchen, he held his breath as he flicked the light switch. Light flooded the dark room. Nothing had changed in the years he had been gone. He walked over to the kitchen sink, wet a paper towel, and washed the dried blood from his face. He sat on the couch and placed the cold rag to his nose and hoped it wasn't broken.

Chapter 61

The task force called for a meeting with Chloe and Sam on Tuesday morning at 9:00 a.m. Chloe was the first one in the door and sized up each member of the task force as they walked into the conference room.

Chloe held her side as she rested in a seat at the round table. After introductions were made, she was the first to speak. "It has been more than forty-eight hours since my grandmother was abducted from the nursing home, and I don't see you guys doing anything about it."

Chloe wanted to take each one of the half dozen or so members of the task force sitting around the table in the Bishopville Police Department and shake them. "What do we have to do to see you guys out there looking for Elizabeth Lee?"

"Ms. Parker," the officer from the Wyoming Division of Criminal Investigation spoke up, "you can't see everything we're doing. I've been able to tie the suspect in the murders of Sheriff Bob McLane and his deputy to Kimball Mitchell. And the investigation has turned up a definite connection between Kimball Mitchell and the sheriff in Snow Valley. We know these men are all linked."

"That's why you have to arrest Mitchell," Chloe said as she took Sam's hand. "His employee has not only threatened me but attacked me. He told me Kimball Mitchell would trade Elizabeth for the evidence I had against him which I gave to one of your officers. Does this matter to you people?" Chloe asked as she raised her voice. The wound in her side began to throb, and she placed her hand over the bandage. She tried to calm herself down.

"We understand your frustration, but things take time. We can't rush into something without knowing what we are getting into," an older man sitting next to the WDCI officer said. "Right now, we only have the word of an old man that Kimball Mitchell has Elizabeth Lee. Where's the evidence?"

"Where's the evidence?" Chloe mocked. "Are you kidding me? Isn't it your job to get the evidence?" Chloe stared at the man and wished she could concentrate hard enough to fry his worthless brains.

"Gentlemen," Sam said as he stood up, "a solid connection has been established between Mitchell and the man positively identified by nursing-home residents as the one who abducted Elizabeth Lee yesterday morning."

"My grandmother doesn't have time for you, men, to get every detail down," Chloe interrupted. She glared at the older officer again. "She is seventy-eight years old. Please do something. We know Mitchell attacked Elizabeth's friend, Willie B." Chloe propped her elbows on the table, crossed her arms, and leaned forward. In the most controlled voice she could manage, Chloe said, "Can't you see Mitchell knows where she is?"

Sam walked around the table. "Is it possible for you guys to obtain a search warrant based on what you already know?" Sam asked. "The abductor, after all, has known affiliations with Kimball Mitchell and is a wanted criminal from Wyoming. I mean, you guys are looking at him for the murderers of two of your own," Sam said as he looked at the WDCI officer.

"That's what we called you in for," the WDCI officer said. "We are waiting for Judge Harris to sign off on the warrant we wrote earlier this morning."

"It's about time," Chloe said. She leaned back in the conference-room chair. "What will happen next?"

"We are going to search Mitchell's property for your grandmother as soon as the warrant is approved," the local sheriff said.

"We should know anytime now," the youngest officer on the task force spoke up. The young man looked at his watch, stood, and walked around the table toward the door.

Chloe noticed the officer's badge and realized he was part of a SWAT team. He was the only one in the room wearing a uniform which came with unique matching leg holsters.

"Because of the nature of this case and your grandmother's condition, we have an ambulance on standby," the local sheriff said. "Also, we will call you the second we find her."

Sam walked over to Chloe and pulled her chair out. She stood and went around the room with Sam as he thanked the gentlemen for their help. She went to the older officer without saying a word but left him with a glare as she went out the door.

"Sam, do you trust these men?" Chloe asked as they walked to his car. "Are they really going to do anything? She's going to die if they don't help her."

"I have confidence in most of those guys and believe they are legit. I only have doubts about one of them, but I think we are in good hands. Let's allow them a little time to see if they can acquire the warrant, and if they don't—" Sam turned to Chloe and cupped her face in his hands and said, "we'll go look for the evidence together. Promise."

"Okay, deal. I can't stand to think about her dying. I don't really know about this sort of thing, but I think we should try the 'come to Jesus' prayer thing my grandmother was telling me about." Chloe leaned into Sam's arms.

"I know about prayer, and we'll pray when we reach my place," Sam said. "I've already been praying."

For the next few hours, Sam undertook the job of getting Chloe to relax. They said a prayer for Elizabeth and tried to eat. Chloe placed dishes in the dishwasher after Sam rinsed them. As they finished the last dish, Sam's cell phone rang.

Chloe listened as Sam paced around the kitchen's island. "I see," Sam said over and over until he finally said goodbye.

"What's going on, Sam?" Chloe asked.

"The task force received the warrant." He walked over to a cabinet, took down a clean glass, and filled it with tap water.

"And what happened?" Chloe walked around the dishwasher to his side.

"The team searched all the buildings on Mitchell's property, but they didn't find Elizabeth anywhere." Sam emptied the glass and placed it in the sink. "I'm sorry, Chloe."

"Oh, God. Do you think she's dead?" Chloe grabbed Sam by the arm and pulled him to her. She laid her head on his shoulder and started to cry.

"No, I didn't say that." Sam drew her into his chest and wrapped his arms around her. "She's going to be okay. I told you we would go out to the homestead property and look for evidence. Kimball will try to keep her alive until he gets the evidence. When we find it, Mitchell will give her back to us."

"I can't accept she might be gone. I was just getting to know her. This is so unfair," Chloe said.

"We'll get the proof we need, and I'll call Mitchell myself."

Chloe pulled away from Sam and took a seat at the kitchen bar. She propped her elbows up on the countertop and placed her face into her hands. "What would happen if I burned a copy of the cassette Elizabeth gave me?" She looked at Sam. "You remember the one I gave the officer? I saved it to my computer. I could burn a CD and give it to Mitchell."

Sam walked behind her and slowly rubbed both shoulders. "You know a CD won't work. Mitchell will know it's a copy. The cassette was made back in the seventies. He might take the CD, but he would not tell us where Elizabeth is. We have to give him whatever is buried at the homestead if we hope to get her back."

"Well, let's go get it," Chloe said. She turned and fell into Sam's arms.

Chapter 62

Kimball Mitchell smiled to himself as he prepared the old bat's lunch. He wasn't an architect by any means, but his plans for the special room had paid off. The police would never find her. He assembled a bowl of soup and crackers on a tray and took a boiled egg from the refrigerator. He was happy the associate was at the cabin. It was only fitting for him to take the old bat's last meal to her. She was his guest after all.

*****

Elizabeth's head was back, and her mouth opened when Kimball walked in. Kimball slammed the door, and Elizabeth held her head an inch off the pillow. She looked at Kimball for a moment and then dropped her head again. Her once perfectly combed hair was knotted and no longer in the tightly rolled ball. Elizabeth's mouth was drawn, and her eye sockets had sunken in.

"I have your lunch," Kimball said proudly. "I have a busy day planned so eat up."

Elizabeth's head remained on the pillow, but she followed Mitchell with her eyes. She didn't reach for the food. She was no longer hungry.

"What?" Mitchell glared at Elizabeth and then the spoon. "You want me to feed you?" He sat the tray on the end table. "Ain't going to happen." Mitchell walked to the empty wheelchair and took a seat. "Truth be told, I can't stand the stink in this room. I can't believe the cops didn't smell you this morning when they walked right by your door. I had to excuse myself to keep from laughing in front of them. They are supposed to be so highly trained, and yet not one of them saw the seam in the wallpaper around the doorway." Kimball crossed his legs. "What a joke."

Elizabeth spoke in a hoarse voice, "The police were here?"

"Oh, so you do still have a voice." Kimball toyed with the wheelchair, uncrossed his legs, and moved his feet back and forth.

"Barely, but enough to tell you a few things," Elizabeth said. She struggled to find him with her eyes and tilted her head slightly.

"I can't wait. Let me guess. You have a new sermon all ready for me." Kimball crossed his legs again and then his arms. "Well, let me have it. It'll be your last sermon."

"You know Chloe's your daughter, don't you?" Elizabeth said in a raspy voice.

Kimball uncrossed his arms and legs, stood from the wheelchair, and looked down at her. "So this is how you plan on keeping your grudge alive after you're gone. Passing the torch to the grandkid, huh?"

"I only pray this ends with my death. Chloe needs to live her life in peace." Elizabeth attempted to cough, but it was scarcely audible.

"How much is she planning on hitting me up for in order to keep your lies silent?" Kimball walked to the room's door and leaned against it.

"It isn't a lie. Anna told me about the rape," Elizabeth whispered. "She told me how you stopped by the house that hot summer day when she was sunbathing near the side of our home." Elizabeth coughed again. "How could you have done that to her? She wanted a tan before she went to church camp, not a baby." Elizabeth tried to sit up but couldn't. She rolled her head to face Mitchell.

"I never touched her."

"You did. She got pregnant as a result of the rape. She and I fought the night she found out, and it has taken me years to overcome the regrets I've carried with me because of what I said. I made a mistake in telling her she should have known better than be half-dressed," Elizabeth said as she struggled to get her breath. "Anna begged me to move us somewhere else. She said she would never be safe again around Bishopville."

"There isn't one ounce of proof to this," Kimball said in an evenly toned voice. "And besides, the statute of limitations ran out years ago," Kimball scoffed. He propped one foot against the door behind him and crossed his arms. "And darling little Anna is dead, so she can't testify that a rape ever occurred. Can she?"

Using the remaining strength in her body, Elizabeth pushed her skeleton of a frame upward. She finally managed to get her upper body raised enough so she could hold her head upright and watch Kimball as she spoke. "It's always about protecting yourself, isn't it, Kimball?" Elizabeth asked in a whisper. "What about protecting your offspring? A simple DNA test can prove she's yours."

"So what? Chloe will be joining you in the ever after soon, so it doesn't matter." He uncrossed his arms.

"Anna didn't send me many letters or cards because of our fear of what you would do if you found out she had your child. I know you were always snooping around my mailbox acting like you were bringing in my mail to help me out. But I knew the truth. After you found the letter with Chloe's seventh-birthday picture in it, you kept everything Anna sent."

"So you going to sue me for mail tampering?"

"I know you were intelligent enough to do the math just like I did. You had to know all these years she was yours. You used my mail to find her."

"Yeah, I found her. It was easy." Kimball walked toward Elizabeth. "All I needed was a few hunting trips to the area and getting acquainted with the locals. Finding her was fun. The hard part was putting enough fear in her and you to break that stubborn family tie you two had." Mitchell grabbed the wheelchair and sat down.

"It worked, Kimball, because she only called me a few times"— Elizabeth coughed—"after she left home, and that was it. One of those times was the day after she had given birth to Chloe. Your money and power didn't accomplish what you set out to do. When you raped my Anna, you mixed your blood with ours. And the Lee name will go on through Chloe because of you."

"Really. Like I can't take her out anytime I want. You think I'm going to go all soft in the head and confess to killing Morgan, turn you lose, and become friends?" Kimball crossed his legs again and looked at Elizabeth. "Too much water under the bridge, and you know it."

"I want Chloe to live." Elizabeth forced out a strong voice. "I want you to leave her alone."

"So you know you are dying, and you know you can't do anything to save yourself, so you hatch up this story hoping you'll make me feel sorry for your precious granddaughter."

"She really is yours, and whether I'm alive or dead, she'll still be yours," Elizabeth said as she relaxed her head into the pillow.

"Well, this is so touching." Mitchell stood and walked to the edge of Elizabeth's bed. "But evidently your little Ms. Chloe doesn't care as much about you as you do her. She isn't trying to save your old hide," Mitchell said. "Today is Tuesday. I brought you here on Sunday morning. My man told Chloe to get me the evidence, and I'd make her a trade. I haven't seen any indication of that happening." Mitchell walked around the bed to the tray on the end table, picked up the boiled egg, and ate it.

"The evidence Morgan buried all those years ago will only prove your father killed Cotton Joe, not Morgan. The evidence won't hurt you or help you, but it would clear Morgan's name. The only thing I have against you is the tape recording I made of you saying you killed Morgan. If Chloe gives it to you, will you let her live?"

"As long as she's alive, I'll be harassed to the end. I can see it now," Kimball said. "First, she'll want money to finish college then more money, and then she'll threaten me with your death. The list will never end." He picked up the tray and walked toward the door.

"She doesn't need or want your money," Elizabeth said. She sought to make her words sink in, but Kimball continued to walk.

"Right." Mitchell turned and looked at her. "First time her old man thinks his ranch is going to fold under, I'll be the first one she calls. No, thanks. I've had to deal with you for too many years. It's time I was able to enjoy my middle-age years without a Lee in them. Think I'll retire, buy me a boat, and go fishing after the two of you are dead," Mitchell said then laughed as he opened the door. "I desire a vacation."

Elizabeth lifted her head completely off the pillow. Her tiny bones and blood vessels strained as she turned toward the door. "Kimball, please," Elizabeth said, "before you go, I'm asking you to remember Chloe is your daughter. It doesn't matter about me anymore. Just let Chloe—"

"Yeah, yeah. I know, let her live." Kimball walked out into the hall and let the door close behind him.

Elizabeth dropped her head back on her pillow. She prayed God would protect Chloe. She longed to see her again.

Chapter 63

Two ranch hands rode up to the Morton building on horseback. It was already in the low nineties. Kimball Mitchell walked out of the office door and down the grassy knoll to where the cowhands had dismounted.

"Boys," he said. "It's going to be a hot one today."

The two cowhands agreed. The younger of the two unsnapped his long-sleeve shirt, removed it, and stuffed it in his saddlebag.

"Did you boys find anything down by the shack this morning?" Mitchell asked.

"Yes, sir, we did," the cowboy wearing a white hat answered. He held out his hand, and a small section from a woman's blouse covered in streaks of dried blood lay across his palm.

"The tractor was gone this morning, sir," the younger man spoke up. "It's still real muddy down there too. Whoever drove the tractor out had a heck of a time. Ruts everywhere."

"I'm sure I know who owns the old piece of junk tractor, but I can't deal with that now. I've got more pressing matters. I want you two boys to ride out to the hunting cabin and give this note to my man from Wyoming." Kimball held out a sealed envelope which he had folded in half. "Before you head out, stop by the kitchen facilities and fix him a few sandwiches and get some chips and beer."

"Yes, sir, Mr. Mitchell," the younger cowboy said.

"When you have given him the note, I want both of you to go back to the shack. There's been too much activity down there lately.

Whoever's trespassing will be back. You catch them on my property again, you hold them, and give me a call."

"Yes, sir." They answered in unison.

"They're breaking a law, so if you want to shoot them, go ahead. In fact, I'll pay a bonus to the one who nails the first one."

"Will do," the ranch hand in the white hat said. The two cowboys went into the Morton building, and Kimball walked back to the office. He took out his cell and dialed Sam's number. It took him less than seven seconds to tell Sam that Elizabeth was near death. He had no tape and no evidence. They didn't have long to save her.

Chapter 64

Chloe said goodbye to Stump and replaced Sam's phone onto the receiver. "Stump said he would meet us at the Pines Community Café. I can't believe the audacity of Kimball Mitchell. He acts as though Elizabeth is a stray dog. If we don't find the canister today, he'll kill her, or she'll die from neglect." Chloe butchered an apple she had planned to eat. Her voice accelerated. "It's been two and a half days since she was abducted. It would be hard for us to go without food and water for three days. She probably hasn't had any of her medication and no telling what Kimball has done."

Sam walked over to Chloe and placed his hands around her waist.

"Watch the side." Chloe wrenched. "It's tender."

"Sorry." Sam adjusted his arms. "Take a deep breath." He held her for a moment then pulled her long hair to one side and kissed her neck. "Just breathe." He reminded her.

Chloe slowed her breathing and relaxed. She sensed a measure of peace while in Sam's strong arms.

"Don't worry, we are going to find the evidence," Sam said. "It's only 11:30 a.m., and as long as Mitchell will leave us alone, we have the rest of the day. If he shows up at the homestead, I'm going to tell him if he wants the canister, he'd better let us do our work."

"I told Stump we could be at the restaurant in fifteen minutes," Chloe said.

"Then we better get going. It usually takes longer to drive to the Pines Community." He walked over to the key holder near the front door and took his keys. "Are you sure you are up for this?" Sam asked placing his hand on Chloe's side.

"Yes, the stitches will hold, and I made sure the bandages were secure. I'm fine. Now let's go kick some butt and find that canister. Elizabeth is counting on us."

"All right then, let's do this," Sam said.

They left the house, and Sam drove toward the Pines Community as quickly as he could. On the drive over, they talked about the task force and how they were glad the men had kept their word and searched Mitchell's property.

As they left the city limits, Chloe touched Sam's hand as he rested it on the gearshift. "I told you about growing up without my mother, but I didn't tell you I grew up with a lot of anger in my heart."

Sam let go of the gearshift and took her hand.

"On our ranch, there's always more work than one person can do. After my mom died, Dad needed help, and in our part of the world, help of any kind is hard to find. He didn't seem to realize I was a kid when my mom died. He threw more and more work on me right after her funeral."

"I can relate. My folks were both killed when I was young," Sam said. "I started hanging out with a gang at school. I thought that was the answer to the void in my heart. But Elizabeth was a substitute teacher back then. She tried to save all of us in that group. I'm the only one that didn't end up in prison. I'm a lawyer today because of her."

"I can't imagine what my life would have been if I'd always known her. Elizabeth helped me to be able to forgive my dad. I don't think I understood my anger was from the resentment which started years ago when Dad forced me to take on the workload that once belonged to my mom," Chloe said.

"He should have known you couldn't do a grown woman's job. You were so young."

"He didn't see it that way, and now I understand why. He grew up under a hard-nosed old rancher himself. My grandfather didn't care if you had just been run over by a bull and were bleeding to death on the inside. As long as a bone wasn't sticking out, you had better get back up and tackle it with everything you had. I guess my dad thought he was taking it easy on me compared to his life."

"But still."

"He had no one else to count on, Sam. My mom was always at his side. When she died, I think he thought he had to teach me to be able to stand against anything life threw at me."

Sam turned the car into the café parking lot.

Stump was standing in front of the building finishing a double-patty hamburger and drinking a large soft drink. He threw up his hand as the Charger pulled near Willie B's old pickup.

Sam let down his window.

"You're goin' have to leave your sweet ride here," Stump said. "It won't make it. Park over there, and I'll pick y'all up." Stump motioned to the side parking area. He threw his trash away and climbed into the muddy pickup.

A few minutes later, Chloe and Sam were in the front seat of Willie B's old truck. Chloe was surprised at the room in the older model vehicle.

"Y'all have to hold on to the dashboard cause this thing ain't got no shocks under it. And it ain't goin' ride like that baby of yours," Stump said as he looked at the Charger. "It's a little too small for me, but it's a nice ride for someone like you, Sam."

"Thanks," Sam said. "I think."

"I put the chainsaw in the bed of the truck 'cause I know the oak tree is right in the way. Grandpa done told me the canister is under it somewheres."

"Are we going to take the same way we did before?" Chloe asked. "I'm sure the creek hasn't gone down any. The bridge will still be underwater."

"Uh, well, that's something I need to ask y'all. I thought we could take the road out by Mitchell's ranch. I know it's risky, but the ground is higher, and we can make faster time," Stump said. "If it's okay with y'all?"

"I say we do it," Chloe said.

"Sure, we need to save time." Sam agreed.

Within a few minutes, Stump was nearing Kimball Mitchell's property boundary. "We here." Stump turned down a ranch road partially covered with gravel.

Chloe noticed the pines were more crowded than on the other ranch road Stump and she had been on the previous day. The old pickup bounced them across several hills and hollers. As they turned to go toward the homestead place, Chloe thought she saw a rooftop and the side of a log house. "Did you guys see a house back there?" she asked.

"Oh, that's Kimball's huntin' cabin. He brings in some bigwigs and lets them stay there while huntin' season is going on," Stump said. "I've cut many a load of firewood for that cabin over the years."

"But this is the middle of May. What season is open now?" Chloe asked.

Sam shrugged his shoulders, and Stump didn't reply.

"I wonder if that's where Mitchell has Elizabeth?" Sam asked. "I know everyone I spoke to on the task force told me they did a thorough search of Kimball's ranch, but no one mentioned the cabin," Sam said. "Stump, why didn't you tell us about the hunting cabin before?"

"I never thought about it, Sam. He stopped the pickup and pointed in front of them. "Look, over there's the Lee's shack."

"Guys, what are we waiting for? Let's go to the cabin and see if that's where my grandmother is?" Chloe urged.

"Let's make a plan before we go to the cabin," Sam said. "I'm sure Kimball will have a hired man or two on the grounds if Elizabeth is being held there."

The three exited the pickup arguing about what they should do. As they talked, a couple of shots rang out into the morning stillness.

Chloe saw two men on horseback near the back of the vacant shack and screamed for everyone to get down. Sam grabbed Chloe's arm and pulled her behind the pickup.

Stump grabbed one of the shovels from the bed of the vehicle and ran behind a pine tree near the house. A rider wearing a white hat rode past the tree. Stump stepped out and swung the shovel into the man's face. The cowhand slid backward, fell from the horse's rump, and hit the ground. The horse continued on its path.

A bullet whizzed pass Stump as the second cowhand fired in his direction. Stump ducked behind the pine once again as the rider approached him. The man's horse jumped a pile of brush and sped forward. Stump stepped from behind the tree. He swung again, and the rider somersaulted from the horse. Chloe pulled away from Sam's grip and ran in the direction of the horse that had slowed to a walk after losing his rider.

Chloe took the reins and calmed the horse enough to get control of him. She led him back toward Sam and Stump who were standing over the two riders. Neither men had moved from the spot where they had landed. Sam collected their pistols which had fallen to the ground and handed them to Chloe who placed them in the saddlebag.

"What are we going to do with these guys?" Stump asked.

"Here," Chloe said as she removed the lariat from the cowhand's saddle, "we can take this rope and tie them to the pine tree." She tied the reins together and looped them over the horse's head and allowed it to graze in the deep grass. Sam and Stump held the two men against the bark of the pine tree as Chloe wrapped the lariat around their shoulders. Neither man regained consciousness.

The three of them gave each other a round of high fives. Chloe held her side and hoped Sam didn't see.

"Stump," Chloe said, "I want you and Sam to stay here and cut up the huge oak tree. I'm going to take a ride over to the hunting cabin to see if Elizabeth is there."

"Hold it. I don't think so," Sam said. "We don't know who is in the cabin. Elizabeth could be there, but I doubt she's alone. I'll go, and you stay here with Stump."

"Sam, would you stop? I'm capable of taking care of myself. I've told you that before. Besides, I doubt you even know how to ride a horse," Chloe said.

"There's a lot about me you don't know yet." Sam walked over to the other grazing horse, took the reins, and swung himself up into the saddle like he was in a western movie. He rode the horse over to Chloe. "I won every horse competition our summer church camp held, year after year, until they made me stop competing so others could win. Shall we?"

"Let's roll," Chloe said. She attempted to swing herself into the saddle but felt a pull in her side and stopped halfway. She asked Stump for a little assistance and thanked him once she was sitting in the saddle.

Stump picked up the chainsaw. "All right, city slickers, I'll start in on this tree, but if y'all need me, shoot in the air, and I'll be there."

Chloe and Sam turned the horses north and rode in the direction of the cabin.

Chapter 65

Chloe approached the cabin first. Sam was directly behind her. Sam dismounted, but Chloe stayed horseback.

"I hear a television. Do you?" Chloe asked.

"Yes, I hear it," Sam replied. "What do you think is the safest way to handle this?"

"Here, this might help," Chloe said as she handed him the 9mm she had placed in the saddlebag.

"Yeah, that'll do it," Sam said.

"Don't let anything happen to that gun," Chloe warned. "I left the other one with Stump."

"Okay." Sam held the weapon like it was a tainted object.

Chloe shook her head. "Knock already."

Sam knocked on the door and stepped back. He placed his hand on the pistol behind his back. "I hope I don't have to use this thing," he whispered.

Within a few seconds, the door swung open, "Yeah, boss, I got the note—" The associate's eyes widen. He slammed the door shut.

Chloe watched as Sam opened the front door. He followed after the man who had bolted through the log cabin. Chloe heard what sounded like furniture turning over. From where she was positioned, she saw the associate run out of the house into a clearing behind the cabin. Sam chased him holding the gun far out in front of his body.

Chloe leaned over Sam's horse, pulled the lariat from the saddle, sprinted the horse around the side of the house, and swung the lasso in the air above her head. She tossed the rope with perfect precision, and it looped itself around the associate's head. The man fell hard to the ground and lay there gasping for breath.

Chloe rode up to the man as Sam ran up behind her and knelt down on the ground. Chloe tossed Sam the loose end of the rope, and Sam secured the man with the full measure of the line.

The man finally stopped coughing and spitting and looked around. Chloe was kneeling in front of him, and Sam was standing slightly behind her with the pistol pointed toward his head.

"I know you have my grandmother. She's dying," Chloe said forcefully. "I need to know where she is and as quickly as possible."

The associate spat on the ground. "I don't know what you're talking about, lady."

"Don't do this man," Sam said. He stepped closer to the associate. "We know who you are. Winston Cook from Cody, Wyoming, veterinarian assistant aka kidnapper, murderer. I'm sure the list goes on," Sam said.

Chloe took the 9mm out of Sam's hand before he knew she was even reaching for it. She slapped the associate across the face with the handle causing him to spit out a tooth. Then she pointed the weapon at his face. "Do you want to die? My grandmother is about to, and it's because you abducted her. So you tell me where she is now. Got it?" Chloe aimed the pistol between the associate's eyes. She heard Sam yelling at her, but she ignored him. "I'm going to count to three. One. Two—"

"Okay, she's in Kimball Mitchell's Morton building. You can't miss it," the associate whimpered. "I hate him anyway." Blood ran down his chin. "I'll . . . I'll show you where she is. Just don't shoot me."

The helicopter hovered above them. Chloe looked up and realized it was a police helicopter. She raised her hands toward the sky and tossed the pistol to the ground near her leg.

Sam ran over to Chloe. "I tried to tell you," Sam screamed over the whirling wind. "Step away from him, and let them handle it. We know where she is."

Chloe and Sam moved back and ducked their head in the strong wind as the helicopter landed in the clearing. Law-enforcement officers poured from the open side of the helicopter. They handcuffed and loaded the man into the chopper within minutes.

One of the officers told Chloe the associate was crying and asking for a deal. They were taking him to the Morton building, and from there, the associate would lead them to Elizabeth. Another officer told Chloe and Sam to meet them at the Mitchell ranch. Minutes later, the chopper lifted off the ground and was airborne.

Chapter 66

*K*imball *Mitchell parked* his Ford underneath the covering of several oak trees and watched the police helicopter fly over the trees. He was sure there was no need to continue to the lodge to pick up his man as planned. Mitchell climbed out of the Ford and stepped to the edge of the trees. He knew the weasel would spill his guts to save his own skin. He heard sirens wailing in the distance, and he knew he had nowhere to run.

Mitchell opened the Ford's door and pulled out his hunting rifle. He checked to see if it was loaded and then slid the gun onto the front seat. He tried to think ahead. If the task force had his man and he was sure they did, what would the police do next?

He moved the weapon over, climbed back into his Ford, threw it in four-wheel drive, and drove toward the Lee's old homestead. Mitchell knew if the guy gave up Elizabeth's whereabouts, he would be without a bargaining chip. He would have to fight his way out if they found him.

He drove the Ford through the potholes, and water splashed onto the top of his pickup. As Kimball approached the shack, he saw Stump wielding a chainsaw into the branches of a large oak tree.

Mitchell slowed the Ford to a crawl until he came to a stop. He got out of his pickup, propped the rifle on the edge of the hood, and aimed it in Stump's direction. He lined up the large man's head with the scope's crosshairs and steadied his finger on the trigger.

*****

Chloe and Sam mounted their horses, and Chloe took the lead. She knew if they cut through the woods, they would connect with the gravel road that ran in front of Mitchell's ranch. She let the horse fly and glanced to see if Sam was behind her. To her surprise, he was. As she came to the end of the pines, Chloe noticed the fence ahead had no visible gate. She spurred her horse and held on as he cleared the pasture fence with graceful ease.

Seconds later, she was on the gravel road. Once again, she skimmed behind her for Sam's whereabouts. He was nowhere in sight. Chloe decided not to wait.

She looked to the west and saw the helicopter touching down. Several black Tahoes trailing each other turned onto the ranch drive. A line of dust stretched across the road like a brown curtain blocking Chloe's view of what was happening in front of her. She had no desire to wait for the dust to settle. She followed the white board fence which ran along the gravel road. She watched for a place to cut across. She knew it would be difficult for her horse to go down into the ditch and then jump the fence. As she neared the ranch driveway, she noticed a strip of grass running between the fence and the drive. She pointed the horse in the direction of the grass and then spurred it to run with all its might.

Chloe rode the horse alongside the last Tahoe. As the procession came to the ranch, she rode behind the vehicles and up to the Morton building. She swung her body off the saddle, and a pain shot through her side.

An officer standing near one of the vehicles ran over to her. "Are you Chloe Parker?" he asked.

"Yes, I am. Have they found my grandmother yet?"

"Not that I'm aware. I was told to wait for you and let you know the second they find her," the officer said.

Chloe saw him looking at her midsection.

"Ma'am, have you been injured? You're bleeding." The officer nodded toward her side.

She reached around and looked at the blood, which had soaked through the thin cotton shirt she was wearing. *I really don't need this.* "It's a wound that reopened. I'm okay."

"Well, ma'am, there is an ambulance on standby. If you'd like, they can take a look at that for you."

"I'll be fine. I want to see my grandmother." Chloe turned her attention to an approaching horse running up the driveway. As it got closer, Chloe saw Sam sitting in the saddle. He rode alongside her and then dismounted.

"I had to go around the fence to the nearest gate. It's been too long since I jumped anything on horseback to try it today. I didn't think we needed any more stress, so I took the safe route."

"It's okay. I'm glad you made it."

Sam leaned forward to take the reins from Chloe. "Let me take your horse, and I'll put both of them in the barn." He stopped. "You're bleeding again. Are you okay?"

"Yes, it's nothing," Chloe replied. "Stop worrying about me."

The officer spoke something into his mic and walked a few feet away from Sam and Chole.

Sam took both horses and led them into the open end of the barn. He started to tie the horses to one of the stall's black metal bars when a ranch hand walked over and took the two reins and lead the horses away.

The officer ran back over to Chloe and yelled, "They have her."

"Oh, thank God," Chloe said. She raced toward Sam and took his hand. "Is she okay?" she asked the officer.

The officer listened to the voice coming over his dispatch mic and replied, "Copy that." He turned to Chloe and said, "Yes, she's alive."

"When are they bringing her out?" Chloe asked.

"It won't be long," the officer said.

"Please, may I go see her?"

"Give me a minute." He walked away from Chloe and Sam.

"Sam, they have to let me see her." Chloe looked at the officer who was talking into the mic again. She couldn't wait any longer. She ran through the Morton building.

"Ma'am, wait. I'll take you." The officer ran to Chloe and grabbed her by the arm. "Slow down," he said. "Look at me. Let me take you there."

Chloe looked around the open arena knowing she needed to go somewhere but had no clue where.

"Look at me," the officer said again. "Okay, slow down and look at me."

Chloe focused her eyes on his. She saw he was going to help her. She took a deep breath and struggled to slow her heartbeat. "Okay, let's go," Chloe said. "Sam, come on." She motioned for Sam to follow.

Sam jogged over to them and took Chloe's hand. The officer led the way.

They continued through the open end of the Morton building and walked across the dirt. Chloe saw several horses standing in the stalls which lined one side of the building. The two Sam and she had been riding were there as well. They followed the officer across a connecting slab of concrete that led to a doorway. The officer opened the door and directed them up a flight of stairs. As they exited on the second floor of the Morton building, Chloe saw a dozen officers at the far end of the building who seemed to be leisurely standing around. As Sam and she walked down the long hall, a couple of law-enforcement officers moved out of her way. Chloe saw the associate handcuffed and sitting on a padded bench against a wall.

As the trio approached a doorway leading into a room, several officers were blocking the entrance. They moved away from the door and allowed the officer leading Chloe and Sam to enter.

As she neared the doorway in front of her, a terrible wave of fear rolled through her body. She froze. A picture of Sam trailing her in his white Nissan back in Snow Valley, Wyoming, flashed across her mind. The same odd sense of dread swept over her. It had not been Sam who caused the dread; it was this moment. She wanted to go beyond the doorway and follow the officer, and at the same time, she didn't want to enter the room.

"Chloe," Sam said. "You look very pale."

"I . . . I don't think I can do this."

"Chloe." Sam took her shoulders and faced her. "She needs you to be the strong Wyoming girl she met a few days ago. I'll be right beside you." Sam took her hand and stepped into the room first. Chloe followed.

Chloe recognized the WDCI officer who was standing near the end table by the bed. The young SWAT officer was ambling around the room quietly talking on his cell. Sam stepped to the side of the bed. Chloe came from behind him and looked down on a woman she no longer recognized. The once perfectly combed hair was matted and tossed around the pillow. A forehead covered in dry, blotched skin led to a woman's face that had sunken in. Chloe swallowed hard and reached her cupped hand toward the meatless cheeks. Elizabeth's skin was cool and clammy to the back of Chloe's hand as she stroked her grandmother's face.

Elizabeth lifted her index finger at Chloe's touch.

Chloe's knees buckled under her, and she knelt on the floor by the bed. Sam held onto her shoulders as she leaned into the mattress. "Grandma." Chloe rubbed Elizabeth's dehydrated arm. She dropped her head and a tear fell onto her grandmother's outstretched hand. Chloe knew she had to show strength for Elizabeth's sake. She blinked several times and lifted her head. Elizabeth's eyes were looking at hers. "I'm so sorry he did this to you," Chloe said.

Elizabeth spoke, but Chloe couldn't hear her.

Chloe turned to one of the officers and asked him to bring some water with a straw if he could. She looked back at Elizabeth and said, "Grandma, you're going be okay."

An officer walked into the room and announced for everyone to clear the room for the EMTs. Sam helped Chloe to her feet. Officers cleared the hallway and allowed the stretcher to come into the room. The room was completely silent as the EMTs pushed the stretcher near the twin bed Elizabeth had been laying in for three days. One emergency technician started an IV, and the other one hooked her to oxygen and took her vitals. Within a few minutes, paramedics had carefully lifted Elizabeth from the twin bed onto the stretcher and were wheeling her toward the stairway.

Chloe and Sam followed the EMTs outside the building and toward the ambulance. As they approached the back door, Chloe saw Elizabeth move her head left then right. Her grandmother was trying to speak, but almost no sound came from her lips. The closer the stretcher neared the ambulance door, the harder Elizabeth shook her head. Chloe ran around Sam and over to the EMT who was carrying the oxygen.

"Wait, she's trying to tell us something," Chloe said. She stepped to Elizabeth's side, pulled her hair out of the way, and knelt down as near her face as she could. She lifted the oxygen mask slightly off Elizabeth's mouth.

"Home," Elizabeth said.

"Did you say home, Grandma?"

"Home, take home," Elizabeth said again.

Chloe asked Sam to come and listen to Elizabeth.

He walked around to the other side of the stretcher and knelt down to Elizabeth's body.

"Take me home," Elizabeth whispered.

"She wants to go home," Sam said. He looked back to the old woman. "Do you want to go to the nursing home?"

Elizabeth moved her head from left to right. "No."

Chloe bent down over her again. "What home are you talking about?"

"Homestead," Elizabeth said in a soft voice. "Morgan, truth."

"Truth, Grandma?" Chloe asked.

"Yes, Morgan, truth."

Chloe looked at Sam. "She wants to go to the homestead property. I think she's talking about the canister."

Elizabeth nodded her head.

"I don't know, Elizabeth, you need to go to the hospital now," Sam said.

She mouthed "No" and shook her head again.

"Sam, in our visits, Grandma told me how important it was for Morgan's name to be cleared. She's kept that hope alive for more than thirty-eight years even in the face of fear for our lives."

"I don't care. The EMT said her vitals aren't stable. We have to get her to the hospital as fast as we can."

Chloe took Sam by the hand. "Sam, she needs to see if the evidence is still there. It will prove Morgan's innocence," Chloe said. "That means more to her than anything, and she's the only one who really knows where it is located."

Elizabeth lifted her hand from the stretcher and nodded her head.

"But . . . what if . . ."

"There are no what ifs, Sam. My grandmother is trying to tell us what she wants."

The county sheriff walked over to the stretcher. The other task force members were gathered in a huddle near the Tahoes. Chloe saw one of the officers place the associate in the backseat of the Tahoe farthest away from her.

The sheriff reached his hand down and placed it on Elizabeth's shoulder. "Ms. Elizabeth, do you want us to take you to your old homestead place across the road?"

Elizabeth nodded.

A paramedic spoke up and told them he had already administered an IV, and they would have to stay with her.

"Are you okay with this?" Sam asked Chloe.

"Yes. I know it's what she wants."

The sheriff motioned for a couple of officers to come over. "Let's get this little woman over to the homestead and tear the place apart until we find the evidence she talking about, and hurry."

The emergency technicians loaded Elizabeth into the ambulance and closed the door.

"All right, let's get it done." The sheriff walked over to Chloe and Sam. "This is the best we can do for her. It's her wish, and I'm a witness to it. Let's get over there, and I'll get some of my men to dig up this thing she's been talking about."

Chapter 67

Kimball Mitchell held his rifle on Stump who was now tied to the same pine tree the two cowhands had previously been secured to. Mitchell had forced Stump at gunpoint to untie his men. He watched as the taller cowboy picked up a shovel and slapped Stump across the face with it. Blood mixed with Stump's sweat and ran down his bare chest. The other man tied Stump to the tree with the same rope and then kicked him in the side.

Stump let out a yelp.

Mitchell forced the two men to move the sections of the oak tree Stump had cut with his chainsaw. The cowhand with the white hat was shoveling the rich dirt, and the shirtless man continued to saw through sections of the oak and clear the brush away from the area.

*****

The county sheriff took the lead. Chloe and Sam rode in the back-seat. A line of Tahoes followed. The ambulance was at the end of the procession as the group traveled around the road that bypassed the hunting cabin.

As the task force drew near the old shack, Chloe squeezed Sam's hand. "I don't think Elizabeth is going to survive this. I hope I'm wrong," she said.

"I pray we can find the canister for her. It would be a blow if after all these years the canister was gone or rotted away."

"She told me my grandpa had welded the ends closed."

The sheriff pulled to the side of the house. Within minutes, everyone had unloaded the vehicles except for Elizabeth and the EMT who was attending to her.

The sound of a gun shooting in their direction sent members of the task force into a spin. They assumed their positions and took cover behind SUV doors and pine trees. Chloe and Sam ducked behind the back door of the sheriff's car.

The sheriff yelled out, "It's Kimball Mitchell. He's behind the house."

Chloe looked toward the back of the shack to see if she could spot Mitchell. She let her eyes follow the horizontal massive oak tree to its root system which stood vertically after being pried from the ground by the tornado force winds. She remembered walking by the huge hole created from the roots as they were pushed upward. Chloe could see Mitchell standing to the edge of the mixture of roots and dirt. He was holding a rifle and was pointing in the direction of a pine tree. She followed the barrel of his gun to the base of the pine, and then she saw Stump sitting on the ground with his body tied to the tree.

"Don't anybody get any bright ideas," Mitchell screamed. "I can take this man's head clean off from here."

Chloe watched the EMT who was standing outside the closed ambulance door, open it, slip inside and then pulled the door closed again. She wished she had ridden in the ambulance so she could check on her grandmother.

The sheriff made a quick motion with his arm, and the task force SWAT officer moved away from the others, stepped behind a cluster of trees, and disappeared from Chloe's sight.

The sheriff lifted his mic from his shoulder. "Dispatch, we have a hostage situation here." A muted reply came over the speaker. "Hostage situation." Another muted reply, "I'll be negotiating."

The other officers held their stance, and each one positioned their weapons to fire if necessary. Chloe couldn't believe this was happening. She wanted to go to the ambulance and check on Elizabeth, but she didn't dare move away from the car door.

The sheriff stepped a few feet forward from his position near the driver's door. "Mitchell," the sheriff shouted, "we all want to go home here. Let's see if we can do that? How 'bout you put the rifle down."

Kimball shot off another round. "No, not going to happen, sheriff. We all know I won't be going home after this."

"Can't we at least talk about it? We all want to help this situation turn out right for everyone."

Chloe looked toward the pine where Stump had been tied. He wasn't moving his body, but she could see the anger in his blood-stained face. She knew it wouldn't do for him to break the rope that held him to the tree. His bare arms were cut and bloody from struggling to get loose.

The sheriff clicked his mic again and spoke in a softer tone. "Alpha One, you in position yet?"

"Copy that" came back over the mic.

"Mitchell, look at me," the sheriff yelled. "I know you don't want to shoot anyone today. So why don't you put the rifle down."

Mitchell fired a third round into the air. "I'm not going anywhere."

"Calm down," the sheriff said. "We have to find a solution to our problem."

"How about this, everyone gets in their vehicle and leaves," Mitchell shouted.

"We need you to help us help you, okay? So put your rifle down, and let's talk."

Mitchell yelled out, "I would have brought some beverages had I known y'all were coming. Looks like I picked the wrong place to hide out."

"What are you hiding from, Mitchell?" the sheriff asked.

"I know you found the old bat. She's in the ambulance, isn't she? Probably still alive," Mitchell said in a disapproving tone. "She refuses to die, you know."

"Well, the way I see it, that's a plus for you," the sheriff said.

"Yeah, how's that?"

"I don't have to charge you with her murder."

"You say that like it's a good thing," Mitchell said.

Chloe wanted to stand and say something, but Sam held her arm.

"How did you find her?" Mitchell asked. "Wait, don't tell me. That punk from Wyoming told you, didn't he?"

"Doesn't matter. What matters now is you put the weapon down, and let's wrap this thing up." The sheriff turned his head and pressed his finger into his earpiece. "Come again?" he said into his mic. "Did I hear you right? Snakes?"

Chloe watched as the sheriff turned and faced Mitchell again. His neck stretched. He stood on his toes, and then he placed one hand over his eyebrows to shield his eyes from the sun. She attempted to see what the sheriff was looking at. But from her crouched position, she couldn't see a lot.

The sheriff spoke into his mic again. "Are you positive, man?" Seconds later, the sheriff spoke again. "Copy that." He stepped a little closer toward the old house. "Mitchell," the sheriff spoke loudly, "I'm not trying to trick you. I want you to know what I am about to tell you is the truth. One of my men informed me there are snakes all around you."

"Yeah, right. That's lame coming from you, sheriff. I thought you were better at your job."

"I'm not lying to you. Don't move. My man's got his scope on you and can get the snake closest to you, but there are so many—"

A blood-curdling scream came from Mitchell's direction. Shots fired from behind the shack but not toward the task force.

Chloe saw the sheriff directing his team. Mitchell continued to scream in anguish and shoot toward the ground. The men rushed to the area where Mitchell had been standing. Chloe stood, and Sam reached to pull her down toward him.

"I don't see Kimball anymore. I think he's been bitten by a snake or something," Chloe said. They both stood by the car. Chloe stared at the scene playing out in front of her. Kimball lay screaming on the ground near the tree's root system. Every member of the task force, except for one who was cutting the lariat from Stump's body, was standing near the oak unloading their weapons into the hole.

Minutes later, a deathly silence fell over the forest. Kimball Mitchell wasn't screaming any longer. The sheriff dropped his gun to his side. The SWAT officer came running from a row of pines toward the house. Chloe and Sam walked toward the task force.

She gawked in disbelief at the dead snakes covering the roots of the oak tree and the ground underneath. Kimball lay still. Chloe could see bite marks on his arms and face. His eyes were wide open and still.

Chapter 68

*C*hloe *ran to* the ambulance. She banged on the door. An officer joined her and gave the EMTs an 'all clear.' The door opened slightly. "He's down," Chloe said. "It's okay." The policeman nodded. The man swung both doors opened. Elizabeth lay still on the stretcher with an oxygen mask across her face and the IV attached to her arm. "May I sit by her, please?"

One of the paramedics stepped down from the ambulance. He pulled Chloe aside and told her he had been in contact with Elizabeth's doctor. He continued to give Chloe an update on Elizabeth's vitals. Chloe thanked the man and moved into his position. "Grandma, how are you doing?"

Elizabeth nodded her head and raised her thumb upwards.

"They got Mitchell. Well, sort of." Chloe said. "He's gone, and you don't have to worry about him ever again."

Elizabeth smiled and blinked her eyes.

Chloe could see Elizabeth move her lips. She lifted the mask slightly from her nose. "What, Grandmother?" Chloe asked.

"Canister," Elizabeth whispered.

"Did we find the canister?"

Elizabeth nodded her head.

"Not yet," Chloe said. "Do you want me to go check?"

Elizabeth shook her head left and right. She lifted her hand slightly above the stretcher, cupped her fingers, and motioned for Chloe to come closer to her.

Chloe moved as close as she could to her grandmother. "What is it?"

Elizabeth spoke in a whisper and in broken sentences. "I don't want you to be sad, angry, or bitter over this. I'm at peace."

Chloe rubbed her grandmother's hair back. "Don't talk like that. We're okay now."

Elizabeth shook her head. She continued to speak in broken words. "Don't go on mourning for me as someone who has no hope for the future. We can meet again. Ask Jesus for his comfort. You'll be fine."

"No, Grandma, it's going to be okay. You'll see," Chloe said.

Sam ran in view of the open ambulance doors. He yelled in excitement, "The men found the canister. The task force pitched in along with Stump and myself. We've been digging with sticks and the two shovels Stump had. It's still intact. Come see." He motioned to Chloe and realized she was crying. He bent down and entered the ambulance. "It's going to be okay, baby." Sam knelt down and placed one hand on Elizabeth's leg and the other one on Chloe's back. He bowed his head and said a silent prayer.

Chloe held her head up and watched as a tear ran down Sam's cheek. She felt a sense of peace come over her and relaxed by Elizabeth's side.

Elizabeth whispered something, and Chloe watched her lips. "Sam, I think she's saying 'Willie B'," Chloe said.

Elizabeth nodded.

Sam took out his cell and stepped out of the ambulance.

Chloe held her grandmother's hand and sat patiently. The sheriff stuck his head in the ambulance.

"I wondered if I might show Mrs. Lee something?" the sheriff asked. He held up a dirty canister about twelve inches long and ten inches in diameter.

Elizabeth smiled and motioned to Chloe.

Chloe listened as her grandmother asked to touch the canister one more time.

The sheriff handed the container to Chloe. "The welds held together, and I don't think there has been any disturbance to the canister at all," the sheriff said. "We'll log this into evidence, and if it contains proof of Morgan's innocence, I will personally see to it that the case is reopened."

"Thank you, Sheriff," Chloe said. She held the container over Elizabeth's body and then moved it down so Elizabeth could touch it, again. Sandy dirt fell to Elizabeth's duster as she rubbed her finger down the side of the container. Chloe watched tears roll from her grandmother's eyes to the stretcher beneath her. "See, it all worked out okay. It's going to be fine. The sheriff will prove Grandpa didn't commit suicide or murder." Elizabeth dropped her finger back to the bed.

Chloe handed the canister back to the sheriff. "Thank you so much."

The sheriff turned and walked away. Chloe yelled at him to come back. He stuck his head back in the doorway. "Yes, ma'am?"

"Elizabeth is asking for her friend Willie B. Wilson. Is it possible one of your men could go get him?" Chloe asked.

"No problem at all. I'll get right on it."

Chloe walked back over to her grandmother and held her hand. "They found it, Grandma. Can you believe it? Now, reliable law-enforcement officers have the information they need to clear Grandpa Morgan's name."

Elizabeth smiled. Chloe could see she was happy and squeezed her grandmother's hand. Elizabeth coughed but no sound came from her lips.

"I'm so sorry this had to turn out this way. Mitchell should have paid years ago for what he did to this family. I'm glad he's gone."

Elizabeth shook her head back and forth. Her mouth moved, and Chloe leaned in again. Elizabeth spoke slowly, "I have to tell you the last detail before I go but not so your anger will return."

Chloe looked at her grandmother in wonder.

"Kimball is the man who raped your mother. He was your biological father."

"No," Chloe said. "Not him." She buried her face in her hands and shook her head. "No, no, no, this can't be." Chloe looked back at her grandmother, and tears ran down her cheeks.

262

"Forgive . . . forgive . . . ," Elizabeth whispered.

The sheriff stuck his head in the doorway and asked Chloe to come to the door. She wiped the tears away, but they returned like an uncontrollable leak. She got up, bowed her head over, and walked out of the ambulance.

Willie B was waiting around the side of the vehicle holding a single orange rose. "Ms. Chloe." Willie B nodded toward her as she neared him.

"Go on, Willie B, she wants to see you." Chloe and the sheriff helped the old man into the ambulance. He moved to the side of Elizabeth's bed.

"Ms. Lizzie, my, my," Willie B said. He shook his head, leaned into the side of the stretcher, and lifted Elizabeth's hand. He placed a single orange rose between her fingers. "You have always been the rose amongst my thorns. I couldn't have lived my life as fully as I did without you, Ms. Lizzie," Willie B said. I hope you won't mind, but I'd like to give you a kiss."

Chloe stood near the back door of the ambulance. Tears rolled down her face. Sam's arms slipped around her waist. She watched as Willie B leaned over Elizabeth and kissed her softly on the forehead. She admired the love between the two people who had never been in any kind of relationship other than the best of friends.

Elizabeth's hand slipped from Willie B's. The rose dropped to her chest. She closed her eyes and took a final breath.

Chloe turned her face into Sam's chest. She resisted the anger that rose up in her again. She heard Elizabeth's voice in her head telling her not to be angry; she would see her again. Sam guided Chloe away from the back door of the ambulance, and the EMT took Willie B's hand and helped him down. The paramedic at the head of the stretcher pulled the cover over Elizabeth as the EMT closed the doors.

Chloe heard sirens wailing in the distance and lights flashing all around her. She lifted her head and looked into Sam's eyes, which were filled with tears as well. The disturbance around her became a blur of people moving, shouting, and shuffling as Sam walked with her to the sheriff's car. He opened the back door. Chloe started to get in and then stopped. In the distance, she noticed several men loading a black body bag onto a gurney. A bald man in a nice suit stood by with a small notepad in his hand.

Several men rolled the gurney toward the waiting coroner's vehicle. Chloe asked them to stop. She left the car and walked over to a man wearing a suit. She asked if she could see the body once more.

Sam stood behind her and nodded to the coroner, who gave his okay to the attendant. The man unzipped the bag.

Chloe looked at the salt-and-pepper-haired man covered in snakebites. She had only known him as an enemy. He had caused so much destruction, and he was her father. She shook her head. Tears formed in her eyes. She wanted to hate him, but peace settled in her heart instead. She thanked the coroner, turned, and walked back to the patrol car. She slipped into the backseat.

Chapter 69

Wednesday morning, Chloe called her father in Wyoming and told him about Elizabeth's death. She did not tell him about the information Elizabeth had shared with her before she died. Chloe said the funeral would be in a couple of days, and she would be flying home afterward. He didn't argue.

After she hung up, Chloe gave Alice a call. She was happy to hear Alice was madly in love with Hank's son. Alice was saddened to hear about Elizabeth and told Chloe she looked forward to seeing her again.

Sam had offered to handle most of the funeral arrangements and was downtown taking care of the final details. The doorbell rang. Chloe noticed the sheriff's car parked in Sam's driveway as she walked to the front door.

"Hello, sheriff," Chloe said as she opened the door.

"Ms. Parker," the sheriff said, "I wanted to speak to you, if I may."

"Yes, come in. I've been wanting to talk to you as well." Chloe moved aside, and the sheriff walked into the living room. Chloe noticed the folder in the sheriff's hand as he walked to the couch. She took a seat on the oversized ottoman in front of the sheriff and waited for him to speak.

"A couple of things, Ms. Parker."

"Please, call me Chloe."

"All right, Chloe," the sheriff said. "I wanted to share a few photographs with you. These are pictures of the evidence we found in the aluminum canister. Almost everything was as your grandfather had placed it in the canister thirty-eight years ago," the sheriff said as he opened the folder.

Chloe accepted each picture as the sheriff handed them to her. The first couple of photos were of other photos. They clearly showed Kimball Mitchell's father, Corbin, holding a large handgun while standing in front of a skinny black man. The second showed the black man bent over holding his stomach. A third picture was of an assortment of items. Chloe saw a glove, a VHS video, and a shell casing.

"With this evidence, there should be no problem reopening this case and finding your grandfather was framed for Cotton Joes' murder. It should also shed new light on Morgan's death. I suspect the ruling of suicide will be revoked."

"I'm thankful to know this, sheriff," Chloe said.

"There's something else too," the sheriff said. "Seems your grandfather didn't expect this canister to be opened for some time. He treated the container very much like a time capsule. He placed a letter to Elizabeth and Anna in the container. I made you a copy if you would like to read it sometime." The sheriff handed Chloe a sealed envelope.

Chloe accepted the envelope and thanked the sheriff.

The sheriff stood, and Chloe pulled herself from the ottoman. They walked to the door in silence. "Well, Ms. Chloe, if there is nothing else, I'll see you at your grandmother's celebration service on Sunday."

"I do have a question about Kimball Mitchell's death. Have you ever seen anything like that before? I asked Sam, and he said it was common for snakes to den up in tree cavities. Is that true?"

"Yes, I've heard tales of it since I was a kid running around in these woods, but it was my first time to ever witness it firsthand. If Kimball hadn't received so many strikes, he might have lived."

"It was a shocking sight."

"It was at that. Good day, Ms. Parker."

"Goodbye, Sheriff," Chloe said and closed the door behind him. She walked to the kitchen table and placed the envelope on a yellow placemat. Chloe poured herself a cup of coffee and sat down at the table. She held the envelope in her hand and couldn't decide if she should open it. After all, it was written to Elizabeth and her mother.

A few minutes passed, and Chloe decided Elizabeth would not mind if she read it. She unfolded the copy the sheriff had given her and read.

My Dearest Elizabeth,

I fear the witnessing of Cotton Joe's murder will be my undoing. Still, I could not allow myself to stand by with a camera in my hand and not capture what I saw happening right in front of me.

I believe our lives would have gone a different way had the Bishopville Timber Company not asked me to photograph the forest that particular day.

I'm afraid I haven't solved anything by collecting this evidence and storing it away for the future. It was probably a crazy idea, for I wonder if our town will ever have a police force that isn't corrupt.

Yet I am compelled to write this letter to you, for as I said, I fear the worst will come of this attempt to do away with a killer in our midst.

The Mitchells aimed to destroy what we built, but they could not destroy our love for God and one another.

In case I go to my reward before you, I want you and little Anna to know that picking strawberries with my girls was truly the greatest highlight of my life.

My love for you will outlast this lifetime.

Your loving husband,
Morgan

Chapter 70

The closed casket hid the snakebites covering the man beneath the lid and sealed his façade forever.

Chloe sat at the back of the massive church and listened to a well-dressed man boasting about the long list of Kimball Mitchell's accomplishments. Several hundred others sat motionlessly between her and the bronze box that held the man who had caused untold detriment to her loved ones.

A choir, robed in red satin, lined the pews behind the speaker. As the man took his seat, they waited for their cue then broke out in a loud harmony.

At the end of the song, there were no tears in the huge auditorium, no babies crying, no one calling out Kimball's name, only low murmurings and the shuffling sound of expensive clothing as people moved toward the exit doors.

Chloe kept her seat and watched as the hundreds of people funneled their way out of the three enormous exits. As the crowd thinned, she rose to walk toward the lone casket.

Several rows down, she noticed a tall man approach the coffin. Chloe stopped and took another padded bench to observe the muscular man holding a black cowboy hat in his hand. He placed the hat at the head of the bronze box and knelt beside it for a brief moment. The young black-haired man lifted himself, looked around, and walked over to the oversized framed photo of Kimball Mitchell resting on an easel. He placed his large hand on the top of the frame and bowed his head.

Chloe decided she would speak to the man. Seconds later, he had disappeared into the crowd of people exiting the church. Standing at the front of the church alone, she could no longer see him. She positioned herself near the head of the expensive casket, played with the white lace around the hem of her sundress, and stared at the cowboy hat. After a few minutes, she could no longer restrain herself from picking up the black hat. She ran her fingers over the high-quality beaver felt and noticed the sweat stains on the crown. As she turned it over, a small white square of paper fell from the inside band to the floor. She quickly picked up the paper and unfolded it.

Dear Funeral Director,

Please place Kimball's hat in his coffin before lowering him to his final resting place. I know he will feel lost without it.

Bill

As Chloe replaced the square paper, she noticed the gold engraving of Kimball Mitchell's name on the inside sweatband. He must have worn it many a day. She rubbed the lettering. She wanted to hate him. A man she had not known and would never really know. She could carry the hate back to Wyoming with her, or she could lay it down and forgive like Elizabeth had told her to do. She didn't want to carry the weight of hate back to Wyoming. He didn't deserve her grace, but she knew she deserved to be free.

Chloe placed the black hat back on the coffin and walked out of the church.

*****

A hundred orange roses, ranging from buds to full open blooms, adorned Elizabeth Lee's white coffin. The front of the small church was lined with dozens of other arrangements leaving a small space for a single violinist to stand behind the pulpit. As the hymnal rang out across the wooden pews, Chloe recognized the tune. She had heard Elizabeth hum it several times.

The celebration service was one of reassurance. Chloe no longer doubted if she would see Elizabeth and her mother again. She rejoiced in the fact she had come to Mississippi to meet a lady she would never forget.

As one elderly friend after the next stood to tell their fondest memories of Elizabeth, it became clear she was a respected member of the Pines Community as well as Bishopville.

Sam walked with Chloe to the grave-site service and held her hand as the final words over Elizabeth's life were spoken.

Willie B and Stump stood to the left of Sam. The sheriff and a few of the men from the task force stood to the right of Chloe. The elderly pastor spoke a beautiful farewell to what he called his *sister-in-the-Lord*. He said, "The courage and strength Sister Elizabeth exhibited in her final days was a perfect example of a verse in the book of Isaiah. Elizabeth had waited and trusted that God would allow the truth to be made known. God had given Elizabeth the strength to soar in the end, and her husband's good name would be restored." The pastor mentioned that she had never lost hope that Morgan would be cleared from the false accusation, and as her pastor and friend, I'm glad the desires of her heart had been fulfilled.

Chloe was thankful for the time she had spent with Elizabeth. She realized not only had the last couple of weeks brought the knowledge of a wonderful grandmother to her, it also brought the good news of peace and joy God had for her.

The church hosted a time for Elizabeth's relatives and friends to gather and encourage one another. Chloe appreciated what a wonderful example Elizabeth had been to so many.

Sam pulled Chloe away from the group of elderly people to inform her the grave site would be ready for viewing within a few minutes.

"Sam, I can't believe the difference between Elizabeth's celebration and Kimball's service earlier this morning."

"And I can't believe you went alone," Sam said. "You should have told me you wanted to go, and I would have taken you."

"I needed to go alone. I needed to say goodbye to him. I needed to forgive him."

Chloe and Sam walked to the cemetery holding hands while Willie B and Stump followed them.

The earth had been pulled back into its original hole, and the huge family spray of orange roses lay across the sandy dirt. Several other flower arrangements formed a semicircle under the canopy provided by the Bishopville Funeral Home.

Chloe stood at the edge of the freshly closed grave. She took a deep breath and looked around at all the beautiful flowers. She knew Elizabeth would love them. Everything looked so peaceful. She wished she could tell her grandmother what a difference she had made in her life in the short time she had known her. But she would see her again.

The double monument with carved praying hands had waited for many years for the date to be filled in under Elizabeth's name. As Chloe approached the marker, she realized an additional smaller similar stone had been placed next to Elizabeth's side of the monument. She bent down and read the engraving.

Our Dearest Anna

You are not lost to us.
For we know you are in the hands of our awesome God.
Until we meet again.

Mom and Dad

Chloe dropped to her knees. The new yellow sundress fell around her as she crumpled toward the marker. Her long brunette hair draped over her shoulders as she reached out to touch her mother's name. At last, Chloe had found a place to mourn her mother. All the years, she yearned for a place to say goodbye—vanished with the touch of the stone. It wasn't goodbye; it was "until we meet again." Chloe knew she would be buried here as well. The rural Pines Community of Mississippi was where she belonged.

Sam's hand touched the side of her head, and she leaned against his leg. He took the white linen handkerchief from his suit and extended it to Chloe. She sat still for a few minutes and prayed a silent prayer.

As Sam helped Chloe to stand, Willie B and Stump walked to the side of the larger monument.

"Ms. Chloe," Willie B said, "I made this just fer you. I have another one for Ms. Lizzie's tombstone too." He held out one hand, and Chloe saw the wooden dove against his aged, dark skin. She took the dove, admired the craftsmanship, and hugged Willie B.

"Thank you so much. I'll treasure it always." Chloe rubbed the smooth sides of the dove. It was soothing to her hand, and she loved it instantly.

Stump stepped forward. "Grandpa thought we would let you put this where you want to. It's for Ms. Lizzie's grave."

Chloe admired the extra-large dove she assumed had taken Willie B a long time to carve. "Oh, Willie B, this is absolutely beautiful. Grandma would have loved it. I know she thought the world of your folk art."

"Folk art, nah," Willie B said as he blushed.

"No, Willie B, this is art." Chloe took the dove from Stump's hand and discovered it was heavier than she thought.

"Yes, she's right, Willie B," Sam said. He took the larger dove from Chloe and viewed it in several directions. "You should get these in some of our local art galleries. In fact, I don't know why I haven't thought of this before. I know one of the art directors downtown. She's got a gallery near my office, and I'll be paying her a visit this coming week."

"Well, I'd be honored to place this here for Ms. Lizzie."

Chloe found a perfect spot for Willie B's carved dove, and Sam placed it on the base of the monument.

"There you go, Ms. Lizzie," Willie B said. "I made this dove from a chunk of the oak tree that guarded the canister all these years. Now it can watch over you."

"Are you leaving today?" Stump asked as they walked away from the monuments.

"No, Sam will be driving me to Memphis tomorrow morning."

"We goin' miss you around here," Stump replied.

"I'm going to miss you, guys, too, but I'll be back before you know it. I need to have a long talk with my dad, even if it means driving to Montana to find him," Chloe said. She stopped and turned around to face the grave site. "It's time I forgive him as well."

When they reached the parking lot, Chloe hugged Willie B and thanked him again for the beautiful dove. She reached up to Stump to hug him. He picked her up, squeezed her gently, and sat her down again.

Chloe was about to get into the Charger when Willie B spoke up.

"Ms. Chloe, I have to tell you somethin'."

"Yes."

"Mr. Mitchell wasn't always as bad as he ended up. He was a decent boy before his momma ran off with another man. He didn't have much help growin' up after that. His old man was a rough old goat. I wanted to tell you that 'cause I know Ms. Lizzie told you he was your father."

"Yes, she did, Willie B," Chloe said.

"Well, that's the truth. I didn't know if I should bring it up here at the grave site, but I didn't want to let you go off without telling you."

"It's okay, Willie B," Chloe said.

Willie B looked down at the pavement. "I drove up on Kimball when he was with your mother. I have never beat a man before that day or after that day, but I got my hands on him, and I gave him a whippin'. I know why he hated me all these years. No one ever done that to him before. Don't guess they did afterward either."

"Thank you for taking care of business," Sam said. "If I'd been there, I would have done the same thing."

"Me too," Stump said.

"At least Morgan's land will go back to the rightful owner. Yes 'em, you goin' be a wealthy little lady."

"Time will tell," Chloe said as Sam opened the passenger door for her. "I'll be seeing you guys," Chloe said and smiled at the two men. "Be safe."

Within a few minutes, they were on the road on the way to Sam's. Chloe knew it would be harder to pack her belongings than she could ever imagine.

Chapter 71

*M*onday morning arrived *too soon.* Chloe had placed her suitcase in the foyer and was in the kitchen drinking a cup of coffee when Sam made his way into the living room.

"Good morning, princess," he said.

Chloe smiled. "You're not saying that because you think I'm going to inherit a lot of money, are you?"

"If you were down to your last penny, I'd say the same thing." Sam walked to Chloe and put his arms around her.

"If we are going to the ranch before we go to Memphis, we need to hurry," Chloe said. "Are you ready?"

"Yes, ma'am. Your chariot awaits." Sam pointed toward the garage door.

Within a matter of minutes, they were pulling into Mitchell's ranch road that a few days earlier held so much drama. Now that the task force was gone and the helicopter wasn't buzzing the sky, the ranch took on a new feel. Chloe wondered if it was true that the entire spread would be hers. She wondered what her father would say when she told him she would be moving to Mississippi. She was thankful to know she could live her dream, not his. It was time for her to become the woman she longed to be and step out on her own.

Sam drove the car up the long driveway lined with white board fence on both sides. The grass was deep, and lush and horses ran along the side of the south fence. "This is part of your family's original ranch," Sam pointed. "You see those cattle on the hillside to the north?"

Chloe looked to her right and saw the Black Angus cattle grazing. She thought about Wyoming. "Yes, I see them."

"That is the original property where it all started. Now there are seven miles of road-front property in the Pines Community alone belonging to the Mitchell estate."

"Wow." Chloe didn't know what to say.

Sam smiled at Chloe. "I knew you had to see this before you went back to Wyoming after reading Morgan's letter," Sam said. He drove around behind the Morton building and into a meadow lined with pine trees. Sam parked, and the two walked together into a large, open clover field.

Chloe took in a deep breath and decided the air was as clean and fragrant as in Wyoming. It was different but nice. She closed her eyes and for a moment thought of an alfalfa hay field on her mountain ranch. She had no regrets.

"You want to slip your boots off and take a fast run in the clover? There's nothing finer than running barefoot in the cool clover on a hot Mississippi day," Sam said.

Chloe took off her boots and followed Sam across a small section of the field. She found herself spinning in the grass and imagined her mother doing the same thing as a little girl.

Sam grabbed her by the hand and spun her to his side. "There's one more thing I want to share with you. Come on." Sam led her to the west border of the clover field a few yards away. "Look down," he said.

Chloe bent her head down and noticed there were strawberry plants scattered throughout the edge of the clover. She stooped low and gathered a few of the tiny berries remaining on the vines around her.

"These are the remnants of your grandfather's strawberry fields. He raised thousands as a young man. It's how he got his start as a farmer around here."

Chloe tasted one of the small berries. It was sweeter than any strawberry she had ever placed in her mouth.

"Thank you, Sam, for bringing me here. I don't have to wonder anymore about my mom's childhood. I think I've lived a small portion of it. And, by the way, I've found something of hers."

"Oh, really? What's that?" Sam asked.

"A past with roots that run deeper than the pines."

The end.

About the Author

T ammy Partlow combines Southern charm and character-driven suspense to produce novels with rich characters and a strong sense of place. She lives with her husband in the Wyoming Rockies. She invites you to visit her at Facebook: TammyPartlowAuthor, Twitter: @TamyPartlow, website: www.tammypartlow.com.

CPSIA information can be obtained
at www.ICGtesting.com
Printed in the USA
FFHW020027281118
49686005-54077FF